The Opposite Shore

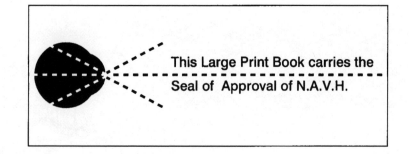

This Large Print Book carries the
Seal of Approval of N.A.V.H.

The Opposite Shore

Maryanne Stahl

Thorndike Press • Waterville, Maine

Published in 2004 by arrangement with NAL Signet,
a member of Penguin Group (USA) Inc.

Thorndike Press® Large Print Women's Fiction.

The tree indicium is a trademark of Thorndike Press.

The text of this Large Print edition is unabridged.
Other aspects of the book may vary from the original edition.

Set in 16 pt. Plantin by Carleen Stearns.

Printed in the United States on permanent paper.

Library of Congress Control Number: 2004103349
ISBN 0-7862-6458-6 (lg. print : hc : alk. paper)

As the Founder/CEO of NAVH, the only national health agency solely devoted to those who, although not totally blind, have an eye disease which could lead to serious visual impairment, I am pleased to recognize Thorndike Press* as one of the leading publishers in the large print field.

Founded in 1954 in San Francisco to prepare large print textbooks for partially seeing children, NAVH became the pioneer and standard setting agency in the preparation of large type.

Today, those publishers who meet our standards carry the prestigious "Seal of Approval" indicating high quality large print. We are delighted that Thorndike Press is one of the publishers whose titles meet these standards. We are also pleased to recognize the significant contribution Thorndike Press is making in this important and growing field.

Lorraine H. Marchi, L.H.D.
Founder/CEO
NAVH

* Thorndike Press encompasses the following imprints: Thorndike, Wheeler, Walker and Large Print Press

Acknowledgments

One Christmas week my then fifteen-year-old son set himself the task of reading five Shakespeare plays. Among them was *The Tempest*, one of my favorites. At the time I was pondering possibilities for a second novel, and being reminded of and then re-reading the play served as inspiration. Therefore I thank my son, Jack, my inadvertent muse.

To the Stevens family who comprise my writing group, Marre, John and Larry, I offer my affection and gratitude. Marre, my spiritual sister, self-appointed public relations agent and cheerleader; John, my sailing encyclopedia and most amiable host; and Larry, our unassuming but convincing model of the artist as contemporary war hero: thanks, y'all.

To my in-laws, Joseph and Evelyn Stahl, whose love for Shelter Island begat my own, I am ever grateful for all the summers and family gatherings at their beloved home.

To my friends at the Zoetrope Writers

Studio — Wendy Vaizey, Jim Devitt, Jai Clare, John Cottle, Donna Storey, Ted Peterson, Robin Slick, David Toussaint, Beverly Jackson, Bob Arter, Melissa Millot, Gabriel Conroy and Andrew Nicoll — as well as my friend Lee Kline and everyone who read chapters and put up with my breast-beating and, importantly, provided premium procrastination opportunities: thanks a lot.☺

Finally, to my editor, Genny Ostertag, for her sensitive and sensible editorial help; my agent, John Talbot, for his guidance and enthusiasm; Dr. Laura Dabundo, English department chair at Kennesaw State; and Kellie Anderson at the KSU book store, for their support: thank you.

Chapter 1

"Boatswain!"

Rose Campbell looked up from her sketchpad and frowned. William was calling to their daughter, Miranda, sunning herself on the cabin roof of their sailboat, the *Ariel*. Characteristically, he was making a reference, probably mythological, one he expected Miranda to recognize. He had been playing this game with her for years. But she hated being treated like a little girl. At sixteen, she considered herself equal or superior to her parents in everything that mattered, and she didn't understand why her maturity so often failed to be acknowledged.

Miranda lifted her head, her long, pale hair catching beneath her elbow. She grimaced and extracted the strands. She answered her father in a flat voice. "Um, what ho?"

Though Miranda's face was turned, Rose knew she was smirking. Miranda had smirked that same half-crooked, maddening-but-very-pretty smirk since babyhood.

9

"What *cheer*," William corrected.

"What*ever*." Miranda gathered her hair to one side and lay down, repositioning herself out of the shadow of the sails.

The wind whipped Rose's braid as she leaned her head back. The sensation was pleasant, and yet there was something almost imperceptibly troubling in it. Rose could tolerate only so much constant physical movement. She liked to be still.

As if to emphasize her discomfort, the *Ariel* heeled sharply to port, Rose dropped her drawing pencil, and Miranda slid, squealing, to the deck. William laughed. He loved to make Miranda scream, though it took more these days than it once had. He sailed closer to the wind, almost to beam ends, and water sloshed up over the railing. He always had to push it.

Rose wouldn't mind sailing if she could paint on board, but that was impossible. Though she appreciated that it was a point of pride with William to sail as efficiently and as swiftly as possible, she found it tedious. All she could do on a trip with William was draw, and shakily at that, when what she really wanted was to mix the tones she saw around her. She had an idea for a new series of paintings evoking the various moods of blue, so she was grateful

10

— and frustrated — to be surrounded by blues today. Her eyes drank color the way alcoholics drank liquor, without a drop to spare.

She picked up her pencil and looked up at the spar, dark against the daylight, and willed herself to remember this for later. The air shimmered like water, the water shone bright as the sky. Rose had to admit that it was a glorious day for a sail, though because of the holiday, boat traffic was heavy on the Long Island Sound. Today was Saturday of Memorial Day weekend, the official start of summer. Rose believed in the importance of family outings, but she didn't get a lot out of sailing; nothing, at least, that an hour on the water couldn't provide. But one didn't sail for an hour only. One barely got out of the harbor in an hour. They had been sailing for two, going essentially nowhere. And William was sailing a bit recklessly.

Anna's blond head popped up at the top of the companionway. "Thirsty?" she asked, and she came on deck carrying canned drinks.

Rose accepted a beer. "You read my mind."

"The gift of second sight exacts a price," William said. He was hamming it up today, in a good mood.

Anna stuck out her tongue at him and handed him a beer.

"You're an angel," William said, and Rose glanced at him to gauge whether he was mocking. But his eyes were shadowed by an old Red Sox cap, and both his beard and the glare of the sun made his expression difficult to read. He sailed off the wind a bit and flattened the deck.

Anna ducked beneath the boom and went to sit beside Miranda, whose shoulders glowed pink.

"Put sunscreen on, please," Rose said. "Both of you."

Miranda pulled the tab on a Coke. It hissed and lightly splattered her. She didn't answer, but Rose knew she had heard. Miranda leaned closer to Anna, saying something Rose couldn't hear, and Anna lifted her chin, laughing. Her hair swung out, catching sun. A shade or two darker and several inches shorter than Miranda's, Anna's hair was the same silky texture. Rose's hair had always been thick and coarse, a dull beige. She rarely wore it free; it got into her paint.

In her sail bag Rose kept a kind of sunscreen that contained insect repellent. She knew Miranda wouldn't like that, but she called, "Heads up," and tossed her the tube.

Anna turned and caught it, smiled, and handed the tube to Miranda, who looked at it and frowned.

"What are you drawing?" Anna had to raise her voice above the deep whine of a passing speedboat.

Rose glanced down at her sketchpad and shrugged. "Lines," she said, considering them. "Angles. Corners. Knots. Surfaces."

Miranda stood, grabbed on to the lifeline, and faced the bowsprit. The *Ariel* rose up and slapped down over the speedboat's wake, spraying the deck. Miranda shouted as she was splashed. She was laughing.

The boat rolled, and Anna tripped forward, knocking into the mast. William jumped to reach for her, and Rose took the tiller, watching as William gripped Anna's arm. Sometimes, lately, his solicitude of Anna was annoying, but not much more annoying than his condescension.

"God, I'm so clumsy," Anna said. She always said it, and she was. Though Anna had been a graceful little girl, at some point during the years of their growing up she had tautened; her limbs now were tense and alert. Rose thought she knew

13

why, though not exactly when Anna had changed.

"Where are we going?" Miranda asked, facing away from them.

Anna looked to William for an answer, and Rose felt the stab of something she didn't want to understand.

"Who wants to decide?" William asked.

No one volunteered. Rose looked past William's shoulder to the *Ariel*'s elegant wake. Swirls of blue and white; wavy lines of violet. She saw the movement of water as shooting lines of light. In the sky behind the *Ariel*, a cormorant seemed to be following them, its dark shape a marker for where they'd been.

"Do we ever actually go anywhere?" Miranda was now lying across the bench on the sunny side of the boat, one leg stretched out, foot flat on the deck ready for the *Ariel* to come about.

"Of course we do," William answered. "We're never in exactly the same place as we were."

Rose looked at the cormorant and knew that William was wrong.

The winding streets of her Connecticut neighborhood pleased Rose, and as she drove home from the marina after drop-

14

ping Miranda at her girlfriend Jai's, she took an unsought but welcome comfort in the flower gardens and the flags, the well-tended yards and tasteful fences. She had always liked this area; it was especially pretty in May, with the dogwoods and the roses and the hedges just greened. And yet, she sometimes wondered if she didn't belong somewhere else.

Miranda planned to spend the night at Jai's — compensation for having had to endure the day with her parents. Anna and William had stayed behind to close up the *Ariel*, and Anna would give William a ride home when they were through. She would probably stay for dinner. Rose had defrosted steaks.

Their yellow clapboard Colonial stood at the bottom of a sloping cul-de-sac, an icon, Rose had always thought, of what a "family home" looked like. William was renting it when they met, and they bought it together when they married. Almost immediately, the place became home to Rose, more home than the house only a mile or so away where she and Anna had grown up, the house in which their mother had peacefully died in her sleep three years earlier, the house Anna had dreamed of escaping. With her share of sales profits

15

Anna had purchased her condo, three miles in the opposite direction.

Rose was thinking vaguely about houses, about roof angles and doorways, as she drove along the curve and pulled up to her mailbox. She visualized a painting of rooftops as she lowered the window of the Jeep. The large oak on her lawn cast a shadow over the front door. The sun was moving into summer position.

She reached for the mail and immediately began sorting through the usual bills, store flyers, magazines — and then she saw it, the signature black stationery of the New Works Gallery.

"Oh God." Rose held the envelope to her chest and let everything blur. She had entered two paintings in a juried show, but she hadn't expected the results so soon. This was how the list of winners was announced, by invitation to the reception celebrating them.

She knew she hadn't won. She steeled herself. It was okay; she didn't expect to win. Her style wasn't anything anyone was interested in these days. No, of course she wouldn't have won, but she couldn't help the bit of excitement in the pit of her stomach. She opened the envelope carefully, trying not to tear it.

The New Works Gallery, in partnership with the Connecticut Fund for the Arts, is delighted to invite you and your guest to the fourteenth annual reception celebrating the Solstice Awards for New Artists, featuring the work of
Helen Francia, First Place for Painting/Oil, "Equinus"
Collin Lahst, First Place for Painting/ Acrylic, "Orkney Lighthouse"
Rose Campbell, First Place for Painting/Mixed Media, "Ginger Lily"

Rose caught her breath and read the words again. She had won! Her skin tingled, effervescence rising in her.

A separate letter from the gallery owner, Wendy Roth, congratulated her and asked her to prepare five more paintings for a group show in October. She was going to have a show! A shared show, but still, a show. She laughed aloud, putting the Jeep in reverse. She had to tell Anna. And William. She wanted to tell the world. *At last,* her career as a painter had begun.

But William had applied for a year's teaching post at the University of St. Andrews in Scotland. If he got it, his course would begin in October, and they had tentatively planned a family trip there in early

August, all of them, Rose, Miranda, and Anna. They would investigate the housing situation, see about getting Miranda into school, then return home to sort things here. The idea was for Rose and Miranda to rejoin William as soon as they could. If he got the appointment.

Rose couldn't possibly move to Scotland now.

Well, they'd deal with that. One thing at a time. What mattered at this moment was *her* triumph.

She drove back to the marina. This time, she saw little of the landscaping as she hurried through the neighborhood. She barely saw the road; she drove by rote.

Though it wasn't a recent effort, the painting that had won was her favorite. A still life, it depicted a subtly off-balance close-up of a blue vase holding a stalk of ginger lily cut from her garden, and its scent had filled her head as she painted. She remembered it vividly, and she thought the work suggested that. She had finished it a year ago or more, just after she began to get serious about her art again. She'd paint it differently now.

But she had won!

She pulled into the parking lot of the marina and found an empty spot next to

Anna's Toyota. Exuberant, she rushed along the pier to the *Ariel*'s slip, all the way at the end.

Rose heard the music before she got to the boat, playing from below. Her Dido CD. No one was on deck.

She climbed aboard and crossed the cockpit. The music blared. Which one of them, William or Anna, liked it turned up so loud, and since when? She glanced down the companionway but did not go down. Instead, something made her go around to the port light and look through, and something kept her still for the half second it took her brain to register what she saw.

She heard someone scream — herself.

Chapter 2

Anna was wiping up in the galley while William fussed with the engine. She moved as though his eyes were on her, feeling the prickle of his stare along her back. She was so nervous. Last weekend they had sailed alone, the two of them, and the tension had been almost unbearable. Disturbing and delicious. All week, at work at the Nature Center, at home in her condo, in the car, in the shower, she had thought of little else but him. She was almost sure he felt the same.

What were they going to do? Well, they couldn't do anything, of course, but should they acknowledge what they felt? Would things between them change? She steeled herself against the inevitable awkwardness.

Anna had put on a CD, Dido's *No Angel*, that someone had left behind. The lyrics thanked someone, a lover, for making this the best day of the singer's life. Anna couldn't wait to have a best day of her life. She was due for one, eventually.

"Thank *you*." William's low, suddenly close voice made Anna turn, and he smiled, his eyes fixed on her face. She raised her gray eyes to meet his dark ones. When he squared his shoulders, she knew he was gathering himself, trying for it to be like always, except that it wasn't.

Anna returned a blue plastic bowl to a cupboard. "You like Dido?" she asked.

"Well," he said, and Anna added, "This singer."

"Aaaah." William was in professorial mode. "Dido was the founder of the city of Carthage, you know. A beautiful widow. It was Juno's wish for Dido and Aeneas to get together, but Venus had other plans."

"Always," Anna said. She and William had an ongoing argument regarding the behavior of the goddess of love.

William shrugged. "So Venus directed Cupid to make Dido fall in love with Aeneas. But she also saw to it that Aeneas' feeling for Dido would never be more than a willingness to take anything she wanted to give."

Anna focused her eyes on the place his beard ended, just beneath his ear. She didn't remember what happened to Aeneas, but she knew he didn't end up with Dido. "Typical," she said.

William chuckled and continued. "For a while they were happy, as she lavished ev-

21

erything possible on him, wanting only that he love her in return." The *Ariel* listed to port as a wave hit, probably from a passing motorboat. Anna reached behind, steadying herself.

"But that wasn't enough to keep him," William said as he shifted his weight. "Ultimately, Aeneas set sail for Italy."

"And Dido?" Anna asked. She looked directly into William's eyes — the color of bourbon, as he'd once joked; he had gone to college in the South. She saw her own miniature eyes reflected in his.

"Tragically," he said, a teasing edge to his voice, "Dido killed herself. Aeneas looked back toward Carthage from his ship and saw the light of her funeral pyre."

The *Ariel* was rocking now. Anna stepped backward for balance.

William stepped forward, reaching for her arm.

The music shrieked as Anna bumped the volume control with her ass. She jumped and William caught her shoulders, steadying her, steadying himself. She looked up at him.

"Anna," he said, and even though the music was deafening, she heard his voice distinctly, each rise and dip. His lips pressed her forehead. Her stomach dropped, as though someone had cut its cable, as though she were falling. She knew he was going to tell her that he loved Rose, that he was flattered but couldn't possibly return her desire.

How could she bear it? It had taken her years to realize that she loved this man, her sister's husband, to surrender to this feeling, to want to feed it, to gorge on it. "William," she heard herself say.

His beard tickled her cheek, softer than she expected, and neither of them closed their eyes, as though they had to see what would happen next. Their eyes locked, his lips brushed hers, their hands were in each other's hair, and then they kissed, deeply, and their eyes closed and they sighed into each other's mouths.

A butterfly folded and unfolded its wings in Anna's hollow stomach.

She felt something break in her chest and her eyes began to burn.

And then she heard Rose scream.

Anna leapt out of William's embrace, knocking the CD player off the chart table, the plug pulling free as it clattered to the floor.

"Shit!" William tugged at his jeans.

Rose was there, at the top of the companionway, hissing down at them. "How could you? How could you?" Looking wildly around as if for further evidence. Screaming into the cabin as though it were on fire. "You fucking traitors!"

She was waving a dark envelope, trying to tear it up. "Both of you!" But the envelope was too thick for her to tear, and she threw it down the steps.

Anna rushed to the stairwell. "Rose. My God."

Rose held on to either side of the hatch, her face blazing, but at Anna's words she let her arms drop, leaden, as though suddenly emptied of blood and bone. She closed her eyes and shook her head, softly keening, "No."

Anna glanced toward William, who stood staring at the silent CD player, wordless, frozen.

"It isn't . . ." Anna began, but Rose collapsed backward into the cockpit.

William started toward the steps. "Rose . . ." His foot kicked the envelope, and he looked down. "Christ," he said as he bent to pick it up. Beads of sweat glistened on the back of his neck.

Anna read the engraved return address for the New Works Gallery.

She bounded up the steps, reaching the

cockpit just as Rose jumped from the boat to the dock.

"Please!" Anna shouted, but Rose was running. Anna watched her sister sprint along the pier as though chased, watched the gulls around the trash bin fly up in a great winged mass at her approach, circle, and return, watched Rose disappear into a small, dark sea of cars. Anna watched until there was nothing to see, and then there was nothing for her to do but return to the cabin and her sister's husband, the man she loved, whom she now despised.

They closed down the boat and drove back to the house in near silence, William behind the wheel of Anna's Toyota. In her lap, Anna held the crumpled announcement from the gallery. She tried to remember what Rose's prizewinning painting, *Ginger Lily*, looked like, but instead she saw her sister opening the sleek black envelope. Rose had returned to the *Ariel* in a rush to share her happiness.

A wave of nausea pulsed through Anna and she moaned a little, squirming under the seat belt. She wasn't used to being a passenger in her own car. But when they'd reached the lot, she had thrown William the keys.

Anna couldn't recall the painting. In truth, though she admired her sister's talent and dedication and almost always loved her work, she didn't know the names of any of her paintings. She hadn't realized they had names. *Oh God.*

William reached to cover her hand with his, and she let him, for a moment, before she drew it away and turned to open the window. She needed air. She felt stretched inside, like the thin, burst skin of a balloon. Everything that had been building in her these last weeks, the excitement and tenderness and joy, the sum of it had become its negative, the headiness of love now a solid black despair.

"It's awful," William said as he pulled the car to a stop along the curb outside the house. "It's horrible, but it will be all right." He sat there, the car running, as though he didn't know how to turn it off.

Anna looked at him, at the features she had long memorized, now strange. She didn't think she had ever seen such pain in his face. "Will it?" she asked. "How can it be?"

He dropped his head back onto the headrest, exposing his throat. Anna thought of guillotines.

"It's my fault," he said. And though his

words sounded trite, the wretchedness in his eyes was enough to make Anna bite back a nasty reply. She leaned forward, head against the dash. Maybe it would be all right, if Rose believed that nothing had really happened between them — and how could she not? It was, after all, the truth. Nothing could ever happen between them. Ever.

"Fuck," she whispered.

"Yeah," he said.

Then, infused with a kind of gallows giddiness, Anna imagined the scene they made to passersby, how they looked with their heads thrown melodramatically asunder. "Let's face the music," she said.

And in an apparently similar burlesque state of mind, William added, "And dance."

But Rose was anything but giddy when they found her seated in the living room with a cup of tea. She was coldly determined.

"Get out," she said to Anna. Then she turned to William. "Get your things and then you get out, too."

William held up his hand. "Look."

Rose spat her words at him. "I don't want to. I don't want to look or see or know or hear. I just want you gone." Her voice was tight and hard. The skin around her eyes had gone a pasty gray.

Anna grew unreasonably frightened. "Where's Miranda?" she asked.

"Fuck you," Rose replied. "My daughter is no longer any concern of yours."

Anna looked to William for help. He was tugging at his clipped beard, staring at the carpet. She turned back to Rose. "You can't say that."

Rose glared at Anna, her eyes burning the way their father's had, her mouth a sneer. "Yes, I can. Now leave me alone."

The blood in Anna's veins pummeled her ears. This couldn't be happening. How had they allowed this to happen, to change everything?

"Rose, this is ridiculous." William raked his hand through his hair. He shook his head. For the first time since Anna had known him, he apparently couldn't think of what to say.

Anna felt a wail rise in her chest. He was wrong. It wasn't ridiculous, it was horrible. They were horrible.

Rose placed her tea mug carefully on a magazine atop the coffee table. She stood, her forehead tilted down to emphasize the three inches she had over Anna in height. "Get out of my house." She gestured at

William without looking at him. "Take him. Go ahead."

William stepped forward. "For God's sake, let's talk this out like adults."

"Like adults?" Rose laughed in a high, false voice. "Like adulterers?"

"Stop it!" William banged his fist into the sofa and Rose jumped, sending tea flying from the mug.

Anna cried out, panicking. "Don't do this!" She lifted her hands to cover her face, sobbing into them. "Don't!" she cried. "I didn't do anything wrong!"

"Oh, please." The bile in Rose's voice was familiar. Anna recognized a tone from long ago.

"Grow up," Rose said, and then she left the room and went up the stairs.

Chapter 3

The earliest moments of waking are amnesic, so Rose felt a burdenless pleasure when the first rays of morning sun struck her face. Her limbs were warm and heavy with sleep, but her head, when she lifted it, pounded. Then she remembered.

William was gone. His foam pillow — he was allergic to down — lay plumped where his head had not lain. The sheets did not smell of him. His bulk did not fill the doorway to their bath. He was gone, and he would never again share her bed. She no longer had a husband. Oh God.

Oh God, oh God, how could he have done what he'd done?

A twist in her gut and a freeze-frame in her head, and Rose was peering through the *Ariel*'s port light again, staring at William's ear. Her eyes had focused on the folded curve of it. When Rose remembered this moment, she remembered first the whorled image of his ear. Then, even harder to bear, she recalled the slide of a teardrop, watching as it traced a thin silver line down Anna's cheek, like the slime of a snail.

Stop! She heaved herself onto her stomach, pressed her face into her pillow, and let the tears come. All the tears she had managed to hold back the night before now came boiling up from her center.

As though it would help, she clamped her hands flat against her ears. *Get out, get out, get out of my head,* she screamed inside, much the way she had finally had to scream out loud to get them to leave last night.

As soon as William and Anna had arrived, all sniveling and full of lies that Rose refused to hear, she had told them to leave. Rose had left them openmouthed in the living room, gone upstairs and shut herself in the room she used as her studio. She intended to wait out their departure in there. William would pack a few things, and he would leave — they would both leave. It couldn't take long. And whatever he left behind Rose could trash. She might slash his clothes, shatter his photographs, burn his books.

She had paced from her easel, past a stack of stretched canvases to the long pine table where she mixed her paints. She picked up brushes, rolls of paper towels, screwdrivers, all of which she threw across the room at the wall, one by one. *Get out!* She growled to the floor as though her words could penetrate through wood and plaster to shower those below with vitriol. She would never be able to bear the sight of either of them again, for as long as she lived. She kicked at a table leg; a jar of pencils and scissors fell over. She picked them up, briefly considering murder, if only for the base gratification of the idea.

Then she had lifted her long braid in one hand while the other reached around with the scissors and cut it off. She'd rushed through the hall, down the stairs, and into the living room where, unbelievably, William and Anna remained, talking quietly.

"Get the fuck out!" she had screamed and thrown the plaited hair at them, a weird sort of serpent — or spear.

Now Rose touched her fingertips to her neck where it lay bare. A hollow ache shot through her chest to her stomach, which cramped around it. My God, how she hurt. She understood how someone could die from heartbreak. Or get very ill. What if she couldn't get through this? She didn't see how she could manage the simplest tasks.

The bristly, uneven ends of her hair

caused Rose to sob. Bawling into her pillow, soaking it with tears and mucus, Rose cried because she had cut off her hair. She cried because she would never be the same without it.

Jai's family went to church, so on their way to services her dad dropped Miranda at her house. Miranda walked around to the back and took the key she kept beneath a flower pot by the back door. She liked to let herself in but she preferred not to carry a key. She imagined the house was hers and a handsome husband awaited her.

The kitchen was empty, and the house was quiet. At 11:00 on a Sunday morning, Miranda expected her father to be making pancakes, the one meal she could look forward to all week. He always threw in something different: chocolate chips, blueberries, pieces of apple, chopped nuts. Once he'd sprinkled in peanuts and she had nearly broken a tooth. Almost always her father's pancakes were delicious, and not knowing what kind they were going to be was fun.

But the air didn't smell like browning butter, there was no griddle soaking in the sink, no splatters on the stove. Nobody had eaten; maybe there was still hope for pancakes. Miranda dropped her canvas sail bag to the floor and walked into the hall.

She called up the stairs, "Hullo!" Her mom was probably still in bed or else in her stupid studio, but where was her dad? If not for the sharp May sun slicing through the front windows, a house this still might seem kind of spooky, especially after the slasher movies she and Jai had watched late into the night.

Miranda wished her family had a dog. She'd never cared about having one before, but lately she'd been worried about safety, probably because of all the crap on the news. Plus being alone in the house with her mom felt different than it had when she was little and they were rarely ever more than a room apart, if not in the same room. Miranda didn't want to hang out with her mother anymore, but even if she did, her mother was always painting in her studio. Miranda was aware of being physically alone.

From the window of her bedroom overlooking the street, Miranda had lately begun to notice people walking dogs, mostly suburban-mom types, but every once in a while a cute guy she had never seen before came by, usually with his dog off leash, running ahead of or beside him. If she had a dog, he'd rush to welcome her the moment she walked in. That would be nice, being greeted, and thinking of it brought Aunt Anna to mind. Where was she? It was a holiday and a Sunday. Normally she would have shown up by now, even if only to read the Sunday paper in their hammock.

Miranda called out once more. "Anybody home? Ma?"

From the second floor came the sound of footsteps and the creaking of a door. Her mother appeared at the top of the stairs, still wearing the T-shirt and shorts from the day before. She looked like a zombie. And — she had cut off her hair!

"Mom!" Miranda was scared. "What did you do?"

"It's all right." Her mother kept touching the back of her head as she descended toward Miranda. Her face sagged. "I'll go to the hairdresser on Tuesday and get it shaped. I just wanted it gone." Her eyes were swollen. She had been crying.

"Where's Daddy?"

Her mother stopped three steps above her. "He's not here."

Miranda stared. She didn't have to say anything. Her mother replied to the question in her eyes. "I have asked him to leave, and he has."

"What?" That wasn't the answer Miranda expected. She thought that her parents must have had a fight. They didn't argue often, though when they did it was usually bad. Once they had stayed angry for weeks. But her father, gone? Yesterday afternoon they were all out sailing, and this morning her parents had split up?

"Why?" Miranda asked. Her voice scratched. "You can't mean it."

Her mother ran her hand over her chopped hair. "I'm sorry," she said. Her voice sounded thick in her throat. "I just can't talk about it now."

She continued down the steps and Miranda moved aside, scowling, giving her mother a wide berth. "What did you do?" she called after her mother, who was heading toward the kitchen. And what she read in the droop of her mother's shoulders told her all she needed to know. "Why did you make Daddy go?"

Her mother turned at the entrance to the kitchen. Her face was in shadow, but Miranda could hear the tears in her voice. "We're separating. That's all I can tell you for the moment," she said. "That's all I know myself."

Chapter 4

Miranda stared at the sky; summer trees spread dark against light, green against blue. The combination was gorgeous in real life, in nature, but would be hideous, say, in an outfit.

She and Jai were lying on beach towels on the flat tar roof over the sunporch of Jai's house. Miranda wore a black bikini; Jai a cutoff boy's muscle shirt and rolled-down boxer shorts. Jai had a small, boyish chest and she was as unself-conscious as a boy. Miranda's own boobs weren't huge, but she was very aware of them, which felt nice sometimes but also weird.

"Where did you say your father was?" Jai sat up on her elbows, drinking a lemon diet Coke.

Miranda closed her eyes behind her sunglasses. "Sailing." She hadn't told Jai about her parents breaking up; she hadn't told anyone. They would get back together, so what was the point?

"Is college finished already?" Jai said. She made rude noises through her straw and laughed.

"Yeah," Miranda said. That wasn't a lie. College had ended the first week in May. Her father had been teaching summer session for weeks. But she didn't say that. A bird let out a long, warbling call, a shadow passed over her, and she saw through her closed eyelids the sun slip behind a cloud. She sat up.

She screwed her eyes at her arm, turning it, comparing the white underskin to the rosy forearm. "Did I get any color?"

Jai tugged at a coppery corkscrew of hair. She was always doing that, playing with her curls. She pressed her arm against Miranda's. "Yeah. I think so." Her own skin was golden brown from mornings spent in tennis camp.

"I can't stand being home alone with my mom," Miranda said.

"She bitched out because your dad went off sailing without her?"

"Yeah." Miranda considered telling Jai part of the truth. She knew Jai wouldn't tell anyone — she wasn't interested enough in such things to repeat them. But she couldn't bring herself to say the word her mother had dared to suggest might happen: *divorce*.

"But your mom doesn't really like to sail,

38

does she?" Jai slid into an REI T-shirt.

Miranda reached for her Shakespeare Festival T-shirt. With the sun gone, the air was chilly. "Not really," she said. "She doesn't like anything anymore except her stupid painting."

"Like my mom and tennis," Jai said. "I can't wait to get away from my family when I go to Outward Bound."

"Yeah, that should be a great time," Miranda said. Though she couldn't imagine what would be great about doing something so hard and dangerous and, let's face it, pointless, she knew mountain climbing was great to Jai. "When do you leave?"

"A week from tomorrow."

Miranda pulled her T-shirt over her bent knees, down to the tops of her ankles. "Damn," she said.

In April, she and her boyfriend, Jimmy, had broken up. His parents had sent him to another school, a private school for kids with learning disabilities, and after a few weeks, Miranda felt him drift from her. She missed him more than he missed her. When he stopped calling and hardly ever e-mailed, she had to face the fact that he just didn't care.

And then, out of the blue, she had come

home from Jai's one morning and found her father gone and her mother all weird. Miranda could remember her shock as though it had just happened, though a couple weeks had passed. Her mother wasn't the type to make those kinds of jokes, but Miranda had been certain she must be kidding.

She hadn't been. And she hadn't really ever explained why. One minute their family had been sailing, just like usual, boring but everyone getting along, and then, *wham!* Something had happened. Something her mother wouldn't say. Her father had a girlfriend was the obvious answer, but Miranda knew, she just knew, that he didn't. If he did, wouldn't there have been some sign? Wouldn't he go out nights or weekends? But he never did that. He was always home. Until now.

What more could go wrong in her life?

"Oh God," she said aloud.

"What?" Jai was rubbing coconut lotion into the heels of her feet.

Miranda clutched the hem of her shirt and rocked. Maybe her parents had had a fight over her. About her spending the night at Jai's? About her not helping out around the house when her mother bugged her? They'd had some of their worst fights about her, actually. She'd hated it. She would crawl under the blankets on her bed and cover her ears with her hands so she couldn't hear. But she did hear; her father's booming voice made her stomach drop.

"Nothing," she said. "I was just thinking how my mom has been hassling me to clean my room."

"Tell me about it," Jai said. She reached over her knees and grabbed her ankles, stretching, head to one side.

Miranda felt tears begin to build in the backs of her eyes. "I feel like a cigarette," she said.

"Don't!" Jai was an athlete. Miranda hung out with the yearbook crowd. They had little in common, outwardly, and other girls at school were amazed at their closeness. They had been friends since fifth grade.

"Don't worry," Miranda said. "It's a figure of speech." What she'd said had *not* been a figure of speech, but she knew Jai wouldn't care what excuse she gave.

Miranda wouldn't really smoke again. She had tried smoking, first one cigarette, then another a few weeks later, then another the next Saturday. Then she bought a pack. But her entire smoking career had lasted less than two months.

Jai stood up, stretching toward the sky where the sun shone around the edges of a cloud. "Let's make popcorn," she said.

Miranda followed Jai to the open window that led into her bedroom and climbed in after her.

Rose was meeting Luis in the linen department at Bloomingdale's. He had a full day of meetings and depositions, and he needed to spend his lunch hour buying towels for a birthday gift. But he wanted to talk to Rose about something, quickly. Could she meet him?

Yes, she would meet him at Bloomingdale's. She knew she needed to get out. She couldn't grieve forever, if only for Miranda's sake. She had to keep herself together. But she hadn't yet been able to paint again.

She strolled the aisles, stopping at the Ralph Lauren section. His summer line featured a light blue chambray bordered by ecru lace and coordinated with a muted red ticking stripe. Rose ran her hand along the folds of a pillowcase, touching the fabric. She took the folded edge between her thumb and forefinger and rubbed. Good cotton threads rubbing against themselves made a comforting sweetness.

"Rose." Luis appeared, carrying a Big Brown Bag. "How are you?"

"I'm okay," she said as they embraced. "Have you already done your shopping?"

Luis set his bag atop a patchwork coverlet. "Yes. Look what I've got him." He flashed her a rolled-eye glance. "Ivan. Yes, a new friend. He's redoing his bath."

Luis parted thick tissue paper to reveal a stack of fluffy, tweedy, expensive-looking bath towels.

"Lovely," Rose said.

"I can buy you a latte," Luis offered, folding tissue paper back over his purchase. He looked at his watch. Patek. "Or we can wander around here and chat."

"Let's do that," Rose said. She started toward the escalator. "Cosmetics?"

"Lead the way." Luis dipped his long torso slightly. His blue-black crow's hair fell across his eyebrow.

He looked more actor than lawyer, a Latino leading man of a certain age. His eyes appeared to be rimmed with eyeliner, though Rose knew he didn't wear it. His mouth, his own favorite feature since a date had told him he had "the lips of a hustler," was shapely and soft looking. He was quite a specimen — and naturally, heartbreakingly gay.

They had met in college, stayed in touch through the years. Luis had represented Rose when she'd sold her mother's house, he had executed her mother's will, and he would represent her in her divorce, should she decide on one. He was the only friend or acquaintance she had told about her split from William thus far. She simply couldn't face talking about it. How could she tell anyone the truth? And lying would take more effort than she could spare.

They rode the escalator, Rose watching Luis in the mirrors they passed. She stroked the lapel of his black silk suit jacket. His shirt was black, too. "Nice," she said.

"Thanks. Listen, sweetie." Luis patted her hand on the black rubber rail. His fingernails were in far better shape than her own. "I've been thinking, why don't you take Miranda and stay at my place on Shelter Island for the summer?"

Rose looked at him.

"Seriously. I'm not going to be able to use it, at all." He frowned at her, pursed his lips. "Ok, I don't *want* to use it. Too many memories of David." They stepped off the escalator onto the second floor.

Rose searched Luis's face for a sign he

was joking. She couldn't possibly accept his offer of his summer house. It was out of the question. She needed to concentrate on painting. She had a show to prepare for. Miranda wouldn't want to leave her friends, though her best friend would be gone for most of the summer.

Rose headed toward the Estée Lauder counter, hoping they'd be having a promotion. She had a collection of makeup cases of all shapes and designs, all freebies. She used them to hold small paint brushes and other supplies.

"I want to stay in town this summer because of Ivan, in case you haven't guessed." Luis shook the Bloomies bag. "I hope to put these to good use."

Rose laughed, glad Luis felt free to be himself.

They stopped in front of lipsticks. Rose selected Earth Red and tried it on the back of her hand.

"The thing is," she said, replacing the sample in the display, "I haven't been able to paint lately."

"It's too soon." He checked himself in the mirror, slipping back to lawyer mode. "And you need to get away from the scene of the crime."

"Away from that boat? I haven't gone

near it." Rose swiped a band of Plum Perfect at the base of her thumb.

"Not just the boat. The house. The bed." Luis paused, and Rose steeled herself for him to say, *Your sister*. But he didn't. He said, "I like that color."

"I don't know," Rose said. She meant about the lipstick. She also meant about leaving the house, her fortress. She had banished William from it, so it was the one place she felt safe from running into him. Of course, it was half his house.

"Take your time," Luis said. "Sleep on it. Think it over. But my house is yours, if you want it."

"Are you sure?" she asked.

"Quite sure. Really, you'll do me a favor to air it out and run water through the pipes."

"Okay," Rose said. "Thanks. I'll think about it." She didn't suppose she would take him up on it, but she knew better than to reject an offer out of hand. Especially in her current state of mind.

They kissed cheeks, and Luis promised to phone Rose in a couple of days. Then he dashed off.

Rose meandered away from cosmetics toward the fine jewelry counters. She looked down at the hammered gold wedding band she still wore. She had stopped wearing her diamond because she didn't like to take it on and off to paint. Perhaps she should buy herself a ring. Something stylish or unusual. Or a bracelet. She knew she shouldn't spend the money, but she was so angry at William; she deserved an indulgence. She stopped at the case containing pearls, June's birthstone.

Black pearls had been in vogue for a few years now. Rose caught sight of a pair of plain, single pearl earrings — but what singles. Black pearls as big as small grapes. Or a bird's eggs. Or eyes.

William's dark eyes. His eyes following Anna as she walked out their front door, instructed never to return. That anguish in her husband's eyes hurt Rose more than anything he said.

She turned away from the jewels and left the store.

Chapter 5

He had e-mailed her:

Dearest Anna,
I wouldn't hurt you for the world. Or Rose or Miranda. And yet I have, and I don't know how to begin to apologize.
Will you consent to speak to me, in person, ideally, but on the phone if that's what you want?

W

She hit Reply and typed an answer: *Yes, of course. I accept my portion of the blame.* Then she deleted the words and typed again: *No, I don't see what good it would do.* She deleted those words, too.

Now she stared at the screen, at his name, at his .edu e-mail address. Her office on the second floor of the Nature Center's administrative facility was a windowless cubby directly over the gift shop. She longed for air.

She had not spoken to William since that horrible night. But she had replayed and replayed the last message he had left on her voice mail, confirming the time to meet at the marina for their holiday sail. She waited each day until she absolutely needed to hear his voice, most often in the late afternoon, then she'd listen to the saved message and try once more to determine from the sound of his syllables whether he loved her.

If he didn't, there was no point in ever speaking to him again. He had cost her her sister. If he did . . . what would she do? What could she do?

Anna shook her head. She was deceiving herself. She had cost herself her sister; she couldn't blame William. After all, Rose was her blood.

She did want to see him. Should she answer him, agreeing to meet? She had loved him for years, though she hadn't allowed herself to know it. Perhaps he had loved her all this time as well? She remembered a Bible story from grade school, the story of Jacob, who loved Rachel but was forced — tricked, if she recalled correctly — into marrying Leah, the older sister. William hadn't been forced or tricked to marry Rose, of course, unless he had tricked himself. Maybe he had.

Anna dropped her head into her hands,

as if in prayer. She must stop this romantic fantasy. She must stop thinking of William as her lover. *He was her sister's husband.* He would always be her sister's husband. They had kissed, yes, and they had been caught, but surely that wasn't enough to wreck a marriage. Maybe he and Rose were in counseling.

She deleted William's e-mail.

She needed to talk to Rose. If only Rose would let her.

But she needed William, too.

Theo, the staff botanist, knocked at the open door to Anna's office. He stuck his blond head into the room. He was pudgy and wore glasses and reminded Anna of a cherub.

"Need you at the learning center," he said.

"Okay." Anna clicked off her e-mail program. She rose from her desk and walked numbly to the stairs.

Comparative Mythology had fit Anna's schedule — she'd needed a class to fill the Tuesday-Thursday slot at four o'clock, and ballet, her first choice, was closed. The instructor, Professor Campbell, new to the English department, wouldn't have taught Rose, who was five years older and had graduated with honors in Art History, nor necessarily known that Anna was the daughter of Pauline, secretary to the university president. All good. Anna preferred anonymity.

She took her seat in the back of Campbell's classroom expecting little more than to achieve her B and her three credits. Another class closer to graduation and the day when, armed with a liberal arts degree and a few saved dollars from her job at the Nature Center, she could begin a life.

Anna wanted to travel. As a girl she had sent away for free brochures from the backs of magazines, and her adolescent intention had been to leave home immediately after high school. She daydreamed Rose would journey with her, and together they'd escape the walls that seemed to press the air out of their lives. The plan sustained Anna through times she would no longer allow herself to recall.

When, unexpectedly, their father died, dropped to the street as he hailed a taxi in midtown Manhattan, Anna changed her plans. She shouldn't give up a chance for a near-free college education. Rose had availed herself of the tuition remission their mother was eligible for; why shouldn't Anna? Her reasons for leaving seemed less urgent with *him* gone. She decided to stay on at home four years more.

Though she had had but a few dates in high school, Anna dated regularly in college, one guy at a time, each for a few months at a time. Sometimes the relationships ended painfully, but often they just seemed to fade. Instead of girlfriends, Anna had ex-boyfriends to do things with. And she had Rose.

That suited Anna. Unlike most girls, she didn't dream of emerald-cut engagement rings (like the one Rose eventually wore) or lace veils (which Rose didn't). She dreamed instead of architecture as ancient as history, of favorite flowers thriving in unlikely climates, of birds with calls she didn't recognize. She yearned for strange hills, for unfamiliar scents, for tides in other hemispheres. She imagined the postcards she would send to her old boyfriends, tinted photographs from places with names such as Cephalonia or Micronesia. She dreamed of leaving everyone but Rose behind.

She sneezed the moment she walked into Campbell's classroom. "Gesundheit," he said as she passed. Later he would remind her that his first uttered words to her had been a blessing.

Even at the second class meeting, Anna's attention was only half on Campbell's lecture. The other half was on the new position she'd been offered at the Nature Center, overseeing the wildlife rehabilitation clinic on weekends, when they were busiest, and whatever hours she could manage during the week.

When the third class session came around, however, Anna had mustered sufficient attention to be irked by Campbell.

He was a brute, she decided, partly because of how he looked — rather like a bear — and partly because he gave no lip service whatsoever to prevailing feminist theory. He spoke of the mythology of love as a transcendental, selfless experience of "oneness." To Anna this sounded a lot like the female being subsumed.

After the Romantics, hadn't the *individual* begun to count? Hadn't contemporary thinkers given up the idea that one had to lose oneself in order to love?

She raised her hand. "Doesn't one have to put oneself first, in order to survive? Doesn't selflessness lead to self-annihilation?"

Campbell stepped toward her row of desks and lowered himself to the edge of one, as though prepared to spend time discussing this. She'd meant her question rhetorically.

"Does it?" he asked. He crossed his leg so that his jeans hiked up his ankle. It was late September, and he still wasn't wearing socks with his deck shoes. That, too, annoyed her. "Explain," he coaxed, gesturing with an open hand.

His palms were rough, blistered. Maybe he was a fisherman on the weekends. "You cite the Persian representation of Satan," she answered, not sure whether he was baiting her. She met his dark eyes but saw only a hint of irony. "How he loved God so much, he couldn't serve man."

Campbell smiled at her. She felt her face flush, aware she was acting the sycophant, parroting back his words. And he was arrogant enough to enjoy it. Well, she would make her point. "That just proves he sees himself as separate, doesn't it? If he can distinguish between his love for God and God's love for man?"

"In point of fact," Campbell said, "his refusal to be one with God's will *guaranteed* his eternal separation from his love object — thus, Hell."

"I thought," Anna struck back, "Satan's downfall was his *pride*."

He punctuated the air with a finger —

and Anna was glad, though she had no idea what he meant by it — and strode back to his desk. There he read aloud a passage from *The Golden Bough*, one of their texts, leading the discussion toward concepts of Heaven.

The following week, Campbell announced that because their group was small and the hour was late, he would hold their class in one of the far tables of the campus dining hall. He, for one, could use coffee and a pastry around that time. The class happily adapted to the new location, which helped forge a quick intimacy among them. Invariably, those who had no next class or job or family expecting them stayed, talking. As the weeks passed, Campbell often stayed with them.

One evening Anna found herself the sole lingerer, alone with Campbell, who began to question her about her life. What was her major, what were her goals, what was her passion? Though her irritation with him had by this point all but disappeared, replaced by a kind of awe for his intellectual enthusiasm, Anna didn't want to discuss her future with Campbell. To divert him, she brought up Rose.

"My older sister is an artist," she said, trying to decide whether ordering another cup of coffee would seem pushy. "A painter."

"Is she any good?" Campbell's blunt question, delivered in a low and gentle voice, sent a small thrill through Anna, like a warning.

She answered honestly. "I like what she paints."

Campbell asked about Rose's work. He was in need of art for the walls of his house, he said, though he couldn't afford to spend much. Anna found herself giving him the address of the gallery where Rose worked. She never expected he would follow through and ask her to take him there.

Later she learned William Campbell was a man who followed through in almost everything.

Chapter 6

It was Bloomsday, June 16, and William's afternoon class, which was reading Dante, had suggested commemorating the occasion with a pub crawl through downtown New Haven. He had laughed and distributed the quiz they'd hoped to avoid, but for a moment he'd been tempted. Back during his own college days, drinking with one's professors was a common if not necessarily flaunted rite of academic passage. But the drinking age was older now, and, correspondingly, the students seemed somehow younger than he remembered himself at eighteen.

His office on the second floor of the Humanities building looked directly over the main quad, where bare-legged coeds and shirtless young men gamboled and languished in the clear summer light. He watched, envying them their boldness, their tirelessness, their endearing ineptitude as they tossed Frisbees to one another across the lawn. Were the girls getting ever more beautiful, as they seemed to William, or was this perception just another sign of encroaching age?

"Starbucks?" Rupert Jones, William's best friend and office mate, stuck his shining bald pate through the open office door. Rupert refused to drink the muddy coffee that Sheila, their department secretary, made. He made runs to the new, on-campus coffee kiosk several times a day.

"No, thanks." William did drink Sheila's coffee. A cold quarter mug of it sat beneath his lamp. He gestured at an open folder of papers. "I want to finish grading these." First he'd have to force himself to start.

Rupert's long, thin hands gripped either side of the door frame. "See you at the faculty senate meeting, then."

William groaned. "Shit. That's today."

"Or not," Rupert said. "If you don't show, I'll say you took ill and see you back at the house." William had been staying with Rupert since Memorial Day weekend.

"Thank you." William lifted an exam. "I'm really swamped."

"No problem. Sure you don't want a break?"

William shook his head, waved his friend away, and returned to staring out the window. A lithe blonde caught his eye. She was dressed in a long, flimsy peasant skirt, her shoes were off, and something in the way she ran reminded him of Anna.

He saw her clearly in his mind, Anna as she had been nearly twenty years ago, as his student, and he felt the sickness in his gut that was longing and guilt and confusion. He couldn't look away.

The girl fetched the Frisbee from the grass — she had yet to catch it — and let it fly, a toss clearly intended to move the disc forward but resulting in its sailing backward over her head. She flailed her arms in animated despair, and William laughed to himself. Anna was awkward like that. Awkward and graceful at the same time.

"Christ," he muttered.

"Contemplating the aesthetics of the female form?" It was Rupert, returned.

"Can't a scholar conduct his research in peace?" William tried for the proper note of mock misery. Not even Rupert knew the true nature of his grief.

"I just remembered I won't be going home after the meeting. I've scheduled a senior thesis tutorial. You have your key?"

"I do," William said, touching his pocket. "Which senior?"

Rupert winked. "I'll tell you later. In case Katrin calls. This way you don't know." Rupert's wife, who taught in the sociology department, and to whom he was so devoted he felt compelled to make jokes about other women, had taken off at the end of May for a month of research in New Mexico. Rupert thus was happy for William's company.

Though he knew he would have been welcome in the Jones house even with Katrin at home, William was grateful for her absence, relieved to avoid the chastising, you-bad-boy looks he knew were inevitable. He deserved the looks — he deserved worse — but he'd have been hard-pressed to put up with the affectionate kindness Katrin would have heaped upon him. For despite his guilt, his shame, his sorrow, and all the piercing nuances of his regret, he ached to see Anna. And he knew he deserved no mercy.

He hadn't spoken to her since that night. The more time he allowed to elapse, of course, the less likely it was she would speak to him at all. But, though he had sent her a few brief, self-flagellating e-mails, he couldn't bring himself to phone. He hoped she would answer his e-mails, knowing she would not. His misery compounded.

At a shout from outside, William lifted his eyes to the window. Against a carpet of early-summer green, a young man and woman played keep-away with a Frisbee. They were probably cutting class. *Good for you,* he told them silently. *Gather ye Frisbees while ye may.*

Anna wanted a Frisbee dog. William winced as he recalled how she had been saving up to join William and his family on a trip to Scotland at the end of summer, intending to find herself a Border collie puppy. Now, obviously, that trip was out of the question. William wondered whether Anna would get a puppy anyway. Perhaps he could phone her to offer his assistance. It was his fault the trip had not worked out. His fault for ruining his marriage. His fault for kissing her. His fault he couldn't regret doing so, even now. Even though he was trying to save his marriage — for Miranda's sake, if nothing else.

So far, Rose had rejected every offer William made: to talk things through, over dinner or the setting of her choice; to seek counseling, jointly or separately, as she preferred. "I'm not ready to talk to you," she said the last time he had phoned her. Whereas he felt the opposite; he was eager to set everything right again, if only there were some way he could.

William understood Rose's anger, but he

didn't understand what she wanted. Did she want to save their marriage; did she not? And what did it mean that for the life of him, he couldn't tell? To think he had lived with this woman, this generally lovely woman, for more than seventeen years and yet he could not read her — what did that suggest?

Of course, William didn't understand what he himself wanted, but his desires mattered least of all. He would do what was best, what was right. And that, he supposed, meant waiting for Rose to decide, for however long she needed to take.

He scowled. He loved Rose, of course he did, but it was Anna he missed, damn it, and it just got worse. He hadn't grown used to being without her as conventional wisdom suggested he would. Every day he missed the sight of her, her awkward smile. He had taken her presence in his life for granted, but it hadn't been his to assume.

Mostly, William missed talking to her. He missed her laugh, the throaty wonder in her voice, the suggestion that anything was possible. He stared out the window, remembering.

The phone on his desk rang sharply. Damn thing, he hated it; there was no way to adjust the volume. He took a breath to clear his head, coughed to clear his throat. The phone rang again as he reached to pick it up. "Campbell."

"Professor William Campbell?" He heard a chipper male voice with a broad brogue on the other end.

"Yes." The rolling lawn outside his window were Scottish moors. "This is he."

"Professor Kenny Mac Bride here, from St. Mary's College."

William's heart hammered his chest. He had dismissed the idea of Scotland because of what had happened. Somehow, he hadn't expected to get the position now.

"Congratulations!" Mac Bride was pleased to offer Professor Campbell a one-year post as a visiting professor at the Institute for Theology, Imagination and the Arts at the University of St. Andrews, Scotland. Would he be accepting the position?

Mac Bride waited on his side of the Atlantic, *across the pond*. His heavy breathing — William thought he must be a big man — sounded so close he might be in the room.

"Thank you," William said. It struck him to accept this opportunity as his fate. If Rose would have him back, she could join him in Scotland, for a new start. If not, she would be better off with him gone. Both Rose and Anna would be better without him.

Mac Bride described William's post in enthusiastic detail, but William lost a part of what he said to the brogue and another to the haunting question of Miranda. What would be the best thing for her?

Chapter 7

If Miranda was upset to hear William's news, she didn't show it. She lifted her Coke to him and toasted. "Cheers!"

They were at Cato's, their favorite pizza place. William had already eaten four slices.

He felt a certain trepidation — or maybe it was his stomach acting up. This was his first weekend alone with his daughter since the night Rose had thrown him out. Though Miranda seemed in good enough spirits, he couldn't be sure what she knew about the split, nor what Rose had told her. Not much, Rose had said, not many details, just that they were separated. Not that *he* deserved protection, Rose had assured him; she was thinking of their daughter.

He believed her. And he was grateful.

"Can I still go?" Miranda asked. She had asked for pineapple topping on her pizza, which she was now picking off and arranging in a pile on her plate.

William gulped beer from a plastic cup.

"Well . . ." How could he refuse her the trip he had promised?

"She'll be sorry," Miranda said.

"Who?" William pinched up a mouthful of warm pineapple. Talking with their mouths full was something the two of them did whenever Rose wasn't around.

"Mom," Miranda said. She separated the pineapple pieces and stood them on their sides, a soggy Stonehenge.

"She can still go to Scotland, if she likes," he said, but he knew Rose wouldn't. She had been furious, at first, to hear he'd accepted the post in Scotland. No, she would not consider going with him. All else not withstanding, she had an art show coming up in October — or didn't her life count for anything? If he wanted to go to Scotland, he should go.

Miranda rolled her eyes. "You know what I mean. Sorry for dumping you!"

Wasn't that just like a female. Stroking his ego and making him feel terrible at the same time. William surprised himself with an urge to insist Rose hadn't actually dumped him. He placed a narrow piece of pineapple atop two standing ones to form a lintel. Immediately, Miranda flicked it over with a fingernail and laughed.

He wanted another beer, but he would

wait. Miranda would be learning to drive soon; William didn't want to set a bad example. Instead, he allowed himself the pleasure of saying Anna's name aloud. "Have you seen your aunt Anna recently?"

Miranda took a large bite of a stripped-down pizza slice, mostly dough. "Uh-uh." She swallowed, shaking her hair away from her face. "I think Mom's mad at her, too. She's gone off the deep end."

"Anna?" Acid singed a hole in William's stomach. He patted his pockets for his Tagamet.

"No. *Mom*." Miranda made a face. "I told you, I haven't seen Aunt Anna."

William reached for her Coke. "May I?"

"Go ahead," Miranda said. "You get free refills."

William's throat felt thick. He drained the Coke and then signaled to the nose-ringed waitress for another. The place was filled with locals, youth sports teams and their parents, teenagers on dates. William saw himself as an intruder, a stranger in his own town. He didn't know the community the way Rose did, had never cared to. She raised Miranda and kept house while he went off to college every day. His world was the campus.

The campus and the sea. The *Ariel*. With

Anna as first mate. He'd come to take that world for granted, and now he had destroyed it. Would his daughter lose all respect for him if she knew the truth? When she knew.

Miranda pushed her plate away, her sign for being done with her meal, unchanged since her babyhood. Remarkable, really.

William sprinkled red pepper on a piece of crust. "Has your mother been painting?"

"I don't know," Miranda said. "I just want to get away from her!"

William didn't think Rose deserved that, and he was pained. "Surely you don't mean that." It was his fault, this deepened rift between mother and daughter, and that knowledge only added to his burden of guilt. He bit the crust in half.

Miranda looked at him sideways. Where had she learned that? "Well, can I still go to Scotland with you?"

"I'd love you to," he answered quickly, swallowing, then added, "providing your mother doesn't object."

Pensive, Miranda cut the pineapple into tiny pieces with the edge of her fork. The waitress delivered her Coke.

"Thanks," Miranda said without looking up. Was she addressing him or the waitress?

William's jaw ached, and he became aware that he was clenching his muscles. He focused on relaxing, rubbed his beard with his hand, stroked his neck beneath his chin. He envisaged wind and waves.

"You must be glad school is over?" He spoke the words as a question, the way Miranda often did.

She shrugged. "I guess."

William picked up the last slice and began gnawing. Miranda's mood had turned prickly, and he steeled himself against it. "How's your friend Jai?" he asked, reaching for a subject she would like. "What are her summer plans?"

Miranda pressed the pineapple flat against her paper plate. "Visiting her grandparents, then climbing Mount Something-or-Other with Outward Bound, then doing some other wilderness camp."

"Impressive," William said. "Would you have wanted to do something like that?"

Miranda sighed, annoyed. "I wasn't going to *do* a camp this summer, remember, because we were going to Scotland for our family trip if you got the job?"

"Right." He reached once more for her Coke.

Miranda gathered her hair into a ponytail on top of her head, and William saw the toddler Miranda, whose hair Rose had often fixed that way. Pebbles, they'd called her for a while, after the *Flintstones* cartoon baby. He had loved coming home to her cookie-breath kisses. To Rose's stories of their day together. And, more often than not, to Anna in his kitchen, helping out.

"Mom is so selfish," Miranda said, and she let her hair spill down across her shoulders. "Why does she have to separate? You don't want to, do you?"

William took a third of the slice in one bite and swallowed by way of an ambiguous answer. What did he want? "I don't know whether we'll get back together," he said, reaching for her hand across the table. "I'm sorry."

Miranda's eyes filled; the tip of her nose turned pink.

"You come first, you know," he said. "Always. To us both." How on earth could he have risked losing her?

She stood, sniffing. "I'll be right back," she said and headed toward the unisex bathroom.

William knew exactly how he'd kept Miranda so far, and the knowledge burned in his gut like too much red pepper: His daughter had no idea of what he was capable, nor any inkling of what he had done.

And therein lay his dilemma, classical in its symmetry: For Miranda to forgive him, she first had to know him; but for her to know him, she must despise him.

The waitress with the nose ring caught his eye and smiled, and he nodded, gesturing toward his empty beer glass.

Chapter 8

The Greenport ferry blasted its horn, swung out of the dock, and plunged into mist. Bargelike, with a small, central pilot's compartment and identical car ramps at either end, the vessel was entirely symmetrical. It looked the same whether coming or going — which was, of course, a matter of perspective.

The ferry engine's deep hum vibrated through the wooden deck and the metal frame of Rose's Jeep as though to shake her, to say, *You're almost there.* No denying it now, she was leaving what had been her life and going toward — what?

She didn't know. Toward painting again some day, she hoped. Toward trying to get along with her daughter. Rose knew Miranda blamed her for the separation, but there wasn't anything she could — or was willing to — say to convince her daughter otherwise. She wouldn't lie; she couldn't tell the truth.

Besides, Rose was still furious with William, and she couldn't hide it. Miranda felt sorry for her father. So be it. Nothing Rose could do about that. Their father-daughter relationship had always been strong, and Rose had cherished it. William had been in many ways the opposite of her own father. He had been their safe haven.

Something tugged in the pit of her stomach. What good did all this ruminating do? She must get on with her life.

The sunny June morning that had greeted her in Connecticut had grown into an increasingly gray afternoon on the eastern shores of Long Island. Miranda was stretched out dourly in the backseat, refusing to ride up front with Rose. Now she yawned. "How much longer?"

Out of habit, Rose glanced down at the directions she'd handwritten on the legal pad beside her. She hadn't really needed them, and she certainly didn't need to read them to know that, once on the island, she could get almost anywhere in less than thirty minutes. "We're almost there."

"I'm getting out," Miranda said. "Other people are." She opened her car door slowly, careful of the Lexus SUV beside them. She was always considerate of other people's things. Rose supposed she should be grateful for that. She *was* grateful for that, and for so much else.

So why must it be so difficult between them?

Rose watched Miranda wind through the rows of cars, heading toward the railing. Miranda stood, looking out into the mist, deliberately separate from the family of four that had gathered a few feet to her right. She looked like a wraith, with her long pale hair and loose, white cotton minidress. She looked so alone. Anger simmered in Rose's chest. It was William's fault their daughter wasn't at camp or at home this summer, William's fault Rose was unable to paint. He wasn't like her father, indeed, not nearly so blatant in his aggression. His blows were the invisible sort that would take much longer to heal.

A tap at the window startled Rose. She lowered the glass, and a blast of wet air greeted her, only half unwelcome. She needed to snap out of this ill temper.

"Hello." A bored monotone accompanied the chapped hands that held a stack of colored tickets at Rose's eye level. "Coming back today?"

Rose had to think for a second. "No." Her throat tightened as though she were telling a lie about herself, but she was staying on the island — the Rock, as she had been told the islanders called it. She *was* doing this. The entire rear of the Jeep was filled with her and Miranda's clothes, their computer, her art supplies.

The hands pulled a white ticket and punched a hole through the date. "One way. Three fifty. And turn off your engine."

Rose paid the fare, and the fare collector disappeared. She looked up through the windshield at Miranda. A tall, African-American woman stood next to her, a gray parrot perched on her shoulder. Rose got out of the Jeep and slowly made her way across the rocking deck.

"So, can he talk?" Miranda was asking the woman as Rose reached them. "Would he talk to me?" Her eyes cast her mother a look of antipathy so brief Rose wanted to see it again, to be sure. She knew Miranda thought she was following her and hated it, but her words were polite.

"Dr. Duval, this is my mother."

Dr. Duval turned toward Rose. Her skin was the color of cinnamon, her thick, plaited hair a few shades darker. "Hello, Miranda's mother," she said. Her eyes, crinkling with humor, were a startling turquoise.

"Rose Campbell." She shook a warm and muscular hand.

"Dr. Duval is a vet," Miranda said,

75

clearly wanting to get the introductions over with, perhaps hoping her mother would go away. Rose smiled, fighting the tightening knot in her stomach.

"Daphne," Dr. Duval said. "Please. And this is Simon." She nodded at the parrot.

"Hello, Simon." He cocked his head, looked Rose in the eyes, and shifted from one foot to the other. The feathers beneath his tail were a bright, surprising red.

She crooked a finger at him, a bird wave. "Simon is a parrot?"

"Yes," Daphne Duval said. "He's an African grey who belonged to a man I knew, a client who died."

The ferry pitched, and Rose reached for the railing behind Miranda, grasping it. "I'm sorry," she said.

Daphne nodded. "Thanks. It's my honor to have inherited Simon. I'm working with him on vocalizations."

"That's so cool," Miranda said.

Daphne grinned. "It sure is. Moving house may cause a minor setback in our progress, but" — she shrugged — "that's cool, too." Her long silver earrings moved against her neck. "We're in it for the long haul, we two." Simon walked around her neck to her other shoulder. He was tethered to her wrist by a thin leather strap, and Daphne lifted it over her head, then kissed the bird's beak. Rose liked her.

The ferry pierced through the cloud that hung over the middle of the harbor, and they were enveloped in the mist. "Wow," Miranda said. "How can the captain see?"

The horn blasted.

The family across from them grew agitated. Other passengers began moving back to their cars. In the distance, the light and dark shapes of the opposite shore began to emerge, a developing photograph.

"Do you live on Shelter Island?" Daphne asked.

"We'll be there for the summer," Rose said. "Staying at the house of a friend."

Miranda stared straight ahead, frowning. "God knows why," she said.

Rose turned her face to keep from responding. She pulled her lip between her teeth and bit it.

"Same here," Daphne said. "I'm on the island for the summer, covering a friend's veterinary practice while he's away on a sailing trip to the Caribbean."

Rose felt her stomach sway. For all she knew, William was off on a sailing trip, enjoying himself. Truly, his mistress was that boat. Though he hated when she said such trite things, he loved what he called the "tradition" of the sea-as-mistress. He even liked tacky pop songs, if they had to do with sailing.

"What brings you here?" Daphne asked. "I mean, besides your friend's house." Simon nibbled at the leather strap.

Rose liked the question. "I'm an artist."

Daphne scratched Simon's head. "So you're here for the light."

Rose laughed a little. "Among other things."

Miranda, looking mortified, began to edge away. She had proclaimed recently that anyone who called herself an artist was pretentious. Only other people could make such judgments.

The ferry blasted its horn again, and the dock loomed into view.

"Time to go back," Daphne said. She pointed toward a white van with green lettering on the side: DOCTOR DAPHNE DUVAL, MOBILE VET, WADING RIVER, NY. "Nice to have met you both."

Miranda hurried toward the Jeep.

Neither Daphne nor Rose moved. Instead, they remained at the railing, watching the sun melt like apricot butter. The ferry horn sounded once more as they approached the dock, where a pair of swans paddled anxiously by. Then the

78

broad hull hit a line of rubber tires hung from pilings on the leeward side, the ferry man motioned them back to their cars, and the women went their separate ways.

"Here we are," her mother said.

Miranda felt the car slow down and she opened her eyes. Her mother was turning left past a mailbox marked NAUFRAGIO, a weird last name Miranda knew was Luis's but wouldn't have guessed was Spanish. They drove up a narrow, gravel road through a thick stand of trees that opened onto a circular drive in front of a modest blue cottage. So this was it. Miranda had never been here before, though her parents had.

The house wasn't what she expected, and she wasn't sure whether to be disappointed or glad. Small and ordinary, it looked nothing like the big, cedar-shingled faux-Victorians they had just driven past.

Miranda liked the word *faux*. She especially liked when she thought of ways to use it, as she had this morning while packing the car. "No, I'm *not* looking forward to this faux-vacation," she'd said to her mother. Well, her mother had asked for it.

Now they pulled up outside a weathered

gray front door. "We're here," her mother said, and Miranda answered, "Duh."

"Well, what do you think?"

"What do I think about what?" Miranda unlocked her door and opened it. She sat there, smelling the air.

Her mother removed her keys from the ignition and dropped them into the cup holder between the seats. "Shelter Island," she said, opening her door. "Isn't it pretty?"

"I guess," Miranda said. "So's Hawaii."

When her mother told her they were going to spend the summer at her lawyer's beach house, Miranda had immediately objected. "What for?" she'd asked.

Her mother had gotten all righteous. "Because we've been offered the opportunity to spend the entire summer at the beach."

Miranda reminded her they had beaches in Connecticut, and her mother replied by saying she thought they could both use some time away.

"You mean *you* could," Miranda said.

Her mother hadn't denied it.

"Why can't we go someplace cool?" Miranda had insisted then. "Take a *real* vacation, if you want to get away. Like normal people."

80

Her mother had taken the bait. "What would a real vacation be?"

"Hawaii," Miranda had answered.

Now Miranda took her big suitcase from the back of the Jeep while her mother unlocked the house and pushed open the front door. Miranda followed, entering a perpendicular hallway. The house smelled kind of musty, but it was cute. Well, Luis was gay; of course he could decorate. Miranda set her suitcase onto a woven rug.

Across from the door, the hall opened onto a living room with large plate-glass windows looking out over water. "Huh," Miranda said without meaning to.

"Isn't it lovely?" Her mother touched her shoulder, and she shrank away.

Miranda looked around. "Where's my room?"

"That way." Her mother pointed left down the hall, indicating the stairs to the second story. "And the kitchen is this way." She pointed to the right. "And the deck. Come see."

The deck was weirdly shaped, a prow deck her mother had called it, like the foredeck of a boat — and it overlooked a cliff above Gardiners Bay.

"That's Gardiners Island." Her mother indicated a dark blob on the horizon straight across the water. "And can you see over there to the right? That's Montauk Point."

Miranda knew a girl, a friend of a friend, whose house in Greenwich had a view like this. Not even this nice, really. Not as private. Not as lonely. "Where's Connecticut?" she asked.

Her mother smiled her sad smile, and Miranda turned so her mother wouldn't see the triumph she felt warm her cheeks. "That's Orient Point to the left," her mother said. "Connecticut is way out there." She pointed, then ran her hand through her short hair, a new habit. "But it's hard to see today."

Right after the big fight with her father — Miranda still didn't know what it had been about — her mother had chopped off her long braid, and Miranda had hated her for it. "You look like a soccer mom," she had said by way of insult. But now, looking at her mother in profile, Miranda had to admit that the haircut emphasized her mother's small features. She looked pretty.

A scrabbling sound arose from beneath the deck. Miranda turned toward her mother. "What's that?"

Her mother shook her head, shrugging. "A raccoon?"

Miranda saw it then, crawling out from beneath the steps. "Look," she said, excited. She walked to the edge of the deck. A large, brindle-coated dog looked up at her with soulful brown eyes.

"Hullo," Miranda said.

The dog just stood there, not growling, not wagging its tail, just looking at her. His eyes seemed to size her up, as though deciding what she was doing here — and what use he would make of her.

Her mother stood beside her. "He doesn't have a collar," she said.

Miranda dropped into a deep knee bend and reached over the steps, extending her hand out flat. The dog cocked its large square head. Then it sniffed her palm.

"What an odd-looking dog," her mother said.

Miranda let him lick her. "Part yellow Lab, part something else weird."

"Bulldog, maybe?" her mother offered.

That seemed right, if sort of strange. The dog had the head of a Lab, almost, and a Lab's long tail, but short, muscular legs and the orange and brown and white stripey coat of a bulldog. The dog looked at them neutrally, then ducked back beneath the deck. Within moments he reappeared, carrying something in his mouth.

"Ew! What does it have?" Miranda thought she could make out a tail, and that was definitely fur. "Cannibal!" she said as the dog trotted off toward the woods.

"I wonder who it belongs to?" her mother said. She turned toward the unlit house. It was beginning to get dark.

"Maybe us," Miranda said.

Chapter 9

Anna's phone rang. She had been almost out the door, so she flicked the light switch back on and picked up the phone from her desk.

"Anna."

She sank into her chair. His voice warmed her blood, like drinking cognac in a darkened room.

"Hello."

She stared ahead, in a stupor.

"I just wanted you to know," William said. "I've got the appointment. I'm going to Scotland."

"Congratulations." Anna's tones were low and soft, a balm.

She knew William would be restless to share his news.

"Thank you."

She imagined him holding his black plastic phone, hunched over his desk. "I'm happy for you," she said. "You really wanted this appointment."

"Yes, I did." She saw William in his chair beneath the Buttersworth schooner print on the wall.

"It's best for everyone, really," he said.

"Mmmm," said Anna, in her not-quite-buying-it way.

He forged ahead, seeming to sense that her time and her tolerance were limited. "Anna." He drew out the syllables of her name. "Will you accept my apology?"

She answered immediately. "Of course."

"Then, I am deeply sorry."

"Well, you needn't be."

She realized he'd worded his apology wrong, as though he regretted her, but that wasn't what he'd meant to say. "I'm an adult, you know," she said.

"True." His having been Anna's professor had been the primary obstacle to a relationship between them.

"I'm responsible for my actions," Anna said. She scraped her chair closer to her desk.

"As I am responsible for mine," William said. He paused, as though listening to the sound of her breathing. "And for certain of them, for selfishness that has caused terrible hurt, I apologize."

"Okay," she said. "I accept your apology, though I doubt my sister will. Will you accept that I — Oh, this is morose!" She broke off.

"Anna," he said. "I miss you."

"Don't." She was past being able to deny that she wanted him. "I can't see you until I sort things out with Rose," she said.

Anna knew that she risked losing Rose forever if she didn't make herself clear to her sister. But she risked more by pushing her.

"Of course," he said. "I'm being selfish again."

"It's okay."

Through the phone wire, she felt the muscles in his back relax. "Okay," he said.

She was convinced they had some kind of psychic or karmic or destined connection. He professed openness to the possibility — well, he would have to, given the course he taught. Whatever the contributing causes, including seventeen years of building intimacy, Anna longed for William in a way that felt new, multilayered, and surprising. Although reason told her she was more than likely delusional, still, the excitement was exquisite. She didn't want to fight it, but she must.

Good God, she was his sister-in-law.

"So," she said. "Scotland."

"Yes. Still seems unreal."

She asked him about the course he had designed. He answered her as though he were speaking to a colleague. Was all chance for them lost? It had to be. His duty was to his wife and daughter.

Anna made a little sighing noise. "Well," she said, "I envy you."

"Don't," William said.

"Why not?"

He didn't have a good answer. "You mustn't envy me anything."

"I've been wanting to go to Orkney since I was twelve," she said. She let her bitterness tighten her voice.

"In that case," he said. "You may envy me."

"Gee, thanks," Anna said. *Come with me,* she wanted him to say, although she knew she couldn't.

"Well, I've got to go. I'm glad your life is working out for you." *Since you've ruined mine,* she didn't say.

She would be better off when he was gone. Either that, or she might not survive.

"Right," he said. "Take care."

Miranda spent the weekend with William in Connecticut. He was living in the house again. She had asked to come home, desperately needing yet more of her stuff. The fact that Jai was in town, in between trips, didn't hurt. But he didn't mind that Miranda wanted to see her friend as much as — more than — her father. That was normal; normal was good.

Rose had agreed that he might as well keep up the house while she and Miranda were on Shelter Island. William slept in their bedroom, ate sandwiches at the kitchen table where he and Rose had fought bitterly and made love tenderly and had important conversations with and about Miranda. He avoided the living room, however, the place where he had last seen Anna.

A few times, William had stood outside Rose's locked studio, staring at the oak door as though waiting for a revelation. Rose hadn't locked the room against him, she'd said in an odd moment of pity. She had locked it against intruders of even the most innocuous kind. She couldn't risk anything happening to her paintings. William believed her, except he suspected she saw him as an intruder now — and he was.

The first of their three nights together this weekend, Miranda spent at Jai's, and the following night Jai spent at the Campbell house. William was fine with that. He wanted Miranda's life ordinary. He wouldn't allow guilt to produce in him an obligation to entertain his daughter in her own home.

Still, there was no denying a shift in power had occurred between them. Miranda, whom William figured gained a point of moral superiority for each of his sins, was skillful about using her increased sway with subtlety. He admired that.

Rose had never been subtle. Just beyond reach.

On Sunday William drove Miranda back to Shelter Island. She slept nearly the entire ride, and William, not wanting to disturb her with music, drove in silence and thought about Anna. He replayed their last phone conversation, imagined a future one. He wanted to speak to her again. He wanted to see her. He had even tried to run into her, shopping for groceries where he knew she shopped, at hours he thought she might be there. But their paths had not crossed.

He drove through Greenport toward the north ferry, hoping for a short line. The majority of cars would be traveling the other way. He would turn right around after dropping off Miranda, and he would hit traffic on the drive back to Connecticut. Rose certainly would not invite him to stay for dinner.

The ferry line was indeed short, William's Honda the third car behind an Explorer and a Mercedes.

Miranda stirred beside him as the car engine idled, yawning without opening her eyes. William knew she was awake but not in the mood for talking. That was okay with him. Their weekend together had gone well. Miranda had displayed little of the acting-out behavior Rose had described to him over the phone.

But he knew that she blamed her mother for their breakup, and he knew he would have to set her straight about that, eventually. Soon. But how could he do so without losing her?

The ferry arrived, and a stocky young man in a Mets cap began waving the cars on. William bumped his Honda onto the ramp behind the Explorer.

Miranda sat up. "Are we there?" Like a little girl.

"Almost." William leaned sideways to kiss her forehead. She smiled with her eyes closed.

The fellow in the baseball cap (maybe he wasn't such a kid) directed William to a spot at the bow, if a ferry could be said to have a bow. A white pickup pulled in beside him. A seagull sat on a piling, squawking at them.

The weekend had gone by fast, the

91

swiftest days he'd spent since Memorial Day weekend. The long days of June were dragging endlessly on, and July promised to be no better. He spent every moment, every day, struggling not to think about Anna. This weekend with his daughter had revived his spirit and distracted him from his misery.

The backseat was piled with bags and boxes — a denim jacket, a curling iron, a Ouija board — items Miranda couldn't live without. Also back there were a large box of dog biscuits and fifty pounds of kibble she had wheedled him into buying. A feral dog, which Miranda was calling Cannibal, had apparently staked a territorial claim under Luis Naufragio's deck. William was amused at the thought. Rose had never wanted a dog.

Miranda leaned her head against the window glass. William checked that her door was locked. The ferry blared its horn. Miranda grumbled and recurled herself around the shoulder strap, making her body smaller.

While she had been off with Jai this weekend, William had gone over their family finances, always tight, now critically so. Their checking and savings accounts, credit cards, mortgage, and investments, all of it funneled down to one fact: If they didn't reconcile, they would have to sell either the house or the *Ariel* by the time William returned from Scotland. He could not support both plus his own dwelling if Rose didn't work. And he didn't expect her to. Her career had just begun. She had an art show to prepare for, he understood that. Miranda, who had only two more years at home, had already informed them she wanted to attend college someplace faraway, someplace different. That was integral to the college experience, according to her, as was a year abroad.

If William and Rose stayed together, he understood Miranda's implicit point to be, there would be more money available for her college. His failure should not preclude her opportunity. So which of them should sacrifice? Clearly not Miranda. She couldn't be made to pay for his choices. And Rose still had not given him any indication she was willing to reconcile.

No. It was up to William to sell the *Ariel*. He recognized the simple truth with a jolt, as if he had been the only one in a room who couldn't see the hidden drawing in an optical illusion. Of course that's what he must do. They couldn't sell the house — Miranda needed to continue in her high

Chapter 10

Rose drove along Manwaring Road, a map of Shelter Island spread open on the seat beside her, just in case. Getting around the island was actually very easy. Manwaring connected Ram Island Road to Route 114, which ran in a north and south diagonal across the center of the island between the north ferry, which went to Greenport, and the south ferry, which went to North Haven and Sag Harbor. That one road was the main reference point on the eight-thousand-acre island, and one could follow signs to 114 from pretty much anywhere.

Though it had been to some extent discovered by the "beautiful people" of the renowned Hamptons, Shelter Island retained an isolated, pastoral character. One still had to go to the mainland to get to a movie theater or a hospital. Roads rolled gently along woods and fields, farms and estates. Long stretches of rocky shoreline basked beneath the midsummer sun, often empty of people, even on weekends.

Change came slowly to the island,

"probably because it has to take a ferry to get here," Luis liked to say. He would smirk then. "Keeps the undesirables away."

Rose's house — Luis's house — sat on a bluff near the tip of Big Ram Island, which was connected to Little Ram Island and then to Shelter Island proper by a narrow causeway. At one time, before the Army Corps of Engineers built it up, the road would often wash out during storms, with fast-rising tides that sometimes were higher than a tall adult's head. Luis, who had spent his childhood summers on the island, told an impressive story of swimming home from a friend's one night, against the terrible current.

He had inherited the house from his father. A weekend getaway built in the 1960s and renovated in the '80s, Luis's modest saltbox had little in common with the postmodern airplane hangar or ersatz shingle-style homes being built down the road, but his property, two acres of high bluff overlooking Gardiners Bay, was among the island's most valuable parcels.

"Could you get any more isolated, Mother?" Miranda asked daily, a never-ending admonishment. But every day she went off on her dump-rescued bicycle, and she looked healthy and she was eating reasonably. Thus went the unscientific method by which Rose evaluated her daughter's adjustment: her physical stamina and the clarity in her eyes. The fact that she found fault with everything her mother did was predictable and of little importance.

Miranda's hostility was just part of the package. Separation not withstanding, Rose knew her daughter was supposed to hate her guts at this age. Hadn't Rose hated her own mother at sixteen? For a moment she tried to recall, then realized the futility of it. Hating either of her parents wouldn't have made a difference. She just endured them, and did what she could.

And she had her sister. Past tense.

Focus and physicality check: Rose felt the moist, fleshy pads of her hands pressing the steering wheel, her warm back sticking to the leather seat, her face stroked by gushes of air through her open window. She observed the road ahead of her, the trees and the fields, the patches of sky. She breathed.

She wouldn't allow herself compassion for her sister, her betrayer, no matter what had happened to her as a child. Rose had been Anna's ally back then, had protected her sister the best she could, though admittedly that hadn't been enough.

Just ahead, a hand-lettered wooden sign announced a honey and tomato stand. Rose envisioned red tomatoes in Luis's blue bowl on an outside table, against a deep green background. For the first time since she'd arrived, Rose conceived a possible painting, one that she felt a sharp urge to paint — not unlike her desire to taste the tomato.

She pulled to a stop and got out of her car. The farm stand, though well stocked, was untended. Rose looked around, but there was no nearby building, just a long driveway through trees. Bees droned in the clover.

Rose called out. "Hullo?"

She ran her fingers along the painted wooden stand, a high table covered by a tin roof. On it were a dozen jars of wildflower honey, two metal containers of zinnia bunches, and a large, flat basket of tomatoes so plumply curvaceous that Rose thought the light must be tricking her eyes. She reached for one.

A blue dragonfly, incandescent and symmetrical, landed on a small sign propped between the tomatoes and a cigar box: PLACE MONEY IN BOX. MAKE YOUR OWN CHANGE. THANKS.

"Wow," Rose said aloud. "Shelter Island." This place seemed from another time. She couldn't think of anywhere else people were trusted to leave the proper money and take their purchase. Was it even possible? Apparently so.

The items were cheap, three dollars each. Three dollars for a small paper bag — a stack of which sat in another basket — of tomatoes. Three dollars for a jar of honey. Three dollars for a bunch of zinnias. On your honor.

Rose took one of each — honey, flowers, and tomatoes (she fit four in the bag) — and left ten dollars. The dollar tip was in authentic gratitude. A gratuity, she would say to Miranda later, telling her about it. Rose had been making a concerted effort to bring her daughter interesting words — anecdotes, aphorisms, ironies, puns — to reach her daughter by giving to her rather than asking of her. She didn't know what else to do.

Miranda didn't like direct questions. Rose had learned this the hard way, after making many mistakes. Miranda was principled, sometimes stubborn, and now she was angry. She blamed Rose for the separation; that much was obvious. But she hadn't asked Rose to explain what had happened, hadn't asked *why* her parents had separated, and so Rose hadn't told her.

Rose returned to her car and began to drive toward town. Avoiding the issue seemed too convenient, which made Rose nervous, but it was possible to do and so Rose continued to avoid it. She knew Miranda wouldn't ask a question if she didn't want to hear the answer. And though Rose argued with herself, citing the case she figured Miranda would make for truth and honesty, Rose couldn't convince herself Miranda would be best off knowing her father had been unfaithful with her aunt. Or had wanted to be unfaithful. Or had partly been.

Oh, who knew! Well, that was part of the problem. How could Rose confess to Miranda things she herself didn't understand? And what was there to be gained by this particular knowledge? Rose couldn't think of anything. The only reason to share such information with Miranda was to damage her relationship with her father, deliberately, and Rose wouldn't do that.

She knew, somewhere beneath the fire of her hurt, that William didn't deserve that.

She drove on toward the Heights, alert now to photographic possibilities for later reference. She had come to understand, in the weeks since her marriage had imploded and she had been all but unable to paint, that much of her artistic impulse was connected to visual memory, and her recent memory was too painful to access.

She needed to paint again. She needed it the way she needed sleep or sex — maybe more than either of them. Perhaps she should face the fact that sex had become a problem in her marriage. She had never considered preferring to paint to be a major problem.

But now that she felt that hunger in her again, she realized that she had declared her true passion to William, silently, in a hundred different ways. She wasn't sure she regretted her choice — if it weren't so damn painful, and if Miranda could remain unaffected. But that wasn't the case.

Still, he hadn't been any more eager than she to bring up the subject of their dwindling sex life. He might have fought for her a bit. Would she have wanted him tugging at her? Wasn't she grateful he respected her painting, that he didn't deride it as a hobby the way she knew some women's husbands demeaned their skills and art?

After years of toil and frustration, Rose had won a place in a show, an opportunity that might mean the start of a real career. But because of them, her husband and her sister, she had stopped painting in Connecticut after one attempt. The only images in her brain were those of William and Anna; she had painted their bodies, together, then slashed the forms with cadmium red and brushed over everything with thick mars black. That canvas was all black now, stashed in a corner of her studio. She hadn't been able to start anything else since. She had hoped that the beauty of the island would be a healing muse.

And now, she was eager to get back to the house, to pick up a brush, to taste a tomato. First she had to stop in town for an allergy prescription she'd had her doctor phone in to the Heights pharmacy. She should stop at Bliss's department store while she was down there. Miranda needed toiletries, again.

Historically, when Rose was working well, she slept when she wanted and painted when she wanted and ate when she wanted. She made sure to keep meals prepared for Miranda but otherwise kept no schedule. She knew Miranda was angry about that, too, and so, here on Shelter Island, Rose had been trying to be the "normal mom" she knew Miranda craved. But Miranda didn't seem to appreciate the fresh strawberries for breakfast and offers of trips for ice cream or games of miniature golf. Rose carried her guilt like a wallet photo, sometimes forgetting it was there and other times whipping it out to show strangers.

Painters were not the easiest sort of people to live with, she'd admitted to Luis on the phone over the weekend. Not for daughters or spouses. William had always encouraged her painting, but still Rose had felt that her art was a wall between them. That *he* felt that it was.

Correspondingly, the *Ariel*, the world of sailing, and the sea William so loved, were not an integral part of Rose's world. She knew she was a disappointment to him. That whereas painting was a solitary occupation, sailing was best done with others. She knew her self-sufficiency had hurt him, had damaged them, yet she couldn't see how to change — or perhaps she wasn't willing to change. When she thought of how she had failed him, she almost understood his need; she almost forgave him. But she mustn't let herself do that.

Rose parked the Jeep in front of Bliss's. Daphne Duval, the vet from the ferry, was standing outside the store, looking through a pile of flip-flops on a sidewalk table. The parrot didn't seem to be with her.

"Hello," Rose said. "Any bargains in there?"

"Well, hey, girl. No. Not much in size ten." Daphne shook her head, cheerfully discouraged. "How are you?"

"I'm fine." Rose wanted to add, *Anyway, I feel the urge to paint.* But she was embarrassed by her own enthusiasm.

Daphne shooed a bee away from her face with a postcard that Rose recognized as one she saw sold all over the island: gingerbread-trimmed Victorian houses that were built, she had read, in the late nineteenth century to form a cross from the chapel to the harbor. Judging by cars in the photograph, it appeared to have been taken in the 1960s. "I love that one," she said.

"I know." Daphne rolled her eyes. In this light they looked more green than blue. Unusual and beautiful. "I'm sending it to my grandmama. She doesn't do e-mail."

Rose laughed. A couple got out of a pickup truck with two kayaks in the back and made their way into the Dory restaurant and bar across the street. Rose thought about inviting Daphne to join her for lunch, but she was eager to get home and pick up a paintbrush.

"Hey," she said. "A dog appears to have adopted us, and I've been meaning to call to make an appointment to bring him for you to check."

Daphne squinted against the sun. "Sure," she said. "Does the animal seem sick or injured in any way?"

"Oh, no." Rose shook her head, then wondered whether she was treating Cannibal properly. After all, he refused to come inside the house, and she didn't urge him. She had never really examined him closely. "He lives outside, under the deck," she said. "And actually I haven't tried him in the car."

Daphne touched her arm. "I'll be happy to come to your house." Rose wondered what Miranda had told her about their lives. "It's not like I'm so busy." She picked up a pair of little boy's flip-flops, printed with sharks.

"That'd be great." Rose smiled at a family walking past who smiled back. She wondered when she'd stopped feeling so bad. She hadn't noticed until now, but some of the usual ache in her chest had subsided.

"Maybe I'll buy a couple of postcards myself," she said.

In Luis's kitchen, Rose washed and dried each tomato and then arranged them in a large blue bowl, which she carried out to the deck. There, she had set up her easel on a drop cloth, had set a yellow vase filled with zinnias on a white iron table. She placed the bowl beside the flowers and smiled. The woods provided the deep green backdrop she had envisioned; however, if she turned slightly to the left, the sky and water shone blue upon blue. She had set herself up for choices.

The brush felt just the right weight in her hand, something that wasn't always the case. Rose didn't know why, but some days, so many lately, everything, even objects she used daily, seemed cumbersome and unfamiliar. She picked up a flat brush, dipped it, and as the bristles soaked up bloodred paint, her brain flooded with pleasure. The images in her head would paint themselves.

There really was a kind of magic in the air here.

Chapter 11

The sky was the color of precious metal. Platinum. Rhodium. Uranium. Miranda wasn't sure about uranium. What color was it, exactly? She pedaled through air heavy with atoms of water. Silver. Mercury. Plutonium. She imagined herself as a glowing fish. *A woman needs a man like a fish needs a bicycle.* Her aunt Anna had that saying tacked up on her computer.

Miranda pushed up from the seat of her bicycle, leaned forward over the handlebars, and pumped harder. At first she'd had to walk the bike up the worst of the hills, but now, after two weeks, she almost never did. She made a point of trying not to look like a tourist like her mother with her stupid camera. Everything her mother did annoyed Miranda.

She wished her aunt Anna would visit; she was a nature freak and would love it here: the uncrowded sailing waters, the empty stretches of beaches, and the Mashomack Nature Preserve, which covered the entire southeastern third of the Rock's eight thousand acres. She probably knew all about it already, but Miranda made a mental note to mention it in an e-mail.

Miranda had spoken to her aunt only by e-mail since coming here. Doing so required a certain amount of subterfuge because she shared a laptop computer with her mom. She had to make sure to delete all their messages. She didn't know why, but her mother had discontinued, if not precisely forbidden, all contact with Aunt Anna. They were estranged, that's all she would say. Miranda knew their fight had something to do with her parents' split. Probably Aunt Anna knew something about her dad. It had to be that. Or maybe her aunt thought her mother was nuts for kicking him out. They would have argued about that.

But when she really thought about it, nothing explained why her family had blown apart so quickly, literally overnight. When she let herself dwell on it, Miranda felt as though she were being abandoned, though she knew she wasn't. Not exactly. But living without her father just seemed wrong.

A gust of wind rustled the trees, and a shower of droplets fell onto Miranda's face and arms. The cracked rubber handlegrips slipped beneath her fingers as she bore down harder on the pedals, her calf brushing the guardless chain.

Back home, riding a bicycle would have seemed ridiculous to Miranda. Kids in Connecticut drove around in older kids' cars or else they walked or took public transportation. But people came over by ferry just to bicycle these country hills surrounded by water. Everyone, even teenagers, rode bicycles here.

The first time Miranda hiked the mile and a half from the house to the end of Reel Point, she had encountered a group of kids her age. Apparently school friends meeting to hang out, all had been riding mountain bikes. That's how kids got around here, she surmised, even in high school.

Her mother had found a rickety but reliable Schwinn at Exchange Place at the town dump, where people left unwanted but potentially useful items, and she had spray-painted the bike flat black for Miranda. How ironic that her mother was the one to provide the means for Miranda's escaping her. Even she must realize that Miranda couldn't bear to hang out with her for very long. She was drippier than ever.

So every day Miranda explored, hours each day spent riding around the island. Sometimes she took Cannibal. Half the time, after following her for a mile or so, he took off on his own, but he always returned to his lair beneath the deck. None of the neighbors knew where he might have come from, and no one responded to the signs she posted. Miranda liked thinking of him as partly wild.

She bore down harder, pedaling up a hill, breathing through her mouth. On either side of the road, old farm pasture steamed under a hazy sun. The dense air parted, a transparent cloud soughing against her skin.

And then, all at once as she crested St. Mary's Road, the shimmering water of Coecles Harbor spread before her. She loved this moment, this spot, this exact point where the world expanded from a tunnel of green to a dazzlingly wide and blue horizon.

Miranda kicked out her heels as she rode through a puddle, splashing. Ahead, dozens of sailboats bobbed at their moorings, everyone in from the storm.

For as long as she could remember, summer weekends more often than not were spent sailing the *Ariel*, first with her grandparents and then, after they died, with her parents and aunt and sometimes friends. But since she started high school, Miranda preferred to live her own life on weekends. Her mother didn't sail much anymore, anyway. She was always painting, or she was online e-mailing her artist friends, or she was out somewhere doing some art thing. Her aunt Anna and, of course, her dad were the ones who liked sailing best. Miranda wondered if the two of them had continued sailing together this summer. She didn't think so, though she didn't know why.

She rode along Ram Island Drive toward Hay Beach. Her mother expected her father to sell the *Ariel*. Miranda had overheard her talking to Mr. Naufragio about it. Her father was going away to Scotland, anyway. They had been supposed to take a trip there, as a family, if he got the teaching gig. Now, her mother said they wouldn't. No matter what. That was so unfair.

If only Miranda could live on her own, could somehow support herself. Maybe her dad would help her out. Jai said she could declare herself independent and get state money for college. But that was two years away. She was only a rising junior.

111

She coasted now, down the causeway between Little Ram and Big Ram, water on both sides, sweat beading on her forehead. Ahead on a hill was the Ram's Head Inn. That was her landmark for *almost home.* She liked to stop to rest here, where the lawn rolled down to a white gazebo. Beyond the gazebo lay a little beach with a dock and moorings for bigger boats in the harbor, a favorite spot for cyclists to picnic, take photographs, and sun themselves on the rocks.

On the verge of the road Miranda pulled over to take a swig from her water bottle, pushing her hair off her forehead and looking up at the clearing sky. The weather had changed drastically from the thunderstorm she had waited out in the library less than an hour ago. She had gone to look at magazines and ended up using the free computer, e-mailing Jai who was mountain climbing and had written her about new friends at Outward Bound, people Miranda would never know. Still, Jai's e-mails were something to look forward to. If not for them, Miranda would have gone crazy by now, alone on this island with her selfish mother.

At least she had Cannibal. He was a weird dog, a loner, like Miranda herself had become. Weird but cool. She wanted to keep him. She would insist they take him back to Connecticut.

A family of four stopped along the road near her, and Miranda rolled her bicycle up the hill to get away from them. Above her, an osprey's swift, broad figure cut the sky. She watched as it plunged toward the water, feet first, spearing a silvery fish with its talons. In a flash, the osprey was high in the sky again, soaring toward a nest atop a platform built on a telephone pole. It must have babies to feed. Miranda wished she could see them, but the big, messy nest was deep. She saw only the osprey, poking at the fish — or something — with its beak.

Miranda finished her water and hooked the bottle onto the pocket of her shorts. Back home, she wouldn't be caught dead wearing a water bottle. That was as bad as a fanny pack. But here, who cared how dorky she looked?

She considered going up to the inn to look around inside. No one would know she wasn't a guest. She gazed up the hill toward the big, white house and there was Cannibal, trotting toward her.

Still straddling her bicycle, Miranda called his name. His ears perked, and he quickened toward her across the grass. She could see that he was carrying something in his mouth. What had he got now? And what was he doing here at the Ram's Head Inn?

She swung her leg over the seat, and, holding the bicycle steady with one hand, dropped to a knee bend and reached out with the other hand to coax the dog. "Here, boy."

The damp grass smelled sweet, as though it had just been cut, and it reminded Miranda of home. She recalled the summer Saturdays when her dad would mow the lawn as she lay reading a Judy Blume book in the hammock between the two big oak trees. Her mother would work in the garden, planting or weeding or pruning something. More often than not, Aunt Anna would stop by. Those were the days before her father inherited the *Ariel* from his father, before her mother did nothing but paint.

Her stomach felt empty. She hadn't really eaten anything all day. She didn't feel like going back to the house, but she probably should take the dog back. He'd follow her. "Here, boy," she called again and snapped her fingers.

Cannibal had stopped a few yards away

from her, his jaws full, his long tail swaying in a low arc. Now Miranda could see what he was carrying, a lobster, large and blue-green, and she felt that small jolt of surprise she always did when she saw a live lobster. Even though she knew better, she expected them to be red.

"Come 'ere, boy," she repeated. "Good boy."

Cannibal wagged his tail with enthusiasm, but he stayed back. Miranda wondered whether he intended to carry the lobster all the way to the house and stash it under the deck with the other stuff he collected. Mostly pieces of wood, she thought, but who knew what else was under there? Or maybe he intended to eat it now. Where, she wondered, had he got a lobster?

"Hey." The call made her look up. A tall blond guy jogged down the hill in her direction. He waved.

She stood up, both hands gripping the bicycle seat. "Hey."

Cannibal dropped the lobster, picked it up again, and edged toward the wooded perimeter of the lawn, his ears and tail pressed low.

The approaching guy looked to be around Miranda's age. He was very tan, not quite as tall as her dad but much thinner, and sandy colored everywhere. His limbs, his hair, even his eyes, Miranda saw as he neared, were a sort of tan. His cheekbones stuck out and his chin had a dimple in it.

He stopped between Miranda and Cannibal, hands on his hips, smiling and shaking his head. His shaggy, sun-streaked curls were too much, and when he crossed his arms, Miranda stared. She couldn't help it.

He was looking at her, too. A weird feeling ran through her, like something was happening she couldn't prevent. Even with Jimmy, it hadn't been like this.

"You know that dog?" the guy asked, jerking his chin toward Cannibal, who had backed up nearly to the line of trees.

"Um, yeah," she said. Her voice caught in her throat, froggily, like it did when she hadn't spoken to anyone in a while. It sounded fake. She looked down to where her hands gripped the bicycle seat; her knuckles were turning white.

"That dog stole one of my dad's lobsters," he said. "*Another* one."

"Sorry." Should she make him give it back? Would anyone want a lobster that had been in a dog's mouth? Could she get him to give it up? She looked over toward Cannibal, but he had disappeared.

"Damn dog gets something about every third delivery."

"He does?" Miranda looked down at her rickety bicycle. What delivery? she wondered.

The guy laughed. "Yeah, he sure does. And his mother did the same thing, probably taught him how. Haven't seen her around all summer, though."

She felt her cheeks flush. "You know his mother?" she asked. "Do you know his owner?"

"Nah. He doesn't belong to anyone." The guy looked around, as though for confirmation, and Miranda looked, too. There were people down on the beach and on the tennis courts, but no one near them. The gazebo was empty. She wished she were in it, instead of standing behind this stupid, cast-off bicycle out in the sun. She had to squint to look him in the face. She probably looked like a freak.

"The mother dog got knocked up and someone ditched her, I guess," he said. "There were two other pups. Or three?" He shrugged, and his shoulders moved slow and easy, not quick and jerky like so many of the boys at school.

117

She made a mental note to describe him to Jai. Finally, she had something worth telling. "Where are they, the other pups?" she asked. Cannibal was hardly a pup, though, was he? Maybe he was.

"One got hit by a car, right out there on the road," he said, pointing. "The other, I don't know. Never really saw much of it."

"How sad." Miranda let the bicycle drop back against her legs and reached for her water bottle. As soon as she lifted it, she realized it was empty.

"You thirsty?" the guy asked. He shaded his eyes with his hand to look at her, and she saw that his fingers were calloused.

Miranda shrugged. "Not really."

He nodded his head in the direction of the inn. "I'll get you a Coke."

Miranda glanced over his clothes, a T-shirt and worn chinos. "You work here?"

"No," he said, stuffing his hands into his pockets. He looked a little uncomfortable now. "My dad delivers lobsters here. He has a fish market. I work there."

Miranda nodded. "Oh." He was looking straight at her. Was he testing her?

She let go of the bicycle and the front wheel wobbled and turned. He caught it before it fell.

"So, come have a Coke," he said. "My

118

name is Danny. Danny Princi."

"Princi's Fish Market," Miranda said. You could eat there, too, at picnic tables outside.

"Right." Danny said. Then he took her bicycle from her and started up the hill.

Chapter 12

The nature center was closed for the Fourth of July but Anna was working. Most people would celebrate the holiday at family barbecues or on the beach — or, if they were so privileged, on their boats. She had been invited to join a group of volunteer staffers in a softball game and picnic, but she had declined. She couldn't envision this holiday spent on dry land. She wanted to avoid all reminders of it.

Of course she had known today would be difficult, that each red-white-and-blue streamer would remind her of Memorial Day weekend, the official start to what had turned into the longest summer of her life. There was nothing for her to do but spend the day alone. Alone, but useful.

She banished all such thoughts from her mind and concentrated on the dark, tiny creature she held in her hand. Soft and furry, with a squashed face like a little pug, the bat lay sweetly still. Its miniature arms were attached to wings that joined to its feet and felt like warm leather. As she lifted the creature upright it made a small squeaking noise.

"Now, now," Anna said as she picked up a headless mealy worm with a pair of tweezers. "Here you go."

The bat first sucked on the worm, then gobbled it down.

"Good boy," Anna said. She selected another worm and then another. Joe the crow squawked enviously from his corner cage, coveting the shiny tweezers more than anything. Anna hushed him, knowing he wouldn't be hushed. She liked his companionship.

The Nature Center hadn't always closed on the Fourth. For years, the Center had been open for the holiday, free to the public, a gesture of community goodwill. Though they never offered a fireworks display — there were too many trees, among other hazards — the Nature Center sponsored a hamburger and hot dog picnic, along with nature walks, canoe rides, lectures, and activities. Children especially enjoyed demonstrations that featured animals they could touch — the turtles, certain snakes, and lizards that had come to live permanently at the Center. Two American bald eagles in the aviary were the honorary guests at the lecture on endangered species. A pair of beavers, raised from birth by a local contractor and then abandoned when he relocated, couldn't be released into the wild. Anna was especially proud of their habitat, and the friendly creatures loved to show off for the crowd.

Everyone seemed to enjoy themselves, and the event was an excellent generator of new and renewed memberships and tax-deductible donations.

But there were two problems. The next-day cleanup was time-consuming and costly, and inevitably, no matter what bag checks and other precautions the staff took, some teenage boy would manage to sneak in fireworks, with predictably bad results. Once, a poor bullfrog with an M-80 in its mouth had exploded in front of her, splattering her shirt with an indelible pattern of guts and gunpowder.

The board eventually voted to close the Center for the holiday.

Now, Anna returned the baby bat to its cage and continued to the next, which contained a great horned owl. In addition to its ever-evolving educational collection of indigenous small mammals, reptiles, and amphibians, the Center housed a variety of injured, un-releasable birds of prey: various owls and hawks and the two eagles,

Liberty and Justice Foreall.

Occasionally the Center was approached to rehabilitate a deer or a raccoon, a beaver or a fox. Sometimes, because she was soft, Anna even authorized the nursing of an injured Canada goose, not among the approved animals in the bylaws. In any event, there were always animals to be fed, twice daily.

Though she could easily have asked a staff member to do it, Anna had volunteered to come in for today's evening feeding. She had nothing else to do and she wanted to be alone, indoors. The feedings took about an hour. When she was done, she went upstairs to her office.

Since she was there, she might as well check her e-mail.

She wanted, as always, to check for messages from William. Once, they'd e-mailed daily, bantering back and forth, discussing their respective work, sometimes even discussing Miranda or, rarely, Rose. But mail from William had been scant since Memorial Day weekend. And Anna hadn't answered any of his messages. She'd wanted to, oh God she'd wanted to, but she just didn't know what to say. Not while she and Rose were still estranged — or while he and Rose might reconcile. She hoped he understood that. And she hoped he wouldn't stop e-mailing her.

She booted up her computer in the semi-dark, not bothering to turn on the lights in the room. Why announce her presence to anyone else who might come by? Volunteers often did, for one reason or another, and Anna didn't want to see or talk to anyone. She didn't want to explain why she was alone and checking e-mail on a holiday.

She opened her mail program to thirty-seven new messages. But none was from William. He was probably busy, sailing or getting ready for his trip to Scotland. Anna wondered what his accepting the position at St. Andrews would mean for him and Rose.

She unwrapped a chicken breast sandwich she'd brought from home. *Would* William be out sailing today? And if so, would he have taken Rose? Perhaps try to make things up to her? Anna read through the subject headings of her messages, frowning at all the forwarded jokes and spam. She opened an electronic newsletter from the New Works Gallery — how had she got on their mailing list? Rose must be responsible.

The sandwich dripped ranch dressing onto her blouse. She wiped it up with a finger, which she licked. She searched the newsletter for Rose's name and clicked on it, calling up images of two paintings she had submitted to the contest. The winning picture Anna recognized, but the other, a fanciful rendition of the *Ariel*, she had never seen. Gentle swirls of vibrant colors gave it a surreal, dreamlike quality.

She imagined William's light, expert touch with the *Ariel*'s rig, the happiness in his face when he got her reaching just the way he liked. Although they'd avoided using the term, Anna had been William's first mate, on that Saturday in May and for months before. Over time they had become first with each other in other ways, the person each of them told things to, the one whose opinion mattered. They had pretended it was all fine; they were close, as close as siblings.

Anna hadn't been able to determine the moment it happened, though she had tried during the last six weeks, many times. But at some moment it *had* happened, or a series of moments had rolled together into a much bigger moment. At some point William and Anna had become essential to each other's lives.

Eating made her hungry. She gobbled the sandwich.

"Hey there." It was Theo, her assistant and botanist. He walked into the room and over to Anna's desk. "Why aren't you sailing?"

Anna had to decide quickly. To hesitate over her answer would give too much away. But she couldn't fabricate quickly enough. "I wasn't invited," she said.

Theo bent over her shoulder and looked at Rose's paintings. "Very nice," he said. "But since when aren't you invited on your sister's boat, not to pry?"

Anna shrugged. "It's not a big deal. I had a few things to get done in peace and quiet." She looked up, hoping Theo would get the message.

He did. "Sure," he said. "I'm off to putter in the greenhouse for about twenty minutes."

"Good." Anna felt transparent.

"Okay, well." Theo jangled his keys in his pocket. "I guess you won't want to get something to eat."

Anna wiped her mouth with a tissue. "No, thanks."

"Later, then." Theo left the office and Anna turned back to her computer, closed the gallery Web site window, and clicked open a sailing listserv she frequented. She read through thread headings and considered whether Rose, who had never really had the patience for sailing, would even want to go out on the *Ariel* now. She bet she wouldn't.

In a funny way, Anna had always understood how her sister felt. She knew exactly how much work sailing was, how uncomfortable and tiring it could be, and how much commitment, and/or money, was required to maintain a boat. She had always been able to empathize with her sister.

And yet, despite that empathy, Anna loved to sail. It was congenital, she and William had decided, maybe atavistic. You were born loving the sea or you weren't. Anna loved the sea, smelling it, hearing it, flying across it. But Rose — had she loved the *Ariel*, too?

Anna signed off the listserv, opened an e-mail from a seed supplier, skimmed it, and saved it in a Pending folder. She deleted spam: Get 250 Business Cards for FREE! Lose Weight by Eating More! Earn One Million Dollars Without Working! She read and saved a notice from the State Nature Conservancy. Then, she went back to the New Works Gallery newsletter and deleted it.

Twice Anna had e-mailed Rose and once been answered, Rose writing that she wasn't ready to talk. So Anna had let it go. How long was she ~~was~~ supposed to wait? Until Rose approached her? What if that never happened? What if William went off to Scotland and Rose stayed on Shelter Island and Anna was left alone, abandoned by those she loved most?

An e-mail from Miranda chimed through. Anna opened it and read:

> *hi. you won't believe it, i met a guy here. he's beautiful, aunt anna, and sweet and smart. i can't believe I'm telling you this. don't say anything to ANYONE! how are you? xxx miranda*

Anna smiled. At least Miranda still talked to her. For now.

Don't love him, Anna wanted to write in reply, but she didn't. She saved the message, needing to think about what to say. She was fairly sure her niece still didn't know what had happened on Memorial Day weekend. Anna wanted to talk to her about it, but she couldn't. She dared not send any e-mail to Miranda that she couldn't risk Rose seeing.

How long would her life remain this way, a series of dully painful days, one becoming the next, almost without separation? She hadn't felt this kind of ache in a long time. It was worse, even, than physical pain. Worse than being whipped with her father's belt, worse than the buckle biting her flesh. Then she had gone away in her head to a place where she couldn't feel. She couldn't do that now.

She opened a Word file labeled TRAVEL. In it, she had secreted significant passages from her correspondence with William, documents tucked into folders marked SOUTH PACIFIC and GREECE and SCOTLAND. Anna reprised the contents of the Scotland folder, reading through the "notes" that were her correspondence with William. Innocent enough, for the most part, they had nonetheless once sustained her heart. She read a recent e-mail she had saved:

From: William Campbell
To: anna@ntrctr.org
Subject: Anna, Diana

I miss you.

W

He had teased her with that name last spring after visiting her at the Center,

Anna, Diana, for the ancient Italian wood-land goddess he said she reminded him of, a patroness of wild creatures, represented by the moon. In Greek mythology she was called Artemis and had a dark side, Hecate. He'd called her *Anna, Hecate* once, too.

He missed her.

Another e-mail from Miranda appeared:

> *his name is danny, btw. the guy I met. we have plans to meet tonight. did I tell you I have a dog?*

Anna smiled. She missed Miranda, her niece, her friend, the girl who made up for both her own childhood and the child she'd never had. *Yet,* she reminded herself. She was only thirty-five.

I love you, Anna said to Miranda in her head, *but I'm in love with your father and I don't know what to do.*

She stared at her monitor. Its screen gave off the only light in the room.

Chapter 13

Crescent Beach, a half-mile strand along the Rock's northwest shore, was, according to the island guide, a favorite with both locals and visitors. (Hareleggers, a term of disputed origin that meant people born on the island, sometimes referred to it by its original name, Louis's beach.) So many came on weekends — in recent years, a spillover of young, trendy partyers from the Hamptons had moved their revels here — that the beach was now also known as Sunset Beach.

"You should get yourself a parking sticker," Daphne said to Rose as she idled behind a silver Mercedes, waiting for its parking space.

"I should?" Rose said. They had come for a Fourth of July picnic and fireworks, but Rose didn't see why she would need access to a public beach after tonight. "Luis's house has its own beach."

"You need to get out more," Daphne said, her blue-green eyes sliding sideways, one of her effective *looks*. Rose was becoming familiar with them. "I need to get you over to the Angel Gallery on Bridge Street."

"Sure," Rose said. "Thanks."

Arriving at a time when some day-trippers were leaving and many of those coming for the fireworks had not yet arrived had been Daphne's suggestion. And it appeared to be a good one. A thin but steady trickle of people from the beach were heading for their cars along Shore Road.

"Yeah, yeah," Rose said. "Going from a private to a public beach is getting out?"

"Yes," Daphne said. "There are *people* in public places." She maneuvered the van so as to let the Mercedes out but no other car in.

"Anyway," Miranda said from her seat in the back where she'd been quiet until now, "that hotel restaurant across the street is *the* place to go."

"For what?" Rose asked.

"Not for what, for whom," Miranda said.

Rose peered out the window and took in the crowded tables outside the gray, shingled building across the street. She remembered reading in the *Shelter Island Reporter* about celebrity sightings. Had they been here?

The Mercedes drove off, and Daphne

claimed the spot. "Here we are, Miz Campbells." She put her van in park and turned off the engine.

Miranda grabbed her beach bag, ready to pounce out the door.

"In a rush to get there?" Rose turned to unbuckle her seat belt.

Miranda rolled her eyes. "No."

"Go on, sweetie," Daphne said to Miranda. "Go find us a good spot." She unlocked the doors and Miranda slid hers open.

"Take a couple of beach chairs with you," Rose added. "I'll get the cooler."

Miranda climbed out of the van. "I don't need a chair."

Rose started to protest but stopped. *Choose your battles,* she reminded herself.

Daphne walked around to the rear of the van and opened its double doors. She removed two of the three aluminum and canvas beach chairs Rose had packed.

"I'll carry the chairs for you," Miranda said.

Daphne caught Rose's eye and winked.

They set up close to the water, as the tide was going out.

Though nearly five o'clock, the sun burned white and strong against a cerulean sky. Boat hulls slashed the glinting bay with color, vermillion and jade, and brightly striped umbrellas dotted the narrow beach like candy wrappers. Rose kicked off her sandals, felt the warm, coarse sand between her toes, and breathed deeply of the soft, briny air she had always associated with summer. It was now high summer; she had hardly noticed before.

On the thin, white tablecloth Daphne and Miranda spread behind the beach chairs, Rose set the cooler. In it were Daphne's fried chicken and potato salad; the local-grown strawberries, gourmet chocolate cookies, and thermos of lemonade that were Rose's contribution; and several bottles of water Miranda had added.

"I'm looking forward to your chicken," Rose told Daphne.

"Recipe comes from my grandmama in New Orleans." Daphne gathered her thick, red-brown hair in her hands and knotted it on top of her head. "I visited her every summer as a girl. I can fix that chicken in my sleep."

Rose smiled. She thought of her Connecticut Yankee grandmother's kitchen, which usually smelled of roasting beef. As girls, she and Anna had loved going there, not for the food but for the calm. Her gran's garden, especially, had been a comforting quilt of color and shadow.

"What time do the fireworks start?" Miranda asked, glancing at her watch.

" 'Bout nine, I think," Daphne said. "When it gets really dark." She was rubbing sunscreen onto her arms and chest. "You wouldn't think so, but I do sunburn," she said in response to Miranda's stare.

Miranda looked away, embarrassed.

"And so do you," Daphne said, good-naturedly poking her arm with the bottle of lotion.

Rose dared not beg her daughter to use it, but she hoped she would. The sun was still strong. Miranda accepted the sunscreen and dabbed a bit onto her face, then returned the bottle and strode the few feet to the water's edge.

Daphne looked at Rose and raised her eyebrows, letting her sunglasses slide down the bridge of her nose. Rose shrugged. Both women lowered themselves into chairs, adjusting them to recline slightly.

Rose had forgotten her sunglasses, and she squinted as she watched Miranda dip her toes in the gentle froth of the bay. The sky, the water, and the sand formed geometric blocks of color, radiant with light.

She framed a painting in her mind.

"She's okay, your girl," Daphne said. Her chin was tilted up, her eyes closed beneath her glasses, but her wide, shapely lips were smiling.

"I hope so," Rose said.

Although they had known each other only a short while, Daphne acted as comfortable with Rose as an old friend. In fact, Rose felt easier with Daphne than she had with any friend in years. Of course, she hadn't had many close friends since college — she hadn't needed any. She and Anna had comprised a two-member club.

"She won't always blame you, you know," Daphne said.

Rose sat up straight. "What makes you think she does?"

Daphne turned her face toward Rose and lifted her sunglasses, looking at Rose straight on. "Doesn't she?"

Rose let out a sigh. "Yes. For the separation or divorce or whatever we do. For everything."

Daphne nodded. "Mm-hmm. Well, it's natural. I may not have kids, but I've been around my share of them, starting with my seven brothers and sisters."

"Good grief."

"Uh-huh, and my baby sister's got three,

including a step. She lives in Wading River, so I see them all the time."

Miranda was coming toward them.

"I'm going for a walk," she said before she even stopped walking.

Rose caught something in her voice, a hollowness, that suggested a lie. "Where?"

"Just down the road." Her eyes slid to her wrist, surreptitiously checking the time.

"The road?"

"Itzhak Perlman has a music camp for teenage prodigies. They give free concerts every night."

Rose glanced at Daphne, who nodded.

"You think I'm making it up?" Miranda shifted her weight, impatient.

"No, of course not," Rose said. "But what about our picnic? Daphne's chicken?"

Miranda shrugged. "I'll eat it later."

"We can eat right now," Daphne said, reaching behind her chair for the cooler.

"No," Miranda said. "I can't eat now. I'll just take a water."

Daphne reached into the cooler and fished out a bottle.

"How far down the road is this camp?" Rose asked. She tried to sound curious, not suspicious. She didn't quite pull it off.

"Thanks," Miranda said to Daphne. "Not far." She rolled her eyes. *"At all."*

"I thought that looked like you two."

Rose turned at the sound of the familiar voice. Luis and another man were strolling up the beach.

"Well, look who's here," Rose blurted as they reached her. Luis had mentioned being on the island this weekend, but Rose had never expected to see him here.

"Nice to see you, too, darling," Luis said, cocking his head to one side. He turned to Miranda. "Hello, gorgeous." He kissed her forehead.

"Hi," she said. "Well, I'm gonna go. Bye." She started off across the sand.

"Don't be long!" Rose called after her. Miranda waved over her shoulder without looking back.

Daphne stood and extended her hand. "Daphne Duval."

Luis took her brown fingers in his pale ones. "Luis Naufragio, and" — he nodded at his companion, a slightly built blond not quite as tall as Daphne — "Chris Peters." They were dressed in long pants and polo shirts, not beach attire.

Rose introduced herself to Chris and offered them something to drink, which they both declined.

"We've had a few drinks already," Chris told her in a wryly confidential tone.

Luis pulled a face. "We had a bite to eat over at the restaurant." He gestured loosely in the direction of the street. Rose wasn't sure which restaurant he meant, but she sensed she was supposed to. "And a couple of cocktails. We were just getting into the car when I spotted you."

"How was the food?" Daphne asked.

"Fine," Chris answered. "But I just had a salad."

"Overpriced," Luis said. "But who cares? Peter Jennings was two tables away from us."

"Gosh," Rose said.

"I heard he was on the island," Daphne said. "Do you live here?"

"Oh!" Rose rushed to explain. "I should have said. Luis owns the house where I am staying."

Daphne looked from Rose to Luis. "But he's not staying there?"

"No," Luis said. "Imagine? I'm having to mooch off Chris for the weekend."

The sky darkened abruptly. Rose looked up at a long, thin cloud covering the sun.

"Please," Chris said. "I've been begging him to come out all summer."

Rose knew she shouldn't, but she felt

139

chastened. She was living in a house not her own, with a daughter who couldn't stand being with her. She had no real career, no husband, no sister. Her only real friend was a woman whom, let's face it, she hardly knew. She'd been reduced to accepting handouts from her lawyer.

Luis looked down at his fine Italian loafers and shook sand off them. "We should get going."

"Not staying for the fireworks?" Daphne asked.

"Oh, we'll see them," Chris said. "We're invited to a party on a spectacular sailboat."

Luis touched Chris's arm. "You want to see spectacular, you should see Rose's husband's —" He stopped. "Not spectacular like Quinton's boat. Antique. Anyway . . ." Luis swept his hands back and forth, dismissively. He gave Rose an apologetic look. "Enjoy. We'll talk."

They kissed good-bye.

"I'm hungry," Daphne said when they had gone. "But we'll wait for Miranda."

"No," Rose said. "She won't want us to. Let's eat."

And so they spread their feast out on the tablecloth and sat at the edges and piled their paper plates with food. The chicken was delectable, crunchy outside and moist inside, not greasy but full of flavor. Rose hadn't eaten a chicken that wasn't oven-baked or store-bought in years.

"This is wonderful," she said.

Daphne thanked her with a shrug. "Just usual old picnic fare."

It wasn't usual for Rose. William had almost always grilled hamburgers on holiday outings — which meant sails. He kept a hibachi and a bag of charcoal — the real kind, not the briquettes — on board the *Ariel*. Charred red meat. She had eaten so much less of it this summer.

The thought should have pleased her, but her eyes welled with tears. Daphne passed her a napkin, wordlessly. Then she broke out the chocolate cookies.

After their meal, Daphne suggested a swim.

"My mother always warned me to wait an hour after eating before swimming, or else I'd get stomach cramps and drown," Rose protested.

"Yeah, and she probably told you to wait until you were married to have sex."

"Of course."

"And did you?"

Rose dived into the water by way of an answer and came up laughing. Daphne was good for her, almost like a sister. But she wasn't her sister. In fact, enjoying her friend's company only reminded Rose how much she missed Anna. She allowed her eyes to fill with tears, then she dove below the surface and they mixed with the salt water of the sea.

Later, they sat wrapped in beach towels, watching the kaleidoscopic western horizon. The sky deepened from blue to lavender, and the sun that had been white and high slid ever lower and grew yellower. Its rim turned orange, then nearly crimson, and streaks of color lit the scattered clouds like flames.

The sun was slipping from the sky, and still Miranda had not returned.

"Should I be worried?" Rose asked.

Daphne didn't answer right away. She looked up and down the beach, crowded now, as if to check for Miranda before she spoke. "It doesn't matter whether you should be or not. You are."

"Do you know where the Perlman music camp is?"

Daphne shook her head. "Did we pass it? I've only been here as long as you have."

Rose stood and pulled on a sweatshirt. With the sun going down came the cool of the shore, even on the Fourth of July. A coil of panic began to tighten in her chest.

Daphne stood. "We'll find the place," she said. "She'll be there. She's probably met . . ." Her voice trailed off. Rose followed the direction of her gaze.

And there, making her way through the couples and the families packed together on the sand, was Miranda — and someone with her.

"A boy." Daphne finished her sentence with a grin.

"It was awesome!" Miranda said unapologetically when she got to them. "These kids younger than me playing violins and cellos like real musicians."

Rose gaped at her daughter, not sure whether to laugh or cry.

Miranda introduced the boy as Danny. When asked whether they had met for the first time at the concert, the teens exchanged glances. Then Miranda answered, "No."

Rose couldn't press the matter, and she was satisfied, for the moment, that Miranda was safe and happy and had a friend. The sun had dropped behind the surface of the water now, and up and down the beach lanterns were being lit. Miranda and Danny ate the rest of the chicken, the potato salad, and most of the strawberries, gulping their food like feral animals. Then, all at once, they were both stuffed. Too stuffed for chocolate cookies, too stuffed for anything.

Soon the sky was black except for stars, pinholes of light through a velvet curtain. Music swelled, people cheered, and the sky exploded, raining fire over the boats on the bay.

Chapter 14

Having finished with the front lawn and half of the back, William needed a break. He had waited until the late afternoon to mow, hoping for relief from the heat as the sun slipped behind the taller trees, but it was still a hundred degrees in the shade. Or so it seemed. He wiped his forehead with the hem of his T-shirt and headed to the garage.

At the yard sale of a neighbor whose son had recently graduated college, William had purchased one of those small refrigerators that kids used, often illegally, in dorms. Installed in his garage, its two shelves filled with Cokes, bottled water, and beer, the fridge had served William well all summer. He didn't like going in and out of air-conditioning, and now he didn't have to enter the house when he was thirsty. Why didn't more people have such things?

He grabbed a bottle of water, closed the fridge, and drank the entire eight ounces in a few gulps. He didn't usually mind the heat, loved the outdoors, even enjoyed the immediate gratification of yard work, but this summer had been brutal. He tossed the empty water bottle in the recycling bin Rose insisted on keeping, though William was skeptical of what actually happened to all that plastic and glass when it reached its destination, then he opened the fridge again and took a can of beer.

William walked the perimeter of the large yard, drinking his beer, picking up sticks and the occasional piece of wind-blown trash. He snapped a few dead blooms off a flowering shrub. He had tried to keep up Rose's garden, but between the merciless heat and his awkward touch, the plants had suffered. Lengthening after-noon shadows crisscrossed the lawn, a cardinal called to its mate, and at last a gentle breeze lifted the moisture from his skin. Wondering, as he had done lately, whether he should shave, he scratched his beard. He stepped on a fallen stalk of lavender, and its scent rose on a zephyr, mingling with that of cut grass and pine bark mulch and the deep musk of the compost pile in the far corner near the fence.

William loved this yard as much as the genteelly shabby house it graced. For nearly twenty years, he had made this place home. He would miss it in Scotland, all the more so for knowing he would perhaps never return to it. Still, he would be able to think of Rose and Miranda here, secure, at least physically, among the comforts they had always known. He would provide for that.

"Damn it," he said aloud, remembering that he needed to begin making calls to the list of yacht brokers that he had compiled over the last couple weeks. He was putting it off, of course. He didn't want to sell the *Ariel*, though doing so was the only way to provide for his family the way he must. There was something else preventing him.

He stopped at the green-and-white hammock, a Christmas present from Rose many years back, and lay in it, drinking his beer. A heaviness infused his limbs, a gravity of sorrow. Though he had pled with her to try to reconcile or consider counseling, Rose had continued to insist she wasn't ready to make a decision about their marriage. And in his heart William knew that there would never be any undoing, no going back; something breakable between them had shattered.

But he wanted what was best for all of them, especially Miranda. No matter what that cost him. He had tried to understand what had occurred in his marriage to mark the turning point. Aside from the horror of Memorial Day weekend, he and Rose had had no truly spectacular rows, no Taylor-and-Burtonesque brawls. And as far as he could recall, there had been no drama with which to mark the last time they'd had good sex. Or the last occasion, for that matter, on which Rose had achieved an orgasm with William inside her. He couldn't remember that, either.

They'd never spoken of it. William hadn't consciously acknowledged the situation to himself until — well, he didn't know when. How long had their routine been their routine? One day he had simply realized that it was, had been, and probably would continue to be the case that Rose came only when he went down on her. Not that he minded the act, more what it suggested, that something between them had ended.

The frequency of their sex had dropped, true, but that in itself seemed less than alarming. Was there a correlation between quantity and desire? And which of them was responsible? At some point, William had wanted Rose less than he once had, and he remembered now that he'd felt guilty about it.

"Is my memory going?" he'd teased her

one Saturday in early spring. "Or was the last time we had sex so extraordinary I've blocked it out?" Rose had laughed, and William's blood had chilled in his veins. His wife wasn't embarrassed by their lack of lovemaking, she wasn't angry, she wasn't smoldering in frustration. She was good-natured about it. Perhaps that was the moment William had given up.

Rose had tilted her chin at him, as though its tip held receptors, and William reached for her that Saturday, afraid what might happen to them if he didn't. He breathed vanilla and lemons from the pores of her skin, lifted the heft of her long braid in his hand. She circled an arm around him — her other hand held a jar of brushes; she was on her way from the bathroom to the room she used as her studio — and he could feel what she held back in her touch. She wanted to get to her painting.

"Will you sail tomorrow?" he'd asked, catching her gray-blue glance with his dark one. He touched a finger to the tip of her slightly crooked nose, an old game of theirs where her part was to bite and then kiss his finger, and then his lips.

When had she stopped doing that?

"Anna will go," Rose had said, and she'd slipped away from him.

Now William crushed the empty beer can in his hand and let it fall to the grass. He closed his eyes, listened to the birds begin their evening songs, and thought about sailing the *Ariel*.

Anna was the reason he hadn't been able to face putting his boat up for sale. He couldn't relinquish the *Ariel* without her. She loved the old cutter nearly as much as he did. The idea of being bereft of his family, his *Ariel*, and Anna was too much to bear. He thought of phoning her, as he had done earlier in the summer to convey the news of his appointment at St. Andrews. But phoning Anna again would be selfish — everything he had thought and done these last months had been selfish. And so he did nothing but go over and over in his mind what had happened and the things they had said to each other and the things that he wished he could say.

Anna had finally answered his e-mails. She had said she missed him as he missed her but that she also missed her sister and her niece. The implication — the fact — was that he had deprived her of them. It was enough that his self-indulgence would to a certain, significant extent cost him his daughter. It was too much that it had cost Anna anything, especially the sister who had been her best friend, even surrogate mother. He knew enough about Rose and Anna's childhood to know that their relationship went beyond ordinary sibling affection. It wasn't something any of them talked about, not for years, but he knew. Or he knew enough.

He let his arm drop, raking fingers through the soft, unshorn grass. Maybe he would leave this section of the yard uncut for a while yet. All of the publicly visible parts were trim and neat. Back here, he might as well let it grow a little. Longer blades were healthier for fescue in this heat.

"Hard at work, as usual." Rupert's affable mockery cut through the stillness.

William sat up hastily, nearly toppling the hammock, and Rupert laughed. "Relax," he said. "It's just me. Or rather, it is I."

"I know it's just you," William said as he stood, wiping his hands on his shorts. "Who else would it be?" He picked up the crushed beer can.

Rupert was wearing a Red Sox cap to shield his pate from the sun. He lifted it, ran the palm of his hand from his forehead to his crown, then pulled the visor low on his brow. He looked around the yard.

"Nice look," he said with a sweep of his hand. "I like it. Very yin-yang."

"*I* thought so," William said. He realized how glad he was to see his friend, whom he generally tried not to bother during weekends. Katrin had returned from New Mexico. A couple didn't need a third wheel.

Except, William realized he had never once resented the presence of Anna, not that he could recall, not since the beginning of his marriage. Back then, of course, Anna hadn't come around as often as she had done the past couple of years. But that was because she wanted to sail, and Rose wanted to paint.

This Fourth of July Rupert and Katrin had joined William for a sail upon the congested waters of the Long Island Sound. The day had been pleasant enough, but William had been miserable. He wondered whether his friends had been able to tell, and he felt guilty for that, on top of everything else.

"Got another one of those?" Rupert indicated the beer can.

"You know where it is," William said. Together, they headed toward the garage.

When they'd opened their beers, Rupert took a long swig and surveyed their dim surroundings. He walked over to a corner where William kept his marine supplies: the varnish and brushes, engine parts, rigging, bronze fittings, cleats, and strips of teak he needed to perform the *Ariel*'s never-ending maintenance. Rupert picked up a sable trim brush and sniggered. William's willingness to spend far more on nautical accoutrements than on his wardrobe was a long-standing joke between them.

"How are you doing on finding a yacht broker?" Rupert asked. He put down the brush and picked up another. He didn't look at William. He drank his beer.

For that, as for Rupert's customary tact — which, despite his penchant for friendly ridicule, was considerable — William was grateful. "All right," he said.

"Good." Rupert lifted a jar of brass screws. "So, you've been getting her in shape to sell?"

William snarled.

"Easy, Kiltie-Man," Rupert said. Another of his running jokes was that William, with his unruly dark hair and full beard, was the picture of a wild Scotsman. All he needed was a kilt. "What are you doing tomorrow? Aside from training for the idle wastrel Olympics?"

"It's a yuck a minute with you."

"Don't believe everything you read in the first floor men's room. I can go for at least five." Rupert punched William lightly in the shoulder. "No, I mean it. Let's work on the *Ariel*. I have nothing else to do."

"You're not serious," William said. "Do you have any idea what you'd be in for?"

"Yes," Rupert said. "I have a very good idea." He slugged his beer.

William remained unconvinced. "But Katrin —"

Rupert interrupted him. "Katrin is away until late Sunday night," he said. "So, are we on?"

William shook his head, his eyes on the floor. "I need to do it."

Rupert crushed his beer can and tossed it into the recycling bin. "I know."

William was dicing garlic, one dish towel thrown over his shoulder and another tucked into the waist of his shorts. Rupert had gone to the cellar for a bottle of wine. William had talked him into staying for dinner — *pollo vino blanco,* a recipe from the front page of the Food section of the paper, one that looked simple and for which, fortuitously, he had all the ingredients: Chicken breasts (from the freezer, de-

154

frosted in the microwave), olive oil, garlic, green onions (they grew wild in the yard), mushrooms (from a can in the pantry), black olives (ditto), dried parsley (from the spice rack; how old was it, anyway?), a tomato, and white wine. He would serve it with fettucini.

He had already put the pasta water on to boil. The whole meal should be ready in twenty minutes. He finished chopping and poured one-fourth cup of olive oil into the large sauté pan.

Rupert appeared holding a bottle of Chianti.

"White wine," William said. "*Pollo vino blanco!*"

Rupert shrugged. "I prefer red," he said. "Can we drink this with dinner?"

"Whatever you like." William wiped his hands on the towel at his waist. "But I do need a bottle of white for the chicken."

Rupert nodded, set the Chianti on the kitchen table, and started back toward the basement.

The phone rang. William answered the wall phone near Rose's kitchen desk.

"Daddy?" Miranda hardly ever phoned, since William phoned her every few days.

"Hello, angel."

"What are you doing?" That was new.

William laughed. "Believe it or not, I'm cooking."

"That's nice," Miranda said.

William steeled himself for a request. Maybe she was going to press him once again about going to Scotland. Rose had said no. Period. He had little with which to convince her. He rifled absentmindedly through papers on the desk. "Dr. Jones is here for dinner," he said.

"Good." She didn't ask what he was cooking. Her mind was clearly occupied.

"What's new with you?" he asked.

"Well," she said. "Did Mom tell you about the art show at the school?"

William searched his memory. "Your school, here in town?"

"No. Here. The Shelter Island School grounds. There's an art show there next weekend."

"I see. No, she didn't. Why?"

"Well," Miranda said. "She's in it."

"Terrific."

"And she needs me to help."

William heard Rupert's footstep on the creaking stairs.

Miranda continued, talking faster. "She needs my help with the art show, but I'm supposed to come to see you next weekend, so, I was wondering if we could

156

change our plans?"

"I guess so," William said. He hated missing any time with her, especially the closer it got to his leaving. But if Rose wanted her there for a show . . . He wondered why Rose hadn't phoned herself. Things between them, though hardly cordial, were not quite as strained as they had been.

"Okay, great," Miranda said. She seemed uncharacteristically enthused about helping her mother, especially with her art. Shelter Island must be doing them good.

"Campbell!" Rupert's shout sent William spinning.

"I'll call you back!" he said to Miranda, dropping the phone to run to the stove. The oil in the sauté pan had burned away, and the pan was in flames. Simultaneously, the pot of water was boiling over, hissing as it spilled.

Rupert had turned off both burners, and William, a dish towel in each hand, began beating at the flames. Rupert grabbed a bowl from the counter, dumped out its contents of keys and packs of gum and rubber bands, and filled it at the sink. "Stand back!" he ordered.

William turned. "Don't!" One never threw water on a grease fire. Hadn't

Rupert ever been a Boy Scout? He looked around frantically, grabbed the lid to the sauté pan, and dropped it over the flames, extinguishing enough of the fire to smother the rest by beating it with Rose's largest, flame-retardant pot holder.

William looked at Rupert.

Rupert held up a bottle of pinot grigio. "Will this do for the chicken flambé?"

"Fuck it," William said, throwing the pot holder to the counter. "Let's go down to Cato's."

Rupert chuckled. "An excellent choice."

Chapter 15

Everything but the reptiles suffered in this heat. A large black snake dozed peacefully on a rotting log, but the beavers hadn't been out in the middle of the day for a week, and even the birds seemed still. With the two permanent members of her landscape staff, Anna toured what was slated to be the new bog garden (dry as dust at the moment), a transitional habitat between the beaver pond and the stream.

"We could bring in a few cacti, call it the Connecticut desert, and be done with it," Joe, the senior of the pair, quipped as he paced off the intended boardwalk area.

"As long as you include an oasis," Anna said. In her mind, she saw a shining blue circle of water, a tall palm, and a backdrop of pyramids. A cartoon vision to be sure, but it reminded her that she had always wanted to see North Africa.

"At least the desert gets cool at night," said Riley, Joe's partner, as he bent to take a measurement. "I slept out on my deck last night, and I think it was hotter than inside."

"But your wife was glad to get you out of the bedroom," Joe said, and they all laughed.

Anna looked at the plans she was holding, sent to her from a nature center near Atlanta. Earlier, she had spoken to the director of horticulture there who had overseen a much larger bog project the year before. Of course, that center was on a river — and it was in Georgia, and still the project had been immense.

Anna had a much smaller piece of land with which to work. The corporate sponsor who had donated the funds had made it clear that the money was to go for creating a bog. He wanted carnivorous plants, blueberries, orchids — he would pay for it all and create a trust to provide for maintenance in perpetuity, so long as the results met his specifications.

Riley stood and wiped his forehead on his shirtsleeve. "Gonna take a shitload of peat, pardon my French."

"Look at that," Joe said, pointing to the beaver pond. Someone had launched a paper boat and it bobbed across the water, set in motion by an unseen bullfrog or beaver tail.

"Be nice to be out on the water today," Riley said. He kicked at a stone, sending it rolling toward the pond where it got caught in the long, dry grass. He turned his sun-browned face to Anna. "You planning to go out sailing on your sister's boat this weekend?"

He might as well have thrown the rock at her. "No," she managed to say. She walked toward the trail. "I've got to get back. I have calls to make."

The pain in her chest was always there, though some things made it worse, and sometimes she almost — but never quite — forgot it. She had told no one about the rift between her and her sister. Not just to protect herself but for Rose's sake, and Miranda's. There was no one she could talk to about it, anyway, though she had considered unburdening herself to Theo one night after work when she joined him for a pizza. But no, she couldn't bring herself to speak of any of it, not even to make up a lie.

She couldn't go on like this much longer.

The trail back to the admin building veered down toward the stream, running beside it for a few hundred yards. Though presently at its lowest and slowest, the water continued to flow at a level that supported a broad spectrum of aquatic organisms. Anna was especially proud of the care she had taken to create and sustain a riparian buffer, the strips of grass, trees, shrubs, and rocks that lined the banks, trapping sediment and runoff before it reached the water. Years ago, when she had been a part-time, hourly worker at the Center, the banks of the stream had been little more than earth and pebbles.

Back then, she had planned to leave Connecticut as soon as she had saved enough money. One thing and another had caused her to postpone her plans; first college, then her sister's marriage, then a promotion at the Center, then the birth of her niece, then a further promotion, and so on, until she had nearly forgotten who she wanted to be.

Now Anna sat on one of the eco-friendly sapele benches provided by the Women's Garden Society. She considered her financial situation, something to which she rarely gave thought. Her condo was paid for in full, thanks to the sale of her mother's house, and her expenses were few. Heading a nature center didn't require an extensive wardrobe, just the occasional blue suit for a board or fund-raising meeting, the odd black cocktail dress for a benefit. She didn't spend much on dining out; why would she, when she took a good percentage of her meals with her sister? The days of vacations with girlfriends to Caribbean singles resorts were long past. She was thirty-five, and the few friends she had were married with mortgages and babies and dogs.

What did she have?

On the far side of the stream, a female mallard appeared, a brood of fuzzy brown-and-yellow hatchlings waddling behind. The mother duck slid into the water, paddled a few strokes, and turned around. The ducklings began to slip their way down the embankment, from one large rock to the next, a few managing quite well, others almost tumbling, and one — there was always one, wasn't there? — couldn't seem to grasp how to proceed. It scurried back and forth, its tiny wing stubs held out, chirping for help. But the mother duck was already swimming upstream, little ones following in a line.

In the pocket of her trousers, Anna's cell phone vibrated. She reached for it, checking the number on caller ID before answering. It was Marcia from the gift shop. Someone had come in, hysterical, carrying a mangled but still breathing baby raccoon whose mother had apparently driven off a coyote. Coyotes were getting to be more and more of a problem in Connecticut. People expected the Nature Center to take responsibility for any and all wild animals.

By the time Anna rose from the bench and returned her attention to the stream, the ducklings were gone, all of them. Had the little, uncertain one succeeded in negotiating the embankment? Had it lost its way? Been swooped up by a hawk?

Anna made her way to the admin building, where she was needed to authorize the services of the on-call vet, who had already been summoned. She would do what she could in the meantime, but she was weary.

The raccoon kit had lost too much blood to make it. Though she had experienced more than her fair share of them, Anna took each animal death to heart. This one especially got to her, perhaps because she was emotionally worn, perhaps because of the violence inflicted on a creature so helpless. She kept thinking of the raccoon mother, her bravery in the face of such danger, hoping she had other kits to tend.

Two quick raps on her open office door were Theo's signature entreaty. He stuck his round, bespectacled head through the doorway. "Got a sec?"

Anna didn't have the energy to get up from her desk; she hoped she wouldn't need to trudge over to the greenhouse or the learning center. "For you?"

Theo stepped in. "Yeah. No biggie. Just a quick personal question."

Though her office had no windows, there was a large one in the hallway, directly across from her door; it was one of the reasons she kept her door open. Standing in the molten afternoon light, Theo was a dark and nearly featureless form. Chiaroscuro, Rose would have called the effect. *A personal question.* Had someone started gossip? Perhaps someone from the marina? Or one of Rose's friends?

"Okay," she said. She liked and trusted Theo; she relied on him. She knew next to nothing about his personal life and he knew only superficial things about hers, yet she felt as close to him as she might toward an old friend.

He pulled a donated wooden school chair to her desk. "You look beat."

Anna managed a thin smile. He was treating her normally, so he must not be here about gossip. She was relieved and vaguely disappointed. She could use some-

165

one to talk to right now. "Thanks," she said. "So what's up?"

Theo leaned back in his chair, lifting the front legs off the floor. That drove Anna crazy; he was bound to break the chair or his back or both. At least, that's what Rose said to William when he did it. She had to stop thinking about Rose!

"You know my cousin Margaret, the nurse, from Scranton?"

Did Theo want to chit-chat? She wasn't in the mood. An e-mail came through on her computer and she glanced at the screen. She could say she had to answer it.

"Anyway." Theo leaned forward, setting the chair legs down. "I don't know if you remember she decided to go to medical school."

Anna said nothing, waiting.

"Well, she got into Yale, to do her residency."

"Congratulations to her," Anna said. She should have gone to graduate school, maybe become a vet, anything would have been better than spending her whole life here as her sister's shadow.

Theo slapped the palms of his hands on her desk. "So, I was just wondering whether you knew anyone in your condo building who might want to sublet for a year. That's all. I'd let Margaret stay with me, but, well . . ." He gave her a sheepish, conspiratorial look. "I keep weird hours on the weekends, and my place is small."

Anna lifted her hair off her neck. "I don't know," she said. But she felt more alert than she had in days. "I'll think about it. I mean, check into it."

"Thanks," Theo said, standing. "That'd be great."

The sun had descended below the pine trees, its blinding light diffuse now. Anna stared at her open door, seeing nothing but the images that formed and reformed in her mind. Every now and then she would turn to her computer. She accessed her bank account, the résumé she had written the year before but never used, and she searched through yachting magazines, regatta schedules, and crewing agencies.

Opportunities for crewing on a variety of yachts, including classic vessels and tall ships, abounded, or so it seemed. All one had to do was fill out a crew-finder agency application, pay a small fee, and wait to be contacted by yacht owners or captains. Of particular appeal was a regatta held in Antigua in the spring; boats from all over the world participated, after which their millionaire owners would jet back to Antibes or Portofino and have their yachts delivered.

What if Anna sublet her condo to Theo's cousin? What if she quit her job? With just a little preparation and coaching, Theo could take over as director. She was confident he would do so eagerly and well. She would leave her beloved but far too familiar Nature Center in good hands.

What if, at last, she combined her longtime dream of travel and her love for sailing and the sea and set out on an adventure? She saw herself on a sixty-foot schooner in the middle of the ocean, long since in sight of land, truly sailing. The idea was thoroughly intimidating, thoroughly exhilarating. Not even William had sailed across the Atlantic.

She turned again to her computer, called up the site for the Global Crew Network, and began to fill in the form.

Chapter 16

The light was changing.

Rose had been working all morning — the first strokes, as always, the hardest — and she was ready to stop. She dropped her brush into a can of water, replaced the caps on the ultramarine blue, the cadmium yellow, and the titanium white, and gazed past her easel, across the deck that jutted toward the bluff and, beyond it, Gardiners Bay.

She had been painting the colors of water, trying to get them right.

Miranda liked to count the one hundred wooden steps zigzagging from the top of the bluff to the sandy bulkhead across the stony beach. She also liked to collect stones, and she had done so this morning, just before leaving for the weekend with her father. From her pile at the top step Rose had selected a stone to include in her painting.

She lifted it now, a gray-green oval that had shone nearly emerald when wet. Rose had chosen to paint it dry.

Sea, sky, stone — these were her subjects, these shades of blue and green and gray, cool colors that she liked to underlay with warm oranges and reds. Rose frowned at the canvas. She had been overworking, trying to lose herself in design, distracting herself with detail. She reminded herself not to evaluate. The work was in a rough stage. What was important was to get paint on canvas, and she had been doing that for hours. For weeks now.

Wind was blowing off the water and the temperature had dropped. The sky darkened. A storm was on its way, perhaps minutes from now. Weather moved quickly out here, though the island was protected (hence its name) from the worst of weather by the North and South Forks of Long Island.

Still, electrical storms were dangerous, especially for bicyclists. Miranda was out there now, on her way to the ferry to meet her dad, riding through heavy woods and wide open spaces, marshes and fields and narrow lanes flanked by water. Dangerous places. Rose turned those thoughts away. She replaced them with an image of Miranda arriving safely at the dock.

She lifted her chin, letting the sea breeze blow through her short hair. She was still getting used to the feeling of lightness and the prickling of air against her neck. Large clouds rolled across the horizon. Thunder rumbled, but Rose couldn't tell from where.

She lifted the two-by-three canvas from her easel and carried it into the kitchen through sliding glass doors. A reflected motion in the corner of the glass caught her eye, and a thin shiver went through her. But when she looked directly over her shoulder, no one was there. Another trick of light.

In its article about the winners of the art competition, the local New Haven paper had praised Rose's work for its "tricks of light." Though she had bristled at the phrasing — *tricks* sounded manipulative to her — the review had prompted several e-mails from people wanting to see more of her work.

Her career had begun as her marriage began to end, or had it been the other way around?

Rose set her painting beside two blank canvases propped against the kitchen's stark white wall. She was grateful to escape the screeching primary colors of her own kitchen. White cleansed, renewed, made possible.

She returned to the deck for the rest of her supplies. Out on the bay, the distinctive white sail configuration of a passing cutter reminded Rose of the *Ariel*. But she had successfully blocked the events of Memorial Day weekend from unthinking access, and her mind immediately jumped back in time to the early years of her marriage, when William and she would sail the waters off Cape Cod during visits to his family. Rose actually had enjoyed those outings. Pop Campbell, who had served in World War II, made a natural captain. The sails were fun without being frightening. And William, she remembered with a small stab of pain, had recited Scottish poetry to her, Robert Burns and Edwin Muir, from the prow. With his father at the helm, William had shown off like a boy. Rose had been charmed.

But when his father died and the *Ariel* passed to William, he spent every weekend tending to or sailing it, long, tedious maintenance schedules and repetitive, uninteresting sails on the crowded Long Island Sound. More often than not, these last few years, Rose had declined to accompany William when he sailed, choosing instead to spend her time painting. William's passion for sailing had never truly been hers.

Of course it had become Anna's.

A knot in Rose's chest twisted in a familiar turn, an urge to have it out with her sister, to extract the truth, to lay blame. No matter what else might be true about her ailing marriage, it was Anna who had killed it. Rose threw tubes of paint into a canvas bag, visualizing her fury as quick-winged gargoyles. *Stop*, she told herself. She imagined wings, frozen in flight, disintegrating.

Whitecaps were forming on Gardiners Bay, moving crests of radiance. Rose watched them, and urged herself to be calm. She never tired of this view, a heart-healing panorama wider than her peripheral vision could span. Along with the ever-changing tides, Rose loved the bigness of the sky, the battling stings of salt and pine. Here, Rose felt perched on the very tip of things, and indeed, the vast blue Atlantic that lay just beyond Gardiners Island extended all the way to Europe.

"Yoo-hoo."

Rose turned toward the driveway to see Daphne climbing out of her mobile-vet van. "Hey."

"Hey, girl." Daphne waved, then bent into the van and came back out holding Simon. She set the parrot on her shoulder, slid the van door closed, and started across the grass. Simon bobbed happily on his perch, his leg tethered to Daphne's wrist. She took him along everywhere she could, she'd said, for bonding. Rose always enjoyed seeing them.

Hearing, and probably smelling, them, Cannibal scraped out from his spot beneath the deck. Before Rose could think to call out a warning to Daphne, the dog had bounded to her, grinning and slicing the air with his tail.

"Good dog," Daphne said, scratching Cannibal's head.

Rose was amazed. Cannibal was not timid, exactly, but he was reserved. Wary. Miranda was able to pet him after coaxing him with food, but mostly Cannibal kept his distance. Now he was wagging his prodigious tail at the woman who'd recently given him a rabies shot. And he was ignoring the bird.

"Hey you," Simon said. Cannibal looked up, cocking his head. Rose laughed.

Daphne continued toward the deck, and Cannibal returned to his spot beneath it. They went into the kitchen, and Daphne approached Rose's canvas in a way Rose, always private about her work in progress, would never have tolerated from anyone in Connecticut. She wondered whether her loosened attitude had to do with painting outdoors, or with Daphne's own open personality and its effect on her; or perhaps, having gone through so much anguish these past few months, she viewed her relationship to her art from a new angle now. Less serious and yet more professional, she hoped.

"I like this," Daphne said. "If I'm allowed to say so before it's finished?"

Rose laughed. "You are." She made eye contact with Simon, who held her gaze as he rocked from foot to foot.

"So, are you ready for the show?"

"Well," Rose said, "this particular painting won't be in it. But I did drop off a few yesterday." Daphne was talking about the community art and craft fair held outdoors on the school grounds every August. She had put Rose in contact with the people who ran it, and Rose had invited Daphne to spend the afternoon with her at the show.

"Good," Daphne said, squinting at the sky through the glass doors. "I think it's going to clear. By the way, the Vaizey sisters — who own the Angel Gallery in town — will be there. I told them all about you when they brought their cats in yesterday."

Arp, Simon squawked.

Chapter 17

Danny had suggested spending the day in Greenport. Miranda met him at the ferry, where they locked up their bikes. She had told her mother she was seeing her dad this weekend, as scheduled, that she was meeting him at the ferry because she wanted to ride her bike, not to miss a day of exercise. Meanwhile, she had canceled her plans with her father, using as an excuse having to help her mother with the local art show. No way her mother would catch her. She'd be down at the school grounds from morning to night.

Miranda was supposed to stay overnight with her dad, of course, which she hadn't mentioned to Danny. She didn't want to suggest spending the night together to him, although the idea of sleeping on a beach seemed really romantic. She would see how the day went. If she ended up going home, she'd figure out some reason her dad had brought her back. Her mother would be all too willing to blame him.

Miranda had traveled through Greenport all summer, coming and going from visiting her dad, but she hadn't spent any time there. It looked like a cool place to walk around. When Danny mentioned he would have this entire Saturday free and suggested going to Greenport, she couldn't say no. This was a real date. She was his girlfriend.

"Are you hungry?" he asked when they stepped off the ferry at the dock on Front Street.

Miranda was so excited to be out someplace new with a boy that she couldn't eat. This was so much better than going to the multiplex or the mall back home. This was the real world, smelling of fish and rubber and wood sealed with tar. Eating would make her sick. Still, she knew that boys were always hungry, so she answered, "If you are."

Danny laughed and took her hand. "We'll walk around first, and then I'll take you someplace that will have something you'll like."

Miranda was floating, there was no other word for it. She had gotten drunk on beer once, at Jai's house before a school dance, and she had enjoyed the feeling of loose-limbed giddiness, if not the headache and queasiness that followed. But that high had been nothing compared to what she felt now. Every pore of her skin was alert to sensation.

They walked past an old hotel, and Danny began to talk about the history of Greenport. He took obvious pride in doing so, reminding Miranda a little of her dad. "In the early seventeenth century," he began, "a bunch of Puritans who had settled in New England decided they didn't like it there, and came by boat from New Haven across the Sound to the North Fork of Long Island, a few miles from here in what is now Southold." Miranda remembered passing a sign for it.

"I came from New Haven," she said, smiling up at him.

"There you go," he answered.

He explained that Southold became the first permanent settlement in New York State. "About forty years later, descendents of those settlers moved out to what became Stirling Harbor. To your right," Danny said.

They turned onto Main Street, and Danny said she had to go inside Prestons Marine Supplies, still housed in the original, one-hundred-twenty-year-old building on its own dock. "It's got everything," Danny said, "from crappy souvenirs to real ships' figureheads and cannons."

They went in, and Miranda was delighted by everything, though now she remembered her father once trying to take her there and her not being interested in the least. Well, she had only recently become interested in nautical things. Danny made it interesting.

Danny wanted to buy her something, and she took half an hour trying to decide between a rope bracelet and a T-shirt. In the end she chose a dolphin toe ring, because it cost the least and her mother wasn't likely to notice. Plus, it was a ring, and that meant something, even if it was for her toe.

They continued down Main Street and stopped in front of the Greenport Tea Company, which, according to the lacy menu in the window, served high tea and lunch. Miranda couldn't believe a boy would even know about such a place. "Think you'd like something here?" Danny asked, and Miranda said yes, if only out of awe.

She was able to nibble at a salad and croissant, while Danny ate a fancy-sounding sandwich that was actually tuna fish. After lunch, they wandered around the shops. They visited the Seaport Museum,

180

where Danny told her more about Greenport's history as a whaling port. The town had once been a center of the fishing and oyster industry, and during Prohibition it had been a major port for rum-runners. Later on, during World War II, the waters offshore had been prime areas for patrolling for German submarines.

As the afternoon eased into evening, Danny asked whether Miranda would like an ice cream cone, or would she prefer to wait a bit and have dinner? They were walking along the harbor, and she looked up to see a large, circular glass building with what appeared to be a carousel inside.

"What's that?" she asked.

"That's where we're going next, the carousel."

"How cool!" Miranda chirped, and Danny laughed and pulled her close. She had never in her life spent a more perfect day.

She and Danny selected the prettiest horses that were side-by-side, hers white and his bronze, holding hands as they rode up and down. Though relatively new to Greenport, the carousel was actually antique, built in the 1920s and donated to the town. Danny reached for the brass ring and got it — "You've done this before!"

Miranda said, not minding at all — and won a free ride, and then another.

They ate lobsters at Claudio's as the sun set. "Don't tell my dad," Danny said. "He competes with this place. Or he thinks he does." Then, they stood on the dock, waiting for the ferry, and Danny put his arm around her and hugged her to his side.

Miranda couldn't remember ever being happier. "This has been the greatest day," she told him, and he kissed her on the top of her head.

"It's been awesome," he said. Then he kissed her cheek, and she turned her face to meet his mouth. After a minute, she pulled away first, though she didn't want to stop.

She wanted to ask him about sleeping on the beach, but she didn't dare. He might think she was easy or, worse, say no. He probably had to get home, and he would assume she did. But he'd kissed her, and that was more than she could have wished for.

They rode the ferry back to the Rock in a kind of twilight dream, not speaking much, a bit chilly, sleepy with food and walking and happiness. Miranda was so dreamy that she didn't even notice the black Jeep in the parking lot near the bicycle rack. She didn't notice her mother get out of the car as the boat docked. She didn't notice, but Danny did.

"Don't look now," he said, "but isn't that your mom?"

Rose was hoarse from screaming. The entire drive back from the ferry, she and her daughter had yelled at each other. She couldn't remember ever having been so enraged, not even when she had walked in on . . . not even on Memorial Day weekend. Her anger then had been mixed with hurt; tonight it was fury and fear. If Miranda hadn't appeared when she did, Rose thought she might have spontaneously combusted.

Now they were home, standing on either side of the kitchen counter, momentarily silent and fuming. Rose paced back and forth in front of a stack of canvases against the wall, the ones she had shown today at the fair. She had sold one, someone was interested in another (consulting with her decorator), and best of all, the Vaizey sisters, owners of the Angel Gallery, had come by to chat and look over her work. One painting in particular, one of her most recent, had piqued their interest.

"If it doesn't sell," the elder of the two

told her, "bring it by the gallery after the show. We'll take it on consignment, if you like."

And so Rose had, and that's when she had seen Miranda's bicycle, from the top step of the gallery. In itself, that hadn't meant anything. Miranda had met her father at the ferry before. But Rose hadn't heard from her all day, so she'd decided to phone the house in Connecticut from her cell. Fortunately, William was at home. If he hadn't been, she might not have called again till morning, assuming they were out somewhere. But he was home, and he was nearly as shocked as she was to learn that Miranda had, apparently, manipulated them both.

Caught up in their own foibles, how easily they had overlooked what should have alerted them.

William had wanted to immediately drive out there, but Rose told him no. She would deal with Miranda, and he could speak to her tomorrow. He'd had to accept. For three hours now, Rose had staked out the ferry, simmering in her car or walking aimlessly around the dock. Surely people thought she was a madwoman, or else a furious wife.

Well, she was that, too.

"What's the big deal?" Miranda asked now for the fiftieth time.

Rose felt the blood quicken in her veins. "You lied!" she said, trying not to scream. Luis's house was set on two acres, but voices carried far in the still night. All she needed was for someone to call the police and for her to make the Police Blotter of the *Shelter Island Reporter*. For all she knew, she would anyway, for the scene they had created at the ferry with Miranda pulling away from her clutch on her arm and Rose threatening to slap her.

Lobsterman's Son Caught in Love Tryst with Underage Daughter of Artist. She could just see it.

"Okay, okay," Miranda said, her voice conciliatory for the first time. "I lied. I'm sorry I lied, but I was going to help you with the art show when I told that to Daddy. I was going to surprise you."

"Please!"

"Well," Miranda sniffed, her eyes filling. "I was thinking about it." She was making herself believe her own lies.

"And I was thinking about joining the circus. You lied. You told your father one thing and me another and then you went off to God knows where."

"Greenport!" Miranda cried. "I went to

185

fricking Greenport and rode the carousel! That's what a horrible person I am."

"But you didn't tell anyone," Rose insisted. How could she penetrate this girl's thick skull? "Do you have *any* idea how worried I was after I spoke to your father?" Her eyes began to fill.

"If you hadn't left him, I wouldn't have to go back and forth like a Ping-Pong ball." Tears dripped down Miranda's cheeks, but her eyes flashed defiance.

"Oh, so that's what this is about? You're punishing me?" Rose lifted a magazine from the counter and threw it down again.

Miranda turned her back to her mother. "Yeah, it's all about you." She pressed a sponge in the sink, and a bubble flew up and popped against the faucet. "I don't care what you and Daddy do anymore, okay?" She spun around. Her face was red. "You screwed up your lives, but that doesn't mean you should screw up mine!"

Rose dropped her face into her hands and rubbed her eyes. She was exhausted. What were they doing? "Miranda," she said softly, "there are two issues. One, you lied. And two, we didn't know where you were. That's what this comes down to."

Miranda crossed her arms over her chest, miserable and trying for sullen. "I was on my way *home*."

"Okay," Rose conceded. "I've said what I have to say. You're here. That's what matters. Go to bed."

Miranda was taken by surprise for a moment, Rose could tell, then she stomped out of the room as noisily as possible. About the bottom of the stairs her footsteps came to a halt. "I *was* on my way home, you know," she said in a voice just loud enough for Rose to hear. "I might have even told you about it."

Rose listened as her daughter climbed the steps and closed the door to her room. Maybe she had finally lost it, but she felt that she and Miranda had made some kind of progress.

She crossed the kitchen to the glass door and slid it open, needing night air. Outside, the big sky was black as licorice, and it was strewn with stars like glittering sugar. Rose had never seen so many stars.

"My God," she gasped. The world, with all its pain and danger, was so astoundingly beautiful.

To the east, a shooting star streaked the sky in a brilliant curve like a gash in velvet. Rose remembered: August was the time for them. She wished she could curl up in a blanket with Miranda and watch the spectacle together, wished all the hurt and anger could burn itself out in a dazzling flash, like a meteor.

Another star fell above the water, as though melting, and as she watched, Rose heard the squeak of a window opening above her. Miranda's bathroom.

Now another star shot across the sky, and soon another. This must be a meteor shower. She would have to check the paper. Rose settled herself in a chair, and as she did, Cannibal came up on the deck to join her. "Let's wish on the next one," she told him. And in her heart she wished that Miranda would be all right. *Just let us get through this,* she prayed.

A huge burst of light just above them made even the dog look up. "Wow" came a voice from above. Miranda was watching from her bathroom window.

Rose smiled as she cried.

Chapter 18

Rose had begun a new painting, *Sunset at Crescent Beach*, inspired by the place but not at all representational. She had gone back to the same spot every night for a week to photograph, each time capturing slightly different nuances of color. Once she got her paints mixed to her satisfaction, she had separated the colors into a grid. Then she had begun laying thin squares of paint onto the canvas in a pattern that she thought suggested the progress of the sun. So far she was pleased.

A fine, late-summer morning had evolved into an afternoon that threatened rain. Rose packed up her paints, watching the clouds move over Gardiners Bay. Once again, a far-off sailboat reminded her of the *Ariel*, and Rose wondered what William would do with it while he was in Scotland. The thought irritated her. Though she knew the boat was William's sole remaining tie to his father, it was an albatross, as far as she was concerned. She wished to God he would sell it. But why

189

should he do that, so she could do nothing but paint — after throwing him out?

Well, he had been living in the house all summer, hadn't he? She had acted impeccably fairly. In a few short weeks, he would be gone, anyway. If he had truly wanted to save their marriage, he would have turned down the position in Scotland. But the thought had apparently never struck him. Rose had waited all summer for it while he thought he was waiting for her to decide. He had demonstrated a willingness to get back together, to do whatever was necessary to save their family, and she didn't discount the value of his intentions. But if he truly wanted her, he would have chosen to stay.

She faced it now: She had chosen her work, her painting, over him, and the hurt that must have cost him saddened her — but she would not choose differently if she had it to do again. She couldn't. He'd done the same, choosing Scotland over her. Painful though that was, Rose was glad he was going. Having William physically out of her sight, across an ocean, would make her new life easier. She preferred to reinvent herself without him a part of her landscape. Perhaps it was time to tell him so.

He would appreciate the truth, but did he deserve it? Had he been truthful with her?

Rose thought she could endure the truth now. At first she hadn't wanted to know the details of what had happened on Memorial Day weekend. But the worst of her pain, the gut-churning, disorienting anguish that had made her feel she'd lost all the bearings she had ever known, that huge, boiling grief had subsided. Her hurt had eased with the cadences of summer, of constantly changing sea and sky and magical, reflected light.

This place was healing. *Did I not tell you?* Luis asked nearly every time they spoke. *The island has got you painting again.* And it had. It had eased her, inspired her, and led her gently into possibility. She had entered an art show, begun a friendship. She couldn't help but feel that she was right here; it was okay for her to be alone here.

Now Rose set her paint box and her easel under the eaves next to Luis's collection of unused fishing poles. William had laughed about them, she remembered, the time they'd visited. She visualized him as he'd been that day, a few years back, another lifetime ago, tanned, with his hair grown long, shaggy, but his beard clipped neat, and she couldn't prevent the regret that washed over her. They had been a couple — had it been an illusion? Had she convinced herself that he'd loved her when he hadn't?

Though she was ready now to acknowledge the part she had played in the demise of her marriage, it was still just a part. She'd needed time alone to paint, a lot of time. Perhaps she'd taken too much, but she didn't deserve what had befallen her. She might have forgiven William a transgression, might have been willing to acknowledge his need. But why had he taken her own sister from her?

Rose leaned over the deck railing, watching the sky move over the sea. She was tired of these thoughts. She wished she could let them go. She wished she could stay here forever. She knew Miranda would like to, but they would have to go back to Connecticut in time for the start of school.

Until either the Connecticut house or the boat was sold, Rose couldn't afford to live elsewhere. Yet returning to that house, to the blue and yellow rooms she had lived in as a wife, meant breathing the air and touching the surfaces and moving through the hallways of the life she'd shared with William. Could she bear going back? For the last couple months she and Miranda had taken solace on this island, had stolen a fragment of time from the progression of hours and days that comprised their lives. But the clock would resume ticking, summer would come to an end, and they would have to move forward.

Cannibal came up from the beach, loping across the lawn, stopping to grin up at her when he reached the deck. Rose knew that the dog, with his unfailing internal clock, was expecting dinner. She routinely fed him early in the evening, before her own dinner, filling the bowl in his place beneath the deck. From the first, Cannibal had refused to come into the house, and Rose had dissuaded Miranda from trying to coax him.

When Miranda was home, the job of feeding the dog was hers. She fed him and brushed him and took him along when she rode her bicycle. He had grown to adore her, slavishly, though he was still wary of nearly everyone else.

In a way, Cannibal reminded Rose of Anna: outdoor-loving and open to adventure, she had nonetheless followed Rose from childhood on. Despite Anna's talk about getting out of Connecticut, she had never gone off on her own to do anything.

Inside the kitchen, the phone rang.

Rose hugged herself against an urge to speak with her sister, a sharp wish that the person calling would be Anna. The person to whom she had nothing to say but was longing to speak. She didn't understand it.

She entered the kitchen, hesitated, and picked up the phone. "Hullo."

"Hello, Rose." The rough-edged voice on the line was William's.

"Oh." She ran her fingers around her ear in a tucking motion, the way she had when she'd worn her hair long.

"Oh," William parroted, gently. "How are you, Rose?"

She pulled herself straight against the counter. "Very well, actually."

"I'm glad," he said. "Look, I was thinking, when I bring back Miranda next time, perhaps I could stay for dinner —"

"You're inviting yourself to dinner?" She made sure to sound as incredulous as she felt. What did he expect, everything nice, all forgiven?

"Or *take* you to dinner, of course." But his voice was tight. He was annoyed. How dare he be?

"I don't care to take any meal with you, William." She felt as though she had scored a point, but she didn't know what game they were playing, nor exactly what winning meant. She thought of Shirley Jackson's famous short story, "The Lottery" — sometimes winning is actually losing.

"Look, Rose," William urged. "Surely it's time we talked about what we're going to do. What you want."

"What I want — wanted — doesn't seem to be an option," she said, staring out through the glass doors. The clouds were moving, the sky brightening.

"If we have any hope of reconciling, we need to begin somewhere," William said, reasonably.

Rose squinted at the boats on the bay, blurring their lines. He didn't deserve to be let off easily.

"When I want to start somewhere," Rose said, "I'll let you know."

Chapter 19

For more than a week, William had immersed himself in preparation for Scotland, completing his course work, making final arrangements for his leave at school, packing up books and other essentials to ship in advance. He had fixed a few things around the house and spent hours preparing the *Ariel*. Labor Day weekend he would sail her to Sag Harbor, Long Island, to a semiretired broker who had known her original owner before her sale to William's father, Sergeant Major Campbell. William was almost ready for his journey, but he had one more thing to do.

He had to speak to Anna.

He wanted her to sail the *Ariel* with him for the last time. She would want to say good-bye to the boat, and perhaps to him. He hoped she would. He needed to sail with her again, to remember her with the wind in her hair and her color high, not ashen and miserable as he remembered seeing her last.

And there was something else. He wanted Anna and Rose to reconnect. They must, before he left. Rose had yet to admit to it, and William understood that she wanted to punish him, but she did not intend to take him back. That much was clear to him. If it wasn't yet clear to her, it soon would be. However, Rose needed her sister in her life; William knew this as well as he knew anything at all.

And beneath all of it there was his selfishness: He wanted to feel alive in the way that he felt only with Anna, just one more time.

He lifted his phone and punched in her home number, the first time he had done that since May. She answered on the third ring.

"It's William." At her intake of breath he felt a tugging in his gut. Oh, yes, alive. She still did it to him.

"Hi." She sounded okay, herself.

Should he bother with pleasantries, ask after her and all of that? No. He never had. He said what he called to say: "I am selling the *Ariel*, sailing her to Sag Harbor the Saturday of Labor Day weekend."

"Oh," she said. "I'm sorry."

He wondered whether she felt to blame. The thought had not occurred to him before, so completely culpable did he feel himself to be for what had happened. "No, it's the right thing to do," he said. "I'm okay with it. I haven't a choice." A laugh rose from deep in his throat.

"Okay," Anna said. "Well, good luck. I guess."

He heard the implicit *Why are you telling me this?* and realized he had not made himself clear. Again. "Anna," he said emphatically, "will you sail with me, the *Ariel*'s last sail?"

"Oh God," she said, and his heart expanded. He felt her as though she stood in the room beside him.

"Please, it would mean a great deal to me." That was all he would say. He awaited her response.

Anna sighed. "It's just all so hard."

"I know."

"And this will be hard for you, selling the boat."

He was touched by her generosity of spirit. "Yes. This and other things." He paused. "So sail with me. I've arranged for a rental car for the return trip to Connecticut."

His eyes were closed, seeing the two of them together, sailing. He would stay focused on the sail itself, not the aftermath.

"How can I say no?" she asked.

"You can't."

* ★ ★

Outside, though the thunder and lightning had passed, it was still raining. Miranda liked the sound of rain. And the smell. Everyone talked about rain smelling fresh, but to Miranda rain smelled old, like parts of every growing thing that had ever been. *Fusty. Sultry. Pungent.* These were words Miranda had memorized, words she liked to pronounce. Words that sounded like the smell of rain.

In Danny's father's fishing shed, in front of the partly opened window, she stood and breathed. The rain-drummed air blowing on her face felt almost cold compared to the hot, sticky air in the shed. Drops played patterns against the metal roof.

From behind her, Danny leaned to kiss the rounded top of Miranda's ear, the hollow where her neck met her shoulder, her collarbone. She felt the rise and fall of her skin against his mouth, and confusion, liquid and warm, in the pit of her stomach.

Danny kissed Miranda's cheekbone, then reached to write his initials above hers in the grimy steam of the window. Miranda drew a heart around their initials. She turned to smile at him, her cheek brushing his neck. "I think it's passing,"

199

she said. "The storm."

"Maybe." Danny moved against her. He slid his hands from her shoulders to her wrists, spreading the droplets of rain caught in the blond down of her arms. "You can't leave," he said.

Miranda closed her eyes. She knew he wasn't talking about her leaving now, but soon, when she would have to go back to school, and she had no reply but to wrap her arms around him. He shifted his weight, knocking into a lobster trap.

She jumped a little, eyes open, looking around.

The eight-by-eight shed was crammed with traps and gear. There was no place to get comfortable, but at least they could be alone in here. This was one of "their" places. Shell Beach was another. Mashomack Preserve was another. That's where they'd been headed when the storm began.

Miranda nestled once more against Danny's chest, which smelled slightly of French fries. She tasted his lips for salt.

"We need to be together," he said.

Miranda's stomach twisted. They had been talking all week about it, being together, *doing it*. But not in the fishing shed, nor the school playground where the junior high kids made out. Not on any of the accessible beaches. This had to be planned. Only a little time remained before Miranda would leave the island to go back to Connecticut. The thought made her miserable. Although her mother had promised to "consider" staying to live here on the Rock, Miranda knew the answer was probably going to be no. Before long, she would have to return to the house where she had lived her whole life, a home that no longer existed because her family as she'd known it no longer existed.

"We have so little time," Danny said. "You know?"

Miranda watched his mouth, the way it moved. *I love you* — she said the words in her mind, not daring to be the first to speak them out loud but relishing the sting of just thinking them. "I know," she said.

He pulled her close. She came up to his chin, which he rested on top of her head. Falling in love was the most important thing to ever happen to her, and Miranda hadn't talked to anybody about it except her aunt Anna, a little. Not even Jai.

Jai was off to a "teen adventure" camp in Colorado. Though they had exchanged e-mails all summer, Miranda had mentioned "this local guy she met" only casually, and Jai had been too enamored of describing her own adventures to pry for more. In fairness, she wouldn't expect to need to pry. Each girl took for granted that the other would rush to report any and all romantic developments. Even — mostly — imaginary ones.

Miranda wondered why she had stopped telling Jai everything, and what it meant about how her life was changing. She thought it might have something to do with her parents breaking up, with her grim discovery that the world doesn't stay the same forever. And the world, as if in compensation, had given her Danny, and she had to protect them.

"I wish I didn't have to work tonight," Danny said.

Miranda knew what he meant. "Let's spend all day tomorrow together. We'll get up early and watch the sun rise from the beach."

Miranda drew her head back, looking up into his eyes.

"Okay," he said, and he kissed her.

Chapter 20

Anna walked nervously down the pier, staring at her feet, hardly daring to look up. The last time she had seen the *Ariel*, her life had changed. The boat looked very much the same, looked its best, all polished and gleaming. It was Anna's life that was changing again, and this time she was changing it. Quitting her job. Subletting her condo. Sailing for parts unknown within a few months. She would pick the proper moment to tell William her plans, glad to have an upcoming adventure to equal his. She was proud, like a schoolgirl who finally gets over her shyness and makes a speech to the class.

Well, that's how she felt, that and an anguish she didn't know how else to bear.

William was waiting for her in the cockpit, ready to help her aboard. She avoided his eyes as he took her hand, but as their fingers touched, the last residue of her doubt evaporated. She wanted to be with him, and she didn't know whether she could hide it, or whether she should.

They embraced awkwardly and briefly.

"I'm so glad to see you," he said.

She nodded. *Yes and no,* she didn't say. Glad to see him but tortured, too. Everything had changed since the last time they'd sailed together on that first weekend of summer, an ordinary outing that had shipwrecked their lives. Yet now she felt as though no time had passed between them. In the time-space continuum that contained them, they had just kissed; they wanted to kiss again.

She was dying to ask him about Rose, about whether they were reconciling, but she couldn't face the answer just yet. She wanted a few hours of pure sailing with him. And so she had them. They sailed across the Sound toward Long Island, and here and there they spoke to each other of how they had been. William told Anna stories of Rupert, goings-on at the college, his summer school classes, and plans for St. Andrews. And between the lines they spoke, Anna heard what he didn't say — what he felt.

She took the tiller from time to time while he navigated, otherwise she trimmed the sails. They worked well together even in near silence. It had always been this way. Anna used to think their compatibility came from William's having been her teacher, but then she noticed him doing things he had learned from her. Stupid things, meaningless things like the way she tapped her fingernail against a Coke can so it wouldn't spurt. Things that meant he was paying attention to her.

They were en route to Sag Harbor where William had somehow discovered a yacht broker who knew all about the *Ariel*. Anna was impressed with his diligence; she knew what parting with this boat would cost him. Well, Rose would be glad. Or would she see her share of the profits as blood money?

Anna grabbed on to a line and looked at the horizon. The early morning weather report had been good, and indeed they'd set out under fair skies, but over the past few hours billowing white clouds had massed into a gray bank. Even a landsman would recognize the gathering thunderhead, and William considered himself a salt. Anna was confident in his sailing skills, but she began to worry they'd have to put in to harbor somewhere before they reached the brokerage marina.

William soon confirmed her fear. "Mackerel sky," he said. "We'll need to take in the flying jib." His dark eyes, shadowed by a Red Sox baseball cap, were unreadable. His voice was calm but tinged with anxiety.

The boat heaved, and Anna threw out a hand, steadying herself against the polished brass of the instrument panel. At her nod, William released the halyard, and she made her way forward, tracing her fingers along the cabin as though it were already a memory.

Sea spray flew back into Anna's face as the bowsprit plunged and rose in the oily-looking waves. Swaying, off balance, she had the sudden, distinct sensation that someone was watching, but no other boats were near. The bow lifted and dropped. She lunged forward, grabbed the sail, and took it in just as a gust of wind would have filled it.

She leaned back against the cabin as she rolled up the sail. The sky looked unreal, dreamlike but familiar. Rose's painting. She remembered the painting that hadn't won, the painting of the *Ariel*; it featured a sky much like this.

Swells in the water grew more and more misty, particles swirling as the wind grazed the tops of the waves. The air felt different, charged. The *Ariel* swung sharply to starboard. They had just rounded Plum Island, off the North Fork of Long Island.

Sag Harbor and the yacht brokerage lay to the west. If they got there, in another hour or so William and the *Ariel* would finally part. As if in protest, the boat reared up and back on a wave.

Anna wound the gasket line around the sail, made her way alongside the cabin to the cockpit, and prayed the storm would hold off. The many hours she had spent on this boat, with William at the helm, rushed back to her, a time lapse of haircuts and beard trims, of deepening knowledge. She let her eyes travel his profile, savoring it. He shot her a glance, his eyes skimming hers. She dropped her eyes, and with her thumb wiped a smudge from the brightwork, the fine-grained teak she'd so often rubbed to a shine.

For years she had sailed and crewed on the *Ariel*, and she couldn't fully grasp that she would never do so again. She shook her head and as she did glimpsed her distorted reflection in a porthole. Her features, blurred in the glass, reminded Anna of her niece. Everyone said Miranda looked more like her aunt than her mother. Anna missed her the way one would probably miss a kid sister.

Waves slapped higher against the wooden hull. Anna gripped the railing. She gazed past William's shoulder, past the tender part of his neck, wanting to touch him but not touching him. He wanted to touch her, too. She smelled it from him. She wanted to bury her face in his neck, near the fur of his chest.

Salt spray burned her eyes, and she squinted. Ahead in the hazy distance lay the shores of Shelter Island, where Rose and Miranda were now. Anna felt a tiny shock at their proximity. She hadn't been this physically close to her sister in months. Maybe Rose sensed Anna near. Maybe she had *willed* the storm.

The storm was close; Anna could taste its metallic bite. The wind blew strands of hair across her lips, and as she plucked at them, she suddenly feared — no, she *knew* — the weather would force them to put in on Shelter Island.

She moved toward William, the wind whipping at them now. "What do you think?" She had to raise her voice above the roar.

His hand reached for her arm, touched her, then withdrew. He cupped his dark beard. "I think we'll have to take her in where we can."

"You don't mean *here*." But it wasn't a question.

"I think we must." William yanked the

208

tiller. The boat heeled sharply, and he headed her into the wind.

The *Ariel* took another wave. Cold spray slapped the cockpit. Anna looked around to see how other boats were faring, but sails on the lopsided horizon were scarce. She breathed through her mouth, gulping vibrating air, and pulled deeper into her sweatshirt.

"Maybe it's time," William said, nearly shouting.

Anna looked up at the grim spectacle of the tall, spruce spar raking an ashen sky. "Is that why you wanted me with you?" she yelled. "To take me to Shelter Island?"

William sought her eyes. He leaned closer and spoke in a lowered voice. "You flatter me," he said, "but I'm afraid I can't quite conjure storms." *Oh yes you can,* she didn't say.

The *Ariel* took a swell cleanly broadside, rising and falling like a toy in a tub. Spray swept the stern, drenching them both, and William grunted against the tiller as he struggled to see through the fog.

The cold shower was half thrilling, like the quick, hollow sweetness in the gut at the drop of an elevator. Or the excitement of a fatal kiss, that instant just before the grief.

For a moment, Anna imagined herself telling Rose the story of her decision to go off to sea, enjoying Rose's shock and surprise, taking pleasure in the ways she could make her sister laugh.

Three months ago, the sisters had told each other everything. Almost everything.

A flash of lightning lit the atmosphere so quickly Anna wondered whether it had happened. Then, an explosion of thunder shook the air. She knew she should go below, but she hated breathing the close, dank air of those quarters during heavy weather. Motion combined with lack of air would make her ill.

Which was worse, she wondered, the threat of seasickness or of lightning?

And which was worse, losing a lover or a sister?

The sky opened and William shouted to take in the sails.

Anna ran forward. The worst was losing them both.

Chapter 21

"May I speak with Miranda?" William never wasted time with small talk. Rose could hear clattering in the background, sounds of a restaurant or bar. She switched the phone to her other ear as though to get farther from the noise.

She said, "Miranda isn't here."

"I see." William's voice dropped.

Rose knew the way his bristled chin would press into his neck. She saw his dark brow furrow. She realized, with regret, she had never painted him.

"There's about to be a storm," he said.

Rose crossed her arms over her breasts, holding the phone between her shoulder and ear. She looked out through the glass doors. Rain had begun to patter the deck. What was William doing, watching the weather channel somewhere? Did he think, because of the Greenport incident, that she couldn't keep track of their daughter? He was the one who was leaving the country. The anger began to simmer in her.

"Right," she said. She wound the phone cord around her finger. William had said he was willing to work on their marriage, but he hadn't done much to demonstrate it. Of course, neither had she.

"I've just come in from the *Ariel*." William paused, irritatingly. Voices in the background buzzed. "I had to come ashore because of the weather."

"That's too bad." Rose supposed William was phoning in a last effort to prevail upon her to permit Miranda to go to Scotland. The argument made her weary. She wouldn't change her mind.

She unfocused her eyes, connecting the silvery droplets that ran down the glass doors. Moving her eyelids made the pattern change. She thought of melting metals on canvas. She grabbed a pencil and scribbled the idea on the edge of a take-out menu.

"Rose, I want to tell you something," William said. He treated her carefully now, and part of her enjoyed it. They had been careless with each other for so long. He took a breath. "I'm on the island."

That news gave Rose a start. "*Long* Island?"

"Shelter Island," William said. "I've just now put in at the Ram's Head Inn."

Rose's anger flared. The inn was just down the road, within walking distance. This wasn't his weekend for Miranda. What was he thinking? "Why?"

"I was sailing the *Ariel* to Sag Harbor," William said, his inflection rising at the end of the sentence as though Rose was supposed to ask for details, but she didn't want to hear his story.

Outside, the approaching storm rumbled.

"Right," she said. "What do you want?"

"Well . . ." Wind keened through the eaves. William seemed to consider something. "As I'm here, I'd like to see Miranda. Take her to dinner."

A bizarre jealousy — of her own daughter — warmed Rose's cheeks. William pointedly hadn't asked to take *her*. Not that she blamed him. Not that she'd go. "In this storm?" she asked.

"Would tomorrow night be better? I might be staying through Monday."

Rain began slashing the roof and windows. Rose pictured Miranda riding her bicycle through the downpour. She saw her daughter pull up to the ice cream store on Bridge Street and run inside. Then the image faded, and Rose imagined William's face, his bearded chin tucked into the palm

213

of his hand, his top lip pressed against a curled finger.

"I'll tell Miranda to call you," she said, and a thunderbolt cracked the horizon in two. She hung up the phone, and then, grabbing an umbrella, hurried outside to feed the dog.

William settled in at the bar of the Ram's Head Inn and ordered a single malt scotch, neat. Anna had declined to join him, saying she wanted to rest, but he knew she was avoiding being alone with him.

"No ice?" The kid with the country-club looks tending bar reached for the bottle of McCallan.

"Practicing," William said, "for iceless drinking in the UK."

"You a Brit?" The kid poured from high above the glass, showing off.

William shook his head. "No. Going over to work for a year." Though he had been born in Edinburgh, he carried no conscious memory of Scotland. His mother, a GI bride, had immigrated to America when he was an infant. His father had been American. William was American. And yet, he couldn't help but think of his upcoming journey as returning home, a circle completed.

The kid placed the shot — *a wee dram,* they'd say in Scotland — on a napkin in front of William and went to take an order from a summoning waitress.

The inn's concierge had called this room the lounge. A shining brass and mahogany bar faced a dozen small tables at which couples, mostly middle-aged or better, sipped cocktails and watched the storm abate. Waiters pulled open the double sets of French doors leading to the dining terrace, and a breeze from the water swayed white tablecloths like summer dresses. From his bar stool, William could see beyond the lawn to the glimmer of silver that was Coecles Harbor.

"So, what kind of business are you going to Scotland for?" The kid was in front of him, filling a bowl with peanuts. "You deal in boats?"

William shifted his weight on the bar stool. Anna had once said his whiskers made him look like a sailor, but he trimmed his beard close now. "Why do you say that?"

The kid pointed to the sheet of notepaper in front of William, a handwritten list of boat equipment to provide the yacht broker.

"Oh," William chuckled, disappointed.

215

"No. I'm a professor."

The kid nodded and walked away to deliver peanuts. William turned his attention to his list, scanning it. *Westerbeke diesel auxiliary* — with a bad injector, he'd had to fix that thing. *New gaff* — replaced three years ago with Sitka spruce from Oregon. *Vintage anchor lantern* — made by Davey, a two-hundred-year-old English chandler.

He sipped his scotch and mentally toasted the *Ariel*, moored just beyond the inn's little beach. Nathaniel Herreshoff had designed her in the 1930s, and in the '60s, William's father had bought the boat from her original owner, a guy whose only son had been killed in Vietnam. The old man had been thoroughly interviewed by the owner, who needed to ascertain that William's dad was an acceptable and properly appreciative buyer, not some Philistine who would make repairs with epoxy. And he *was* properly appreciative, as was William after him. Now, William would demand the same of the *Ariel*'s new owner. He required at least that small comfort in return for losing her.

William gulped his scotch. The *Ariel*, his family, and Anna — he had lost them all, through his own fault.

Well, he had tried to salvage his family,

216

to do the right thing, to repair his marriage for the sake of Miranda, if not the love he still felt for Rose. But Rose was having none of it. He had tried to put his family above himself; he had fought his desire for Anna.

And now she was here, with him, but he knew he'd lost her and, what was worse, he had shattered her life, too. He must try to put things right before he left. Anna and Rose must be brought to reconcile. But Rose was stubborn. Was she deliberately making things difficult for everyone in order to keep William and Anna apart? Well, he couldn't blame her.

He thought of Anna daily, that hadn't changed during the past three months. Even when he concentrated on preparing his upcoming course module, he thought of Anna. She was Aine, the Lady of the Lake, or Cliodna, goddess of the sea. She was everywhere.

He had vowed not to trouble her, not to contact her unless she wanted that, which, clearly, she didn't. He had caused her enough grief, had caused the three women he most loved more than enough grief. He had asked her along on this sail, this last sail, because he imagined she would want to say good-bye to the *Ariel*. And because he wanted her with him when he said it.

William swore to himself again, as he had all day, that he'd set sail in good faith, that he had not known of the storm nor planned this diversion. Nonetheless, here they were, fittingly marooned (in a sense) on the island whose shores Rose and Miranda wandered, as if in exile from their former life, an exile for which he was responsible. What could he do to set things right?

When they'd sailed together that Memorial Day weekend — all of them, wife, daughter, sister-in-law — he'd thought them happy, thought happiness possible, despite the palpable tension between he and Anna. How had he imagined he could traverse that edge, sustain that heightened state, indefinitely? He'd been a fool, a greedy fool.

The blender whirred into its motor song as the bartender mixed a batch of daiquiris. William watched him, envying the economy of his movement, the precision of his pour. The kid carried the drinks to a couple sitting by the piano. Married, William guessed, though he couldn't say whether they were happy. For Christ's sake, he hadn't been able to tell whether *he* was happy. But he knew, now, that he had been going through the motions for a long time. He had loved Rose, yes; he had admired her, always. But despite his best efforts, he longed for Anna.

He turned to examine the possibly-married couple. They wore golf clothes in muted pastels. Probably they'd played as guests at Gardiners Bay Club. The man, tanned and handsome with a thick shock of steel gray hair, lit a cigarette, and then, in a gesture out of an old movie, he passed the cigarette to his wife.

William looked toward the kid, to see his reaction, but he had turned.

The silver-haired man leaned back in his chair, watching the sky through the open doors. He wore the look of someone who was elsewhere in his thoughts, the flesh around his eyes and mouth drawn smooth and blank. William wondered whether the man had secrets, and if he did, whether he admitted them to himself.

How often had Rose retreated to an inner landscape William hadn't shared? She'd had secrets, too. Perhaps she hadn't longed for another man but for another life. Powerless to change the shifting dynamics between them, William had been nearly content to let her retreat, nearly able to convince himself the outer structure of their lives could contain them. He'd been nearly satisfied to esteem his wife and want the best for her, and to continue with their foundering but familiar marriage.

The worst of all his failures was to Miranda. He and his daughter had managed by mutual aversion to avoid talking much about his and Rose's separation this summer. She didn't ask about it, and he didn't volunteer. Incredible how much time could pass avoiding a discussion. A lifetime.

He knew Miranda blamed her mother, and he had tried, in his circumspect way, to convince her otherwise, but it was time, he knew, to speak directly. How? He couldn't very well say to her, *I love your aunt — your godmother, your mother's sister, her best friend — I love her enough to have ruined your life.*

But he had never consented to that choice, never willingly chosen his own happiness over his daughter's. He'd given in, yes, and he regretted it at the same time he held the memory of it in his head the way he had held Anna in his arms, with awe.

But he had been willing to pay the price for his self-indulgence, if only Rose would choose to exact it. She had put him off all summer. It was nearly time for him to

220

journey across the pond, and his life was completely unhinged.

William signaled for another scotch. He must focus on the point of this trip, the important point, which was to sell the *Ariel*. That's what he could do for Rose and Miranda. Though he wasn't sure that the current market was the most favorable, he couldn't afford to wait. The best thing he could do for Rose and Miranda would be to enable them to get on with their lives.

He eyed his list lovingly, proud of the *Ariel*'s refinements as one would be of a child's, though she was twenty years older than he.

The kid brought him a fresh drink. "So, you looking to sell or buy?"

"I'm sorry?"

The kid tapped the list. "This boat, you must be either selling or buying."

"Ah." William sipped. "Selling. Alas. She's out in the harbor." He pointed through the open doors.

The kid squinted, as though he could see from there. "The cutter?"

"Very good," William said. He refolded the list and slipped it into his pocket. "The *Ariel*." Talking about her always filled him with pride, which then embarrassed him.

Anna had understood. She loved the *Ariel* as he did. Where Rose looked upon sailing as William's hobby, a diversion that took up his time and thereby granted her time to work on her painting, Anna's love for sailing matched his own. She loved the wildness of the sea and she loved the beauty of the vessel — the burnished teak of the deck, the hand-rubbed brass hardware, the soft Egyptian cotton sails — as William did.

And she looked beautiful when they sailed, her cheeks in high color, her lovely pale hair blown about.

"Great boat," the kid said. He winked at William.

William was intrigued by the kid's poise. His students at the state university were this age, but William couldn't imagine any of them in such a role. They all seemed so lacking in deportment. So young. Perhaps he needed to see them as inhabitants of a world completely separate from his own, the way he had seen Anna for so long. Hadn't he learned that disaster lurked otherwise?

No point in this endless navel-gazing. In two weeks' time, he would be leaving the country. The timing seemed both cruel and an undeserved blessing. He looked eagerly toward his post at the Institute for Theology, Imagination and the Arts at the University of St. Andrews. He had designed his own course, The Spirituality of Creativity, using texts and ideas from Carl Jung to Joseph Campbell to Dan Wakefield. His academic duties included delivering one lecture per week and student tutorials three afternoons a week, a far cry from his crammed undergraduate course load at the state university.

He would finally have the time to write the article on the role of the artist in myth that had haunted him.

"My uncle's a yacht broker," the kid said, sliding William a business card. "FYI."

"Thanks," William said. He pocketed the card and made a mental note to phone Bud Goss, who was expecting him in Sag Harbor.

Waiters were lighting candles on the terrace beneath the green-and-white-striped awning. There would be no sunset view tonight, and the mosquitoes would be vicious. William tried to remember the last time he'd been here, probably the weekend he and Rose had spent with Luis. He didn't recall the occasion, if there had been one, but he remembered mooring the *Ariel* in Coecles Harbor, Luis meeting them here at the inn for dinner, and then driving them back to spend the night at his place just up the road.

Where Rose and Miranda were now.

William wondered whether Miranda was home yet. Should he risk antagonizing Rose by phoning again? He could have asked Rose to have dinner with him — why hadn't he thought of that? She might be ready for such a gesture. They were managing to behave civilly these days.

Behind the kid mixing daiquiris, the windows brightened.

Clouds were moving in the sky, stippling the room with shadows and light. Patterns ran across the walls; faces shone, briefly illuminated as though for a photograph. Voices quickened, the murmur in the room grew louder. The golfing couple leaned toward each other in conversation.

In the distance, thunder rumbled. The storm was moving out to sea. Anna might expect them to set sail in the morning, to continue their original plan. But William had other plans.

He withdrew a few crumpled fives from his trousers, dropped them onto the bar, and turned toward the French doors. Outside, the sun struggled to make an appearance through the moving clouds. William headed out of the lounge, carrying his drink down the steps of the slate terrace, across the sodden lawn toward the gazebo at the edge of the inn's small beach. There he watched the horizon change color in slow motion.

Anna was accident-prone.

At thirty-five, she had shiny scars on her knees, like a child's. Her arms bore the rose-brown evidence of hot irons. A tiny piece was missing from the side of her tongue. And yet, except for breaking her collarbone when she was nine, she had never been treated in a hospital. So she was lucky, too. Her mother had always told her she was luckier than almost any child in India or Africa. By which Anna knew she meant lucky to be alive.

"Beginner's luck," Rose had said to Anna when she won the first game of hearts after Rose taught her to play. But Rose had been the lucky one at everything else, the one who was praised and rewarded, at home, at school — and spared, too. Spared punishment, spared wrath.

Spared everything except her own sister's betrayal.

Anna sat wincing on the cabbage rose

quilt, rubbing her right shin. She had walked into the wooden bed, knocked into its side panel hidden beneath a crocheted bed skirt. A jolt of pain opened a trapdoor to her stomach; she felt nauseated and dizzy. This was her second injury of the day. Earlier, she had caught her finger in a dresser drawer. She had been getting worse, physically clumsier, with each passing week, while mentally she had grown more and more numb.

And then she had made the decision to quit her job and sail.

And then William had phoned.

And she had gone to him, and now she was here, on Shelter Island where her sister was living, wanting to be with William and not daring to be. Wanting to tell him of her plans, wanting to ask him what his feelings were.

She was here because William had asked her, here although three months of sorrow had nearly paralyzed her, here although she alternated between longing for her sister's forgiveness and her brother-in-law's love till she thought she might as well tear herself in two.

For three months she had walked through the hours of her life scarcely able to distinguish between day and night,

226

grateful for the physical labor her job at the Nature Center sometimes entailed, for the poor creatures to whose suffering she was required to minister. If not for the softness of fur and sharpness of beak against her fingers, she couldn't have kept herself from William all that time.

She could scarcely bear looking at him. Today on the *Ariel* they had spoken only of the boat and the weather and the sea, nothing of themselves apart from their recollections of other sailing trips. Those, a litany of high points, of shared pleasures and accumulating intimacy, had evinced from Anna the inevitable blush or glance away. They'd steered clear of talk of the two of them, though. Avoided the subject that hung in the air like the mist off the sea. There was still time for that.

Or perhaps there was not. Perhaps there was time only to let go.

The room was quieter than it had been. The storm was passing. Light flickered across the walls. Anna thought she must try to convince William to set sail first thing in the morning, even though the canceled reservation they'd been able to take included another day.

William must have planned to stop here all along, Anna decided. Obviously, he hoped she and Rose would work things out. But it was hopeless. Rose hadn't answered her e-mails or phone calls. Rose didn't want to listen, didn't want to believe her.

Believe what? That Anna hadn't slept with William? Or that she wouldn't have? And was that the truth? Anna didn't know. For months — for years — Anna had hidden her feelings for William. That was the worst of it: She had kept no other secret from her sister. Her sister had been her solace; her sister, though only five years older, had been her mother. Her own mother hadn't protected her as Rose had. Only with Rose, and then William, had Anna ever truly felt safe.

She dropped back onto the bed and gazed at the ceiling, the throbbing in her shin forgotten, her eyes focused inward. Immediately she saw pictures in her head. She saw the old house, she saw the fishing pole against the wall, she saw her father's hand.

No!

Why was she thinking about this? Where had this memory come from, full-blown as though out of some malign creature's head — or the warped hull that was the mind of a spinster who had spent all of her free time with her sister's family. Who had never risked anything in her life, except perhaps her life.

But that would change now.

She rolled to her left side. Soon, she would be gone, out of Rose's way, out of Miranda's, and away from William.

She reached her right hand between her thighs, parted herself. She slid her middle finger slowly along her split, rocking her hips a little. She wanted William. She wanted him to come to her room, now.

She imagined kissing him, transporting them to the *Ariel* in her mind, feeling the wind against their faces, the length of his body pressed to hers.

She got up and locked her door.

Chapter 22

Rose entered the Ram's Head Inn through the screen door and walked straight through the hall, across the needlepoint rugs, past the staircase and the ram's head hung over the archway, past the reception desk, and out the French doors. The late-morning sun poured like warm syrup over the stone terrace. Luis was already there, seated at a table overlooking the sweep of dappled lawn and the steel-blue shimmer of Coecles Harbor where the *Ariel* was moored.

The sight of the boat stopped Rose quite literally in her tracks, if only for a half step. She had, deliberately, not set eyes on this vessel of her marriage's undoing, not since she'd spent that last day in contented ignorance, sailing the Long Island Sound with the three people she had most loved, had most trusted. Like a blind fool.

Everyone had been in good spirits that day, Rose remembered as she made her way through the tables. Even Miranda, who'd often sulked when asked to spend a holiday weekend with her parents, had been cooperative. William had seemed relaxed, and, despite the holiday volume of boats on the Sound, their sail had been unusually leisurely. They hadn't been headed toward any destination, which had suited her fine.

Luis stood to greet her, waving.

"Hello." They kissed European-style. Luis's affectations amused her.

"I've ordered you a Bloody Mary." He handed her a celery-topped drink. "But if you want something else . . . ?"

"No, this is fine. Thank you." Rose took the drink, set it down, and seated herself. She glanced at the brunchers around them and then squinted toward where the boats rocked and clanked at their moorings. Unreasonable as it was, she despised the *Ariel*.

"How are you, darling?" Luis reached past the bread basket for her hand. "Are you doing any shopping?"

"I'm fine." She smiled at him. "Not much shopping. But painting."

His hand was pale olive on top of her own golden brown. She thought of Daphne's clay-colored skin and had an image for a painting, three bodies, three skins, distinct and yet fading one into the other.

"That's marvelous, but you know I told you so."

She slipped her hand from his and unfolded her napkin in her lap. She hadn't told him that William was here. She probably should. "Yes, I know. About fifty times."

Luis made a face. "How's the dog?"

"Cannibal?" Rose steeled herself for admonitions regarding dog hair and floor scratches. "Don't worry. I haven't let him in the house."

Luis lifted his Bloody Mary and shrugged. "I don't mind." A waiter dropped menus on the table and floated away.

"Sure you don't!" Rose said.

Luis ignored her. "To you," he toasted. "To the success of your work."

Rose was touched. They clinked glasses. How odd friendship could be. You could know a person so well in some regards, feel close to them, and yet be completely in the dark regarding other, perhaps hidden aspects of their lives.

A fat bumblebee landed on a pink zinnia in a milk glass vase. "The ones with the white faces don't sting," Luis said.

Rose inched closer but saw only fuzzy black with fuzzy yellow stripes. "Does this one have a white face?" She squinted, and then imagined the bee squinting back at her.

"No." Luis sat back in his chair, removed a pair of reading glasses from his shirt pocket, and picked up the menu. The bee flew off into the border garden.

Rose picked up her menu. At forty she didn't need reading glasses, but she knew that she would soon. Everyone did. She wondered how changing eyesight would affect her work. She had already noticed a shift in her technique toward broader strokes.

"Oven-roasted oysters with tomato shallot vinaigrette," Luis read aloud. "Ever had those?"

"No." Rose studied the menu and mentally selected the omelet of the day, crab and asparagus. "Do we have business to discuss, legal stuff?"

Luis lay his menu down. "Yes and no," he said. "This isn't on the clock."

Rose looked up. "Ha! If it were, I'd have a biscuit and be on my way." She reached toward where, just minutes ago, a basket of bread had sat between them. "Where did the bread go?"

Luis scanned the table, as though the basket might be hidden behind the flower vase or the salt and pepper. "I don't know."

"I don't really need any," Rose said. Something buzzed past her ear and she reached up, instinctively, and smoothed her hair.

"We'll get more," Luis insisted.

"I really don't need to eat biscuits," Rose said.

"Oh, hell, darling, you're entitled. And you look fabulous," he said. "Your hair. Your skin. Look at me." He lifted his well-muscled arm. "I'm either at the office or the gym. And the bars, of course. Sunlight rarely shines upon my skin. I wish I looked as good as you do."

Yeah, yeah, Rose thought. But still, she felt pleased.

She reached for her drink but it, too, had disappeared.

When it came time for the check, Luis suggested that "subtle service was best repaid by a subtle tip." Rose laughed. Indeed, dishes and glasses had vanished almost before their eyes. Not the inn's usual style. Well, it was a holiday, the last big weekend of the season, and the restaurant here was an island favorite.

The business aspect of their meeting had taken Rose by surprise. Little needed to be discussed regarding legal matters. Rose was favoring legal separation, though Luis didn't really see the point of it. Why not simply divorce? Was she still unsure of whether she wanted to save her marriage?

Yes, she had told him. But the truth was that William was going away. She didn't have to decide anything. She didn't have to give him an easy out.

Luis asked about the *Ariel* and, chagrined, Rose pointed to the harbor and explained that William and the *Ariel* were in fact here, though she wasn't quite sure why.

"You didn't ask him why?" Luis lowered his chin, cocked his head, and raised his eyebrows.

She had to admit she hadn't. She felt like a fool, and she prayed not to run into William. Just let her finish her meal and get out of here.

Luis had another topic to put forth. He wanted to know whether Rose was interested in staying on in his house. If she remained in Shelter Island, she could put the Connecticut house on the market, which would ease her financial situation considerably. Fall was a good time to sell, if not so good as spring. Rose sat in silent surprise as Luis asked whether she would be interested in doing some work for him, not full time, just a few hours, perhaps ten a week, clerical work on a "sensitive" case he had just taken on and would probably go on for more than a year. The work would serve as her rent.

Rose listened with interest, asked a few questions, and thanked Luis for his generosity. She would consider his offer; it had come as a surprise. She gazed out toward the *Ariel*, struck by the thought that Luis's plan would save William from having to sell his beloved boat. Was it possible Luis and he were somehow in cahoots?

No, of course it wasn't. What was happening to her?

She felt chilled, as she often did after eating, and with a shiver came a sharp need for the bathroom. "Excuse me," she said, touching Luis's shoulder. "Too much coffee."

The cramped, unisex powder room was tucked at the bottom of the hall stairs, next to a closet. The door was locked, so Rose waited. In less than a minute an elegant blond woman emerged wearing pastel golf clothes. Rose thought she looked familiar. The women smiled at each other apologetically, stepping out and in, respectively, through the narrow opening.

After latching the door, she peered at herself in the mirror. There was no window in the small room, and the light was uneven and harsh. She wanted to see what was "fabulous" about her. She hadn't felt fabulous in a very long time.

She ran her fingers through her cropped, sun-streaked hair. Luis liked her haircut, he'd said. She liked not having to think about what to do with it. She wanted to eliminate as many chores from her life as she could. She wanted life to be easy.

Would staying in Shelter Island make things easier or more complicated? She thought about Luis's offer, reckoning back and forth in her mind what she should do. Miranda would be pleased to stay.

She was washing her hands at the sink, mulling over the good things she had heard about Shelter Island High School (small classes, good funding) when two short taps sounded at the door.

"Just a minute," Rose called. She dried her hands and availed herself of a squirt of lavender lotion. She unlatched the door, between hand rubbing, and opened it.

"Shit," Anna said, standing there.

For a moment Rose was stunned. Then she spun back into the powder room and slammed the door. She spoke through the wood as though to prevent her sister penetrating it. "Get out of my sight."

237

Trembling, not looking at herself in the mirror, Rose turned to the sink. She was shocked, and shocked at herself for being shocked. She turned on both faucets and let the water run full force, its sound matching the roar of blood in her veins. Anna was here with William — of course — and the son of a bitch hadn't had the decency to mention it. She squeezed closed her eyes, bent her head, and groaned into her chest.

To think Anna and William expected her to believe they hadn't slept together, and worse, that secretly she *had* believed them — though she wouldn't acknowledge that to them, not now. She had actually begun to believe that the kiss she'd witnessed, though a betrayal of the worst possible kind, had been their first. She had trusted their words, foolishly, and had recently been considering phoning Anna. She no longer blamed Anna for what had happened, she blamed William, and she'd come to think she should let her know that.

God, she was a fool! To think she had even entertained the idea of allowing William to make it up to her. She leaned over the sink and splashed water on her face.

She was furious. Her sister and her husband had followed her to this island to fuck in front of her? She twisted shut the faucets, wiped her hands with a paper towel, and opened the door, ready to confront her sister at last, willing to make an even bigger fool of herself, but Anna was gone, of course, and all Rose could do was comport herself calmly out of the inn and then run, as fast as she could, to her car.

Chapter 23

Anna was stunned, but she was not surprised. Of course she had run into Rose, of course, of course. Had she really expected to avoid her? She'd hung out on the deck of the *Ariel* all morning, alone, castigating herself for not phoning, but not phoning.

She was avoiding William and she ached for him, ached to talk with him, to speak at last about all that had happened between them. Not just of that discovered kiss, the confirmation of what had grown and perhaps always existed between them, but of their futures. Last night, as they'd pulled into the harbor, William had told Anna that Rose had spurned his attempts to reconcile. Of course she would, she had been deeply hurt. Still, the more time that passed, the less likely she would be to take him back. And he would soon be leaving.

A shimmering tinsel thread of hope had dangled before Anna's eyes all morning.

Then, coming up to the inn from the beach, she had suddenly had to pee so badly. That's why she'd stopped at the powder room instead of waiting till she got upstairs to her room. And when the door opened, and there stood Rose on the other side, all at once Anna saw another bathroom door between herself and her sister. A white door in their old house, her ballerina bath towel hanging from a brass hook. Anna had knelt on one side of that door and her sister on the other. *Are you all right?* Rose had whispered through the keyhole. And Anna, bleeding, scared for her life, had had no answer. *I'll never let him hurt you again,* Rose had promised. And he never had, not when Rose was there.

Anna hadn't thought about that day in many years, though at one time it had possessed her. She had carried it in her brain, in her tissue. But over the years she had let it seep away.

After she collided with Rose at the powder room, Anna ran straight up to her room. She had stood in the hallway, breathing hard, hoping no one would come by, and searched for her key card. She had been meaning to organize her purse for months.

As soon as she opened her door she saw the note on the carpet. It was from William, in his bold, severe hand.

Her chest muscles constricted, and she

hated herself for her excitement, but her eyes raced to capture his words as though they were escaped animals, dangerous and rare.

Anna,
    I've gone to take Miranda for a sail.
    Will you have a drink with me later?
                                   W

Anna had to do something; had to put herself in motion. She looked up Luis Naufragio's address in the phone book, asked the concierge for directions, and inquired about renting a bicycle. She was told that the inn kept a half dozen on hand for guests. As it happened, one was available. So she set off down the road in the direction of her sister's house, through the geometric light of early afternoon. In her bag she carried a Shelter Island guide map showing that the route was direct and easy. There was one principal road on Big Ram Island, and on it were both the Ram's Head Inn and the Naufragio house. Straight down about a mile.

Years had passed since she had ridden a bicycle, though she rode stationary bikes at the gym and took hikes round the Nature Center. She felt oddly nostalgic, like a girl again, not least because her hair was gathered into a ponytail that flew in the breeze as she coasted downhill. Except for her misery, she could almost feel happy.

The after-rain air was soft against her face as she pedaled through dappled shade along the edge of woods. Occasional clearings revealed neo-Victorian mansions overlooking marshes and water. To her left, a grassy berm led to the rocky shore of Gardiners Bay. To her right lay the cool density of a mixed forest. She was reminded of the back roads of Connecticut, and something in the combined scent of salt air and piney woods evoked a specific memory of riding to her grandmother's house. She recalled an afternoon when the light had seemed broken as it did now, the sharp-edged patterns jutting through the trees. She had run away from home that afternoon, after her father had hit her again. She had gone to her gran's, and her gran had let her stay in her mother's old room.

The next day, Thanksgiving, her gran had returned her home. Anna refused to taste the turkey that year, declaring that to eat a bird was unspeakably cruel, but she sat at the dinner table and filled her plate with salad. She hated sitting there with him acting the holiday host, but where else, at nine years old, had she to go? That night, Rose took a pomegranate from the fruit bowl and brought it up to their room, though they weren't supposed to eat in bed, and they stained their hands and then their nightgowns pretending the glistening red fruits were rubies. But they hadn't gotten in trouble. Their mother never said anything. Anna had wondered whether Mother thought the stains were blood.

A putrid taste traveled from the inside of Anna's mouth, burned along her throat through her chest to sear her gut. Her thighs ached. She was sweating.

Clearly, William didn't love her as she loved him, not if he had tried all summer to reconcile with Rose. But why had he wanted her with him now? Why did his eyes dissolve hers? She couldn't imagine how to recover from him; she couldn't imagine how sailing would allow her to forget him.

A light film of perspiration tingled along the fine hairs of her arms. Anna pedaled, breathing harder. She saw Rose's face as it had been when she opened the door of the powder room, the burst of pain. She saw that Rose had cut off most of her beautiful hair. Anna felt her throat tighten. She must gain her sister's forgiveness. She would just keep trying.

Twigs snapped. A long-legged doe leapt as though catapulted from the woods into the road just feet ahead of her. Anna cried out, braked, ground to a stop. In two swift bounds the deer disappeared again. Anna straddled her bicycle on the side of the road. She thought of a fawn at the Nature Center, whose mother had been roadkill. A car engine growled from behind her, and then a convertible passed in a red blur. Every road is treacherous, she thought as she remounted the bicycle, no matter how remote.

Rose had walked from Luis's house to the Ram's Head Inn many times this summer — it was her regular walk, and she knew that past the inn a private road looped around to Reel Point and then back up Ram Island Drive. So when she left the inn in a hurry after seeing Anna, her harlot sister, she instinctively turned her car right. Despite the sign that warned RESIDENTS ONLY, she took the private road along the water. Anyone who went looking after her probably wouldn't think to go that way.

Her heart was pounding. A slow drive would calm her down.

A canopy of trees shaded the narrow road, and to the right, ribbons of blue sea glimmered through the foliage. Though they fronted Coecles Harbor, the houses back along here were older and smaller than the homes on Ram Island Drive. Several writers were said to live in the area, though Rose hadn't met any, and a few properties looked to be the residences of artists: somewhat shaggy, imaginatively painted, with yards boasting sculpture or laden with materials. An occasional shed or barn was obviously used as a studio. If she stayed on through the winter, Rose thought she might make an effort to meet some of these people.

But it was Luis's house, after all, in which she would stay, if she pursued a life here, and she had just run out on him, leaving him with the check, when she had meant this brunch to be her treat. She pulled over on the side of the road to call him on her cellular phone. It had been rude and childish to leave him sitting there. She hadn't been thinking.

"I'm sorry," she said when Luis answered on the first ring.

"Where are you? What happened?"

Should she go into it? "I'm fine. I'm on my way back to the house."

"Why on earth?" A note of irritation sounded in his voice.

"I ran into my sister. I don't want to talk now." Rose saw the bathroom door as she'd pressed it shut, the fine crackling in the cream paint. "Thank you for brunch. I owe you."

"Are you sure you're all right? You sound terrified."

"Yes, of course," Rose said. "It was just the shock of seeing her there."

She heard the sound of Luis sucking his lips together. "Mm-hmm."

Though it was illegal to drive and speak on the phone without a headset, Rose resumed driving, her cell phone pressed to her ear. Luis explained how he had a tennis date in Amagansett, otherwise he would insist on coming over. Was she sure she would be okay?

"Of course," she said again.

She pulled to a stop along the sandy verge where the road bent. The same meandering, overpriced, green-shingled house had been for sale for years.

"Call me later. I'm not going home just yet," Rose said, then she turned her cell phone off.

Reel Point, a narrow peninsula of rocks and shells, jutted into Gardiners Bay and formed the channel entrance to Coecles Harbor. People came here to fish occasionally, bicyclists sometimes stopped here to rest, and houses lined both sides of the shore; yet, as she had often been this summer, Rose was alone, and she was grateful. Bone-white shells crunched beneath her feet. The wind brushed the water in feathery strokes, and a fine spray moistened her skin.

Rose felt remote here and somehow free. Were anyone looking for her, she would not be difficult to find, yet no one knew where she was.

High above the water, an osprey rode an air current, looking for lunch. Rose wondered if this were the osprey whose raggedy nest hung off the telephone-pole platform built along the causeway between Big Ram and Little Ram. Ospreys were not the avian world's best nest caretakers, but they were dedicated parents. On a hike through Mashomack Nature Preserve, Rose had observed two ospreys teaching a fledgling to fly. She supposed that counted for more than a smart-looking residence.

The osprey darted to the water, talons extended, and speared a fish, puncturing its neck with his beak. A trill of excitement like the notes of a flute vibrated in Rose's chest. Cruel beauty inspired her, had always done so though she hadn't always allowed herself to admit it. The osprey carried off its meal. Rose gazed at the sky, then at the glistening stones along the tide line and the undulations of the sea, and she felt a pull, a longing, objectless but fierce.

A rock tumbling in the shallows struck her eye. Green-gray, bisected by a curving white line like the swoop of the yin-yang sign, it seemed a talisman. Rose stooped for it. Even wet, the stone's surface was matte, absorbing light. People were like that as well, Rose thought, one way or another. Miranda reflected light, for example; Anna absorbed it.

Gripping the stone in her fist, she recalled her sister as she had been just minutes ago at the inn, when she had opened the door onto Anna's muted face, the gauzy outline of her silhouette. She was maddening, almost, in her visual softness. Rose had never before understood that such boundarylessness could be a threat.

She remembered, again, the evening she had seen her sister kissing her husband, the betrayal like a physical blow, the way everything suddenly hurt, arms, legs, skin. For weeks, she had been in such pain, walking through her life like a zombie. And even when she tried to think things through and realized that she and William hadn't been right for a long time, even when she recognized the dissolution of her marriage as an unburdening, even then, she was devastated.

The fact that Anna would risk their bond for William tore a hole in her heart. Rose had thought her sister closer to her than anyone in the world. True, she had taken it for granted. And she had been preoccupied. She was guilty of those things. But she never would have willingly betrayed Anna. If anything, she would have taken care of Anna, would have given her anything.

And Anna had taken everything — everything but what truly mattered: Miranda, and her art.

The green-gray stone felt hard and cool in her fingers, uncannily hers, as though it had turned up here on the beach specifically for her. Rose often felt this way about the physical world — the tiny blue wildflower that bloomed beside her doorstep, the sharp-scaled double pinecone that lay in her path, the flash of green in the sky so quick she wondered if she'd seen it in the moment before the sun dropped behind the sea. She was proprietary about found beauty; she had often painted it. Lately she had been painting what lay underneath the beautiful, or behind it.

She turned the stone in her hand and realized that, of course, Anna's presence was deliberate. Anna was here to see *her*. She must be. She couldn't possibly be so ridiculously cruel as to stay at the inn down the road for any other reason, not even for William. Rose saw her sister's face again, the shock but also the pain deep in her gray eyes.

She tossed the stone gently into the air and caught it. She felt the air move, felt the wind and the water, all moving.

Maybe she was ready to face her sister now. A part of Rose understood that Anna taking William from her had restored a balance between them, like taking turns — as though now Anna had become the one to watch in horror from the doorway as Rose was given the strap.

Chapter 24

In the shade, the grass was still wet with yesterday's storm. Miranda walked along the bluff, barefoot, remembering how she and Danny had waited out the storm in his parents' house, listening to the rain pounding on the roof. The wind's steady rhythms had created a sensation of motion, and she'd imagined herself as a little girl curled up in her parents' berth on the *Ariel*, the ship rocking in the waves like a cradle. The round, spicy smell of the old wood, the heavy press of the soft, worn quilt about her shoulders — those were comforts she craved. And she'd envisioned, as she had when she'd been little, the many creatures swimming past her head, just outside the hull, distracting her with their imagined colors and shapes.

Miranda would not have expected to miss her father's sailboat, nor would she ever admit to missing it, but the truth was she did. Living here this summer, where sailboats were ubiquitous (a word whose sound she disliked and admired at the same time), presented Miranda with constant reminders of her broken family. But at least they were private reminders. Once she was back at school in Connecticut, she'd have to face all the kids who would suspect her parents were split up — all the rumors why, all the pity.

In the thin green blades beneath the big sycamore, Miranda wiggled her toes. Gardiners Bay was crowded with boats. Her mother loved painting it this way, with all the colors and shapes and in all kinds of light. Her mother could see the same thing more ways than anyone Miranda knew. How incredibly boring.

Miranda was bored now. Danny was busy helping his father with something. Again. Miranda realized that her own parents asked very little of her. But that was because they were so wrapped up in themselves. She tore through the grass with her foot and looked over toward the stairs to the beach. Cannibal was there, shaking himself, a gnarled piece of driftwood between his jaws. Miranda called to him, and the dog turned his big head to look at her, then he trotted off into the woods with his treasure.

"Odd-looking dog."

Miranda turned, struck by the words

and the simultaneous appearance of the person crossing the lawn; in the split second before she recognized his voice, Miranda saw her father's square, wide shoulders as the shape of *a man*.

"Where did you come from?" Her voice quavered, embarrassing her.

Her father put on his shaggy dog expression, eyes wide. Even with yards between them, she recognized the look. The gentle professor. Her girlfriends ate it up; she was humiliated by it.

"From the Ram's Head Inn," he said. "I'm here to take you for a sail — the *Ariel*'s final sail — if you're free."

"You're at the Ram's Head Inn?" Her father seemed so incongruous in this landscape.

"I am indeed." Her father shaded his eyes with his hand. He was always forgetting his sunglasses. "Did your mother tell you I called?"

"Uh . . ." From behind her, Miranda heard the dry rustling of branches, and she turned to see Cannibal loping through the trees at the edge of the property. Her father, as she knew he would, dropped to a crouch and whistled. Cannibal approached him, hesitated. He wasn't a shy dog, but he was discriminating, almost as though he were alert to the value of time and allotted only so much of it to humans. Most of the allotment he gave to Miranda, which made her proud.

"Good boy," her father coaxed. He looked up at Miranda as if to show the dog he was her friend.

Cannibal lumbered forward, his paws heavy with obligation. He licked her father on the cheek, tentatively, as though kissing an uncle, and Miranda laughed. She caught the glance between man and dog as they parted and Cannibal trotted off to disappear beneath the deck.

Her father stood, brushing his hands. He stepped toward her, and she met his embrace, but she reminded herself she was angry with him and pulled away. "Why didn't you let me know you were coming?"

"Sorry," he said. "I planned to call from the yacht broker, but we got caught in the storm yesterday afternoon and decided to stop here."

"We?" she asked.

"I asked your aunt Anna to come along; she's here."

Miranda measured her father with her eyes, perceiving some small but significant shift in her perspective. Her father had not gotten out of the car at this house all summer. When she had visited with him, he usually met her in Greenport, at the ferry. Once she'd taken the train into New York City and her father had escorted her to the NYC Ballet production of *A Midsummer Night's Dream.* But he had never visited her here, on the island. This was a new angle.

"What about the *Ariel?*" she asked. "What final sail?"

He looked past her toward the water, then back at her face. "I've decided to sell her."

"Wow," she said. She didn't ask why. She didn't say she was sorry. She knew her father had done something wrong, though she didn't know what. He was selling the boat he loved, but she didn't feel sorry for him.

He bent his head as he rolled the cuff of his blue Oxford shirt, exposing a wavering white line where the red skin of his neck was creased. "So?" he said, turning the fabric evenly, shooting her a glance. "Would you like to go for a sail?" He switched to the other cuff.

"Now?" Miranda asked. "I'm kind of waiting for someone." She looked toward the driveway. Danny had promised to come over as soon as he could. Miranda had hoped he'd arrive while her mother was still out with Mr. Naufragio.

And now her father was here, staring at her. "That boy?" he asked.

She didn't let herself skip a beat. "Yeah, that boy." She said no more. Why should she volunteer her personal life to him?

The sharp, distinct scent of burning charcoal floated past. A neighbor was barbecuing; it must be lunchtime. Miranda thought about sailing the *Ariel* with Danny. She envisioned him tending the hibachi, grinning. They'd have veggie burgers.

"Your friend is very welcome to come along with us," her father said.

Miranda nodded. Weirdly, she was suddenly eager to introduce Danny to her father and her father to Danny, but she fought it. Still, Danny would almost definitely love the *Ariel*. "I don't know," she said. "We have plans."

Would taking Danny out on the *Ariel* ruin the day or make it special? It was bad enough they'd missed the morning together, she didn't want anything to spoil tonight, the most significant night of their lives. Or at least of hers.

Her father gestured in the direction of the deck. "May we sit down?"

Miranda shrugged. "I guess. How did

you get here, anyway?"

She walked past him, and he let her lead the way across the grass. "I walked," he answered to the back of her head. "It's only a mile."

"I know," Miranda said. She climbed the three steps to the deck and stretched out on a chaise lounge. Her father sat in a plastic chair. "Spectacular view," he said. "I forgot."

Forgot? Did he think somehow this house was part of his life, too? That everything was his in some way?

A scrabbling noise rose from beneath the cedar slats of the deck and then Cannibal's big head and odd body appeared and he was flopping beside the chaise. Miranda leaned forward, nudged the dog with her foot, and saw that grass was stuck between her toes. She recalled a photograph taken by her father on the *Ariel* last Memorial Day weekend, on the last normal day of her life: two pairs of feet, her mother's and her aunt's, dangling side by side as though in conversation.

"Miranda." Her father's voice was solicitous. "You're angry at me. And you have a right to be." She had thought he might still be angry at her about Greenport.

She shrugged.

"I'm sorry you haven't seen your aunt Anna this summer."

"Where is she?" Miranda asked. "If she's here, why didn't she come with you?" She sat up and picked the grass from between her toes.

"She's back at the inn," her father said, his brow furrowed over his dark eyes. He leaned toward her. "She'd love to see you, of course, but your mother would have to agree. She hasn't yet forgiven Aunt Anna for . . . what happened."

Their eyes met. Miranda blinked and looked away.

"I'm sorry," her father said, clasping his hands together, pressing his elbows into his thighs. "I never meant to hurt either of you. Please know that."

Miranda felt immobilized, as though he had taken her picture, had clicked the shutter, freezing her in a white flash, mouth agape, shoulder blades held wide and hard. She saw herself in sharp contrast, knife-edged darks and bled-out lights, part of a composition, as her mother would say, the moveable object.

She stared at him.

"Miranda, I don't know what your mother has told you, but now that I am about to leave for Scotland, I must ask you

259

to absolve your aunt Anna of any blame. If anyone is to be held responsible for what happened, blame me."

Miranda sat perfectly still within a shattered moment of perfect stillness, crazed like a windshield falling apart in slow motion.

"Blame me," he said again, his hands open now, palms up on his knees. "And if you ever can, forgive me."

Suddenly, she knew. *Her father had fucked her aunt.*

Oh God, oh God, oh God.

Gravel on the driveway crunched, and Miranda heard and then saw Danny on his bicycle, pedaling up the hill. His shoulders hunched forward over the handlebars. She imagined lying beneath those shoulders, as she would tonight. She imagined disappearing beneath the dark, fragrant warmth of him.

But — *her father and her aunt?* It wasn't possible. Whatever it was, it couldn't be that.

She called out, helplessly, "Danny," and he looked up from where he was parking his bicycle and waved.

When her face opened that way, unfurling like a flower, Miranda reminded

William of her mother. Transfixing, such a face was, and the young man who was the recipient of its gaze appeared well in thrall. He gamboled over the lawn, grinning, lithe, fair-haired, and tan, a classic summer love. What timing.

"Danny."

Miranda's was the thin cry of a child, though earlier William had been thinking how much she had seemed to grow up these last few months. Something in the upright way she had held her body out there on the lawn, some development of her spine, had made her appear to him as a no longer a girl, nearly a woman. But then, just a moment ago, he had shattered her innocence — the blow of it horribly evident now in her face.

"Hey," the boy greeted Miranda, who had run to his side. They embraced, and William turned away. He knew his daughter would seek in another male comfort from the hurt *he* had just caused her, and he couldn't bear to witness it.

Instead, he watched the odd, brindle dog emerge from the woods carrying a small tree limb. *The log-bearer.* The dog traversed the lawn with a dignified and purposeful carriage, as though he owned the place, then disappeared beneath the deck. William turned back toward Miranda. She was kissing the boy.

Miranda was making a point; let her make it. In a moment William would speak. He would grasp the frayed end of the thread that still connected them and he would pull. But for the moment, he let her demonstrate her new allegiance. The dog reappeared from below the deck and trotted toward the woods once more. Just before entering the scrub, he turned his head to meet William's stare, and that moment of canine empathy was enough to shore William's spirit.

He walked toward the kids. Danny, the boy, had draped a long, simian arm over Miranda's narrow shoulders, and she held the hem of his T-shirt between her fingers. William wore a neutral expression as he approached them, extending his hand.

"Hello," he said. "William Campbell. Pleased to meet you."

"Hey. Danny Princi." The boy offered his long, slim, but calloused fingers and William took them carefully, so as not to engulf them in his own meaty hand. Danny looked William in the face, his eyes unbiased and gold like a cat's.

William was grateful for the boy's presence because Miranda would draw strength from it. Yet she also seemed stronger herself.

"How did you meet?" he asked the teenagers. They were slouched into one another like twins in a single egg. They exchanged glances.

"At the Ram's Head Inn," Miranda mumbled.

"I was delivering lobster with my dad," Danny continued, and William liked him for that. "Miranda was out riding her bicycle and stopped along the beach and walked up the hill." Danny laughed to himself. "She was watching people with this look on her face."

Miranda's gray eyes shone. Now she reminded William of Anna. Everyone said she favored her aunt, even Rose saw it, but this was an expression William had never before seen on his daughter's face. Longing. Not a child's gluttonous craving, but a more complex, less innocent yearning born of pain combined with hope: the desire to merge with the Other. Miranda would see this tawny, unformed boy as the male version of herself, of course. William's heart ached.

"You bought me a Coke that day, remember?" Miranda asked.

"You were thirsty," Danny answered.

A waver in the line of Miranda's eyebrows reminded William again of Anna, and the tremor in his daughter's jaw made him regret for a moment that she lacked her mother's strength. He knew that Danny would detect his daughter's vulnerability, and he was grateful that the boy seemed kind. How quickly and thoroughly William had lost his own claim.

A noisy little helicopter of a bee flew between them and hovered near Miranda's cheek. "He thinks you're a flower," Danny said, and William smiled. Miranda would be okay loving this boy. As okay as first love would allow her to be.

Miranda reached up, slowly, as though to swat the bee, but instead her hand scooped the air and, with a little gasp, she caught it. She held out her arm, slowly opening her fist between her father and her beloved; revealing the bee like a tiny golden crown in her palm. William felt the world grow still, hushed, and then the bee buzzed off and Miranda's laughter tinkled like glass.

"If you hold a bee in the palm of your hand and it doesn't sting you, then your love is true," she singsonged, beaming, infused, proud of herself. How resilient was youth.

The sound of crunching gravel made them all turn their heads toward the driveway. There was Anna, straddling a bicycle, looking displaced.

Chapter 25

Anna could smell herself. Her hairline dripped sweat, her cotton shirt clung to her chest, and her own musk radiated from the damp, dark places between her curves. Secretly, Anna liked her bodily scents, all of them. On weekends sometimes she'd skip a shower, finding an inexplicable comfort in the fragrance of flesh.

She whiffed the air, but the tang of her was gone, a temporary emanation. She leaned the bicycle against a tree, wiped her brow with her forearm, and surveyed the place where Rose and Miranda lived, a beachy saltbox set back in the woods on a high bluff overlooking the bay. God, this was perfect. Even in her lowest moments, Rose got more breaks than almost anyone, but Anna didn't think she begrudged her older sister that. Rose hadn't chosen to be the good daughter any more than Anna had chosen to "have a fresh mouth."

"Anna!" Miranda's voice chirped like an alarm.

There she was, crossing the lawn with

William and some boy. William!

"Hello!" Her own voice sounded strained. She smiled as guilelessly as possible as she crossed the drive, not daring to look toward William but feeling his eyes on her.

As she reached her niece, Anna held open her arms for an embrace, which Miranda accepted, but her arms were rigid and her eyes refused to meet Anna's own. *Oh God*, Anna thought, *she must know*.

"Hey." The greeting saved Anna from having to find words to say to her niece. This must be the boyfriend. Anna offered a warm smile. He was an outsider here, as she was.

"This is Danny," Miranda said, settling under his arm. He was tall but carried himself compactly, probably swam like an otter.

"Hi, Danny." Anna reached to shake his hand and his met hers. The smooth calluses on his palms contrasted with the dry, rough flesh of his fingertips. She recognized the hands of a fisherman. "I'm Anna, Miranda's aunt."

William said nothing, and Anna didn't address him. A pause occurred in which the droning of insects and the calls and twitters of birds and the ambient murmur of the sea grew suddenly loud. Wasn't Rose home yet? Anna wasn't sure she could face her sister now, with all these others around, with William here. Branches rustled and a large, bearlike dog came out of the woods and headed toward the group. William called to the dog — "Here, boy" — but though the dog gave William a grin and a wag of his tail, he came over to Anna.

She knelt and let him lick her cheek, and she put her arms around him. His coat was sleek and exotically patterned.

"Cannibal," Miranda said. "That's his name. I told you about him."

Cannibal wagged his tail. William glanced briefly at Miranda, probably wondering when she had spoken to Anna.

Anna rose, and as she did she cast an upward glance at William. Their eyes caught a half second too long, causing a physical sensation like a sudden stop. She looked quickly at Miranda. "So he's yours?"

"Yes," Miranda said. "Well, now he is. He's been here all summer."

"He lived here before you did, I bet," Danny said. Miranda frowned at him adoringly.

Cannibal sat at Anna's feet.

"Mom isn't home," Miranda said.

Was Anna meant to understand that her company wasn't wanted? Being here was harder than being with William on the boat had been. Then, she had managed to contain her feelings, knowing that at any moment she could change her mind because the boat confined and protected them.

She tried to think of a message for Rose. *Tell her I'm sorry for everything.* But William spoke. "Apparently, Rose is brunching at the Ram's Head Inn."

Anna couldn't keep her eyes from meeting his, meaningfully. "Yes," she said. "I ran into her."

He nodded and looked away, bending to tug on his shirt cuffs. His ears were so round, Anna thought. His neck was thick. She loved the salt and pepper that were beginning to stipple his beard, incongruous against the boyish tenderness of his features.

Months of sailing together had built a tension between them that had become increasingly impossible to endure. By the end of May they'd grown weak, or strong, or true to themselves. Nothing since then had changed.

A car rolled up the drive now, Rose's Jeep.

"Here she is," Miranda said. Cannibal raised his head from his paws.

William turned so his shoulder blocked Miranda from Anna. "Do you want to talk to her?" he asked Anna in a low voice.

For a second she was confused, but then she realized he meant Rose.

"Yes," she said. That's why she had come.

William spoke quickly. "If you let me ride that bicycle back to the inn, I'll take Miranda and Danny out for a sail. Perhaps Rose can give you a ride back later, or —"

"I don't know," Anna broke in. She let her eyes linger on his mouth. She wanted to be with him. She needed to confront and be confronted by her sister. She couldn't think straight.

Miranda pulled William by the arm. "Come on," she said. "Talk to Mom about the *Ariel*."

Rose approached them, ever so slightly shaking her head. The dog nudged Anna's hand, as though in moral support.

"I'm going to take Miranda and her friend for a sail on the *Ariel*, if it is okay with you," William said to Rose before she could speak. "A final sail."

"What?" Rose asked. She glared in Anna's direction, seemingly at the dog.

"I'm selling the boat. Assuming she sells quickly, which I am assured she will, we can sort our finances for the coming year before I leave."

Rose still hadn't looked directly at Anna. "Wow," she said. "Good."

"So, do you want to go?" Miranda asked Danny.

He shrugged. "Sure."

William moved to touch Rose lightly on her arm. "Talk with me a moment."

"All right." Finally, Rose threw Anna a look. Not daggers, though. Should Anna stay or was this her cue to leave? Rose led William to a wide, prow-shaped deck.

"I need to get shoes and a sweatshirt," Miranda said to Danny. She pulled him toward the steps. "Wait there."

"Cool," Danny said and she sprinted off. He began to speak to Anna, so she had to venture closer to the deck to hear him.

"Are you sailing with us?" he asked.

Anna shook her head. "No," she said. "I don't think so." What if Rose refused to speak to her? She shouldn't sail with William and Miranda, in any event. She sensed that much. *The final sail!* Well, it wouldn't be final for her; she would sail to Sag Harbor, alone with him once more for that brief trip, at least.

That would be final.

Anna watched William talk with Rose. They weren't arguing. William seemed to be explaining something, and Rose was nodding. Clearly, she had been pleasantly surprised by the news of the plan to sell the *Ariel*. Of course they needed to talk of many things, but Anna found the sight of them together wrenching. She'd been trying to think of Rose and William as finally over.

She turned away from them toward Gardiners Bay, broad and blue and filled with sailboats. The view was remarkable; the wide horizon set off a spark of excitement in her. Within months, she would be sailing across the ocean. She would finally get to mail those postcards she had dreamed about as a girl.

The screen door slid open. Miranda appeared carrying a sail bag and a bike helmet. She walked over to Danny, who adjusted her chin strap for her. They really were adorable. Anna had never had a boyfriend like that at that age.

Anna felt a surge of panic like a chasm opening between her ribs. She wanted to run. She was so out of place here. How could she have imagined coming here would be a good idea?

Rose and William crossed the deck. In a voice for everyone to hear, Rose said to William, "Just take my Jeep to the inn, go sailing, then drive back here later. I won't be needing to go anywhere between now and then." She withdrew a set of keys from her pocket.

"Thanks," William said, accepting them. "You two ready to go?"

Danny was unfastening Miranda's chin strap. "Guess so," Miranda said.

William met Anna's gaze, briefly, and Miranda caught it. She tramped off to the car and Danny followed. "Bye," William said to the air around Anna and Rose.

Anna watched the Jeep pull away as she had so many times, leaving her, and registered an old, disconnected feeling. She was a part of her sister's family and she was outside them, as she had always found herself outside any circle. She turned to Rose. "Will you talk to me?"

Rose frowned. "Oh, of course."

Anna's eyes stung.

"Come on." Rose gestured Anna up onto the deck. "I suppose we must do this."

Chapter 26

William was mopping the latest seagull droppings from the teak deck. Miranda had yet to speak to him directly. Instead, she and he both had aimed their communication to Danny.

"Where are we going to sail, Mr. Campbell?" Danny asked as he tied off the dinghy at the stern.

"He's *Dr.* Campbell," Miranda corrected, surprising William until she added, "a professor, not a real doctor."

"Probably not too far," William said. "Just a jaunt. A joy ride, as it were. A junket. An excursion."

"An odyssey," Danny offered as he coiled lines.

"Very good," William said, "but not exactly." He stuck the mop in the bucket. "An odyssey would constitute a significantly longer journey."

Miranda muttered something under her breath as she stowed the sail covers. William shot her a quick glance she did not return.

"Have you sailed?" William asked.

"Sunfish," Danny said. "A laser, a bull's-eye. That sort of thing." He ran his fingers over the elaborate Turk's heads — fancy rope work done with a light cotton cord to give a good gripping surface — along the curved, ash tiller. "What else can I do here?"

"You can hoist the jibs. Miranda will show you," William said, looking again in her direction, but her attention was fixed rather doggedly on the halyard in her hands.

"I'm going to tend to my engine — she's temperamental, fragile, but very valuable." He felt his neck redden, as though he had shared some intimate male knowledge with this boy who was no doubt after his daughter's virtue. Instead of competing with him for Miranda's attention, he was trying to bond with the kid. Why? Because he had to leave his daughter to him?

"So you do know basic sailing?" he asked, trying to redeem some authority as he unlocked the padlocked hatch and removed the three boards that stacked in the opening to the companionway.

"I can get by," Danny said. "And what I don't know, I can probably fake." He smiled, pleased with himself.

"Right. Good plan." William stepped down onto the little, three-step ladder into the galley area. "I'll be back."

Once below, William removed the stairway, gaining access to the removable panel that opened under the cockpit. He thought of the engine compartment as the *Ariel*'s tender innards, the mainsail as the winged emanation of her spirit, fluttering and lifting, filling and tautening. Pressing her forward.

And he was about to entrust all of this to some stranger's hands.

A cormorant flew overhead, its shadow slicing across the brightly lit square of the companionway. William looked up and saw himself as from the bird's eye, bending to his task, his shoulders round where they had once been square, the hair at the crown of his head grown thin. How had he become this man, estranged from everyone who meant the most to him, about to give up his prized sailboat, preparing to leave his very country as though in search of something that he knew would turn out to be only another version of himself?

Miranda was disgusted by her father but she was here, wasn't she, showing off his boat to Danny, who was loving it, she could tell. What did that make her? A hypocrite? Worse? She considered her gene pool and decided she might as well do exactly as she wanted because she was doomed. Besides, adults certainly did as they pleased, and she was practically an adult.

Danny crossed the cockpit to her, leaned against the cabin with that look on his face. Through the porthole, she saw her father's shoulders pass by. She reached for Danny's hand, eager for the opportunity to kiss him, always eager for it. God, she loved the feel of his skin and the muscles and bones beneath it, pressed against hers. She wondered whether she was oversexed. She loved making out with him, rubbing and kissing and touching until she was transported, that was the word for it, to a faraway plane of pleasure consisting of only the two of them.

His tongue traced the curving inner line of her lips. She opened her mouth to him and their teeth clicked together. They laughed and kissed.

When they made out at the playground last Tuesday, he'd ejaculated in his boxers and she had touched it. She had rubbed him with it till he sprang to attention again and they laughed. But she hadn't put him in her mouth, and she hadn't let him enter her. That was virginity, as she (and her friends in Connecticut) saw it. Danny said he didn't care whether she was a virgin, but she cared. She cared that she would give herself to him.

Danny kissed the tip of her nose and pulled away from her, jerking his chin in the direction of the companionway.

"He'll be down there a while," she assured him. She slipped her fingers beneath the sleeves of his T-shirt, her palms flat against his biceps, detecting messages that ran between nerves.

"Tonight . . ." he said, looking straight at her.

Miranda nodded, and then she heard the antique engine grumble and sputter as her father cranked it to a start below their feet. He would have oiled all the moving parts and primed it first with an eyedropper of expensive fuel that he bought on the Internet and kept in a stainless-steel bottle. When he got the engine going, he would probably hit his head standing up, on the same deck beam he always did.

She couldn't believe he was selling the *Ariel*.

She laid her head against Danny's chest. "Tonight," she said, her jaw working over his heart. "Here. On this boat."

William, at the tiller, wondered about Anna, worried about her, imagining an emotional bloodletting at Rose's. Anna would say it was because he could sense her, that he felt what she felt, but he hoped that wasn't true. He knew it wasn't. He was concerned for her, worried sick for her and Rose and by extension for Miranda, but he had no idea what might be going on.

He knew there were things between the two women that he didn't understand. Worse, the things he did understand he found impossible to reconcile. Never had he imagined himself the sort of man to break a vow, especially his wedding vow. He respected his wife, always had, her beauty and intelligence, her tenacity and ambition, her talent. He had tried all summer to make things right again, to do his duty, though perhaps, he now admitted, he hadn't tried hard enough. Perhaps his will but not his heart had been in his efforts, and Rose would have known.

Miranda and Danny were clowning around on the foredeck, arm wrestling and teasing each other. Her eyes shone with happiness, and William realized, with gratitude and a bit of regret, that she would be all right without him, despite him. But how would he be without her? Would Rose ever consent to let her visit?

Gardiners Bay would take them to the Atlantic, eventually. William fantasized about sailing the *Ariel* all the way to Scotland. Theoretically, he could do it, though not alone. He could do it with Anna at his side. His heart leapt at the idea, at the picture of Anna in his mind, at the thought of her spirit, her extraordinary combination of courage and tenderness. And for all of that, Anna was anchored firmly to the earth — connected to the animals and plants of her work, to the physical here and now. He admired that in her, had always done so.

Anna was present in the moment, not outside it evaluating it for artistic possibility or literary content. Especially when she sailed, Anna seemed to make everything extraneous disappear.

Rose saw her sister in quite a different way, he knew, for they had discussed it from time to time. Rose found Anna ethereal and indistinct, nearly impossible to paint. Her features were deceptively simple, Rose said, like a child's. William saw what Rose meant, but he saw more. He found Anna luminous, like a phosphorescent sea creature, vibrating with energy.

Once, working side by side in the pouring rain, Anna had teased that they had known each other before, he and she, in a previous life, and that was the reason she was there. Now, as he steered his straight course, he was haunted by images of her. Anna in ancient Greece. Egypt. Persia. Rome.

Miranda squealed from the bow as sea spray showered her, and William banished his reverie, clearing his mind of all but the rhythms of ship hull against sea, wind against sail. "You okay up there?" he called as he came up on deck.

"Aye!" Danny answered with a sweeping salute, and Miranda stood beside him, her face to the wind, hair blowing back. They were beautiful kids, with everything ahead of them. William was soothed by the thought of the happiness they would discover in each other. He could never forgive himself the hurt he had caused his daughter; at the same time, he recognized the foolishness of imagining his anguish would matter very much to her. Daddy wasn't the most important man in her life anymore, that was the fact of it. Even in self-abnegation William took more credit than he deserved. He'd been accused of that before.

The *Ariel* heeled nicely, beating into the wind.

"Where are we going?" Miranda asked, the first words she had spoken directly to William since the boy had shown up.

"Where the wind takes us," William said. He pointed toward the inner of the two triangular forward sails. "Please."

Miranda went to trim it. She was an apt little sailor herself, and William had always imagined her inheriting the *Ariel*. He swallowed against the pang that rose in his throat.

She repeated her question. "A sail to where? Let's go somewhere."

William looked at his watch. The wind was good now but unpredictable since the storm.

"We could go to the ruins by Gardiners Island," Danny said.

Miranda gave him her sweetest look. "Yes," she said. "Let's go to Gardiners Island."

"Have we time?" William asked.

Miranda frowned, giving him her you-spoil-everything look. "Why wouldn't we?"

Gardiners Island was privately owned, the largest estate in America. Invitation only, of course; they wouldn't go ashore.

"To Gardiners Island," William said. "Bear off wind and slack the jib."

Chapter 27

Rose left Anna on the deck and said she'd be right back. She didn't invite Anna into the house, but Anna was glad to be alone for a moment, glad to be outdoors. The deck stretched toward the water, seeming, from certain vantage points, to jut over the water. Anna held the railing and felt that she was moving, imperceptibly, forward toward the horizon.

She gazed toward the distant blue mound that was Gardiners Island. She had never been there, but she knew it had belonged to the same family for hundreds of years, that an elderly bachelor, with the middle name of Lion, presided over it to this day. She knew it was a nature sanctuary all its own. Without predators, ospreys built nests on the ground there.

The sweet, funny dog nudged her knee, as if he had something to tell her, and Anna turned to scratch his head. He trotted off to a shady spot beneath the eaves and settled next to a stack of fishing poles. The sight of them made Anna shudder.

Rose reappeared carrying two blue-glass tumblers filled with ice water. "It's filtered," she assured Anna. "Anyway, I don't have much else to give you."

"This is just right," Anna said. She gazed into the glass, her eyes tracing fissures in the ice cubes. Too much joined her to Rose — blood, memory — too much was between them for them to give each other up. Rose had to know that. And yet, Anna couldn't think how to attempt to heal what had torn between them, or how to justify her desire for William. She couldn't deny it.

"I don't know how to begin," she said. She pressed the small of her back against the edge of the deck railing.

Rose snorted, then sipped her water.

A tear slid from the corner of Anna's left eye. For some reason, she always cried from her left eye first. "I'm not here with William the way you think," she said.

"Oh, please!" Rose threw down her glass, startlingly. It clunked on the wood planks between them, splashing cold water and ice cubes across their ankles, but it didn't break.

"How long?" Rose demanded, fury rising. "I want to know, how long were you and William . . ." She kicked at the glass at her feet.

"We weren't," Anna said, backing away. She held her water close to her chest. "We never slept together, if that's what you mean."

"Spare me," Rose said. "Spare me the details of what you technically did not do!"

"I don't mean it that way." Anna looked toward the dog and the collection of fishing poles. "I mean —" Her voice caught.

Rose tossed her head. She looked alternately older and younger with her hair cut short. "You didn't just suddenly have an urge to embrace at the very moment I appeared."

Anna grimaced. "No. It wasn't sudden." She ran her fingers against the grain of the railing, unconcerned about splinters. "But we had never kissed before."

Rose shook her head, looking toward the sky. "I never for a moment thought I wouldn't be able to trust you."

The shadow of a high-flying osprey passed across her face.

"I know," Anna whispered. "I hope you know I'm telling the truth."

Rose tugged at the blunt ends of her hair. "Oh God."

Anna knew she had to push on, that she had to say everything. "I made this trip with William to sell the *Ariel* — but also, though neither of us admitted it, to see *you*."

Rose rubbed her face with her hands. Her nails were flecked with blue and green paint.

"The last time I saw William was the last time I saw you both," Anna said.

Rose frowned. "We know when *that* was."

"Yes," Anna said. "And I am so sorry." She set her glass down on the railing and reached to touch her sister's arm. "Rose? I am so, so sorry. And I know it's inconceivable I could ask for your forgiveness, but I do."

At last, Rose began to cry. The tears weren't there and then they were, explosive and hot. "Oh God, Anna, how?" Rose jerked away. From her pocket, she pulled a paper cocktail napkin embellished with the green logo of the Ram's Head Inn, and she blew her nose with it. She said, "I lost both of you in one minute."

"No," Anna said, her voice low as if in prayer. "No, you haven't."

Rose balled the napkin and stuffed it into her other pocket. Then she took out a new napkin. Tears dripped from Rose's chin and she wiped them. She took a sip of water from Anna's glass, then she folded the damp napkin into a triangle, then another triangle, and another. She asked, "Did you *want* to hurt me?"

"What?" Anna closed her eyes. Hurt was her father with the fishing pole in his hands, the purple of her own back in the mirror. Did she want Rose to hurt? Rose, who alone had protected her, as best she could?

"You know why," Rose said, tacitly reading her. "Because he hit you and not me."

Anna stopped breathing. She saw everything, her father's face behind her, puffed and red and throwing off a kind of electrical charge while she cowered, throwing up her hands, protecting her head. His anger had been more dangerous than the long, thin weapon in his hands. But she had always known that her own anger, if ever it were released, would be most dangerous of all.

Both women were silent, looking off in different directions.

Anna inhaled, filling up, needing the physical pressure of air against ribs. "No," she said at last, "I didn't want to hurt you. I certainly didn't aim to."

"So, you're in love with him?" Rose asked. Partly an effect of the haircut, her expression was severe.

Anna thought it impossible Rose wouldn't already know the answer. Her big sister had always known how she felt, about everything. In fact, Rose most likely had known how Anna felt all along, all the years Anna had distracted herself from William via a string of bad-boy men, each of whom she had invariably, eventually, either found a reason to leave or provoked into leaving her. Rose just wanted her to say the words out loud.

Anna resigned herself to honesty. What was the point of anything else? "I must have loved him since I first took his course, though I hated him then, too," she said, recalling the sexual crackle of their classroom arguments.

"I see." Rose smoothed her folded paper napkin, staring down at it. She bent each corner of the triangle to a blunt line, her fingers pressing again and again. A tear dripped to its center and spread. "Why did you let me marry him?"

"He was my teacher," Anna said. "I couldn't really date him. Anyway, he met you and you got together right away."

"He came to the gallery," Rose said, "because *you* brought him to see my paintings."

"I remember," Anna said. She remembered Rose announcing their engagement. Anna had felt as though she'd given her sister a wonderful gift; she hadn't resented it. "I was happy for you, truly."

"Ha." Rose scoffed bitterly. But in her heart, Anna thought she must know she told the truth. "All the weekends I've stayed home painting while you two went out sailing, I guess you were doing me a big favor."

Anna reached for the ice water. "I did think I was doing you a favor, sometimes, but I've always liked to sail and you don't. You know I love the *Ariel*." Now was the time to tell her sister of her plans to leave.

But Rose implored her. "*Why* did he marry me?"

As though she had been forced against her will? As though William hadn't been hers to lose? She'd had William in her bed, she'd borne his child. As always, Rose had had what she wanted, what Anna wanted. Hadn't she thrown it aside?

"Why did you push him away? Push both of us away?" Anna asked, summoning her courage. She reached into the water glass and fished out a small raft of ice.

Rose shook her head. "You can't justify this."

"You encouraged us to be together." The ice dripped from Anna's hand, drops bouncing off the deck onto the tops of her feet.

"I require solitude to work," Rose said. "And for that I'm completely to blame?"

"William loves you," Anna said, his name enough to cipher her resolve. Just seeing the letters of his name on an e-mail made the rest of the world fade to black. "Everyone always loves you." She slipped the ice into her mouth and wiped her wet fingers on her shirt.

She looked at Rose, crumpling her napkin. From the beach below, a pair of seagulls called to each other from jetty to jetty. She waited for Rose to speak, and when she did, her voice was measured.

"Sometimes, as sick as it sounds, I was jealous because I thought the way Daddy treated you, even though it was horrible . . ." Rose paused as though her tongue had grown thick.

"What?" Anna asked.

"I thought it meant he loved *you* more."

Anna looked toward the sliding glass doors and saw herself mirrored. She straightened her shoulders. That's what he had said, hadn't he? *I punish you because I love you.*

"I know that's disgusting," Rose said. "I'm sorry."

"It's all disgusting," Anna said. She crunched the ice between her teeth and swallowed the pieces.

Chapter 28

Cannibal following at their heels, Rose led Anna to the house. The dog stopped at the threshold of the sliding glass door and sat, looking up at them. "The dog stays out," Rose said, and the women entered the kitchen. She pointed toward the hallway. "There's a bathroom right through there."

"Thanks." Anna stopped in front of the painting Rose had begun yesterday, now propped against the wall. She touched it — Anna was always tactile — running a finger along a cerulean ridge. Then she stepped back from it and bumped the kitchen table, knocking a magazine to the floor.

"Sorry!" she said, bending to retrieve it.

Rose winced at Anna's clumsiness — a clumsiness she had acquired in later childhood, for she had been a graceful little girl.

"This is wonderful," Anna said about the painting. "Your work has really changed." The afternoon sun lit her skin so that it seemed translucent. "I mean, it was wonderful before, too, but this is new for you."

"Yes," Rose said. "It is." She opened the

cabinet in which she kept the dog biscuits and took one out of the box. She had stopped painting pretty. Was that what Anna meant?

Anna looked around the room, at the dozen or so finished and unfinished canvases propped against the walls — against every available space. "You've been painting a lot."

"Yes," Rose said. "I've been able to work fairly well here."

"That's good," Anna said. She turned to examine another.

"It's been ideal, in many ways, this place," Rose said, not sure why she was telling her this.

"Well," Anna said. "You're a paragon of dedication."

Which meant what? That she was unduly focused on her art, consumed with her self, that she had "neglected" her marriage? Rose had anticipated this theory. It was true she had been concentrating her energy on painting these past several years since Miranda began high school and required — in fact, demanded — less of her. She had very deliberately enforced self-discipline in order to produce the body of work that galleries wanted to see. And she had succeeded. Rose took up the challenge. "I am serious about my work."

Anna continued to the next painting, a complicated series of triangles within triangles in minutely deepening shades of purple and gray. *Sails at Greenport* was written across the bottom of the painting.

"Fractals," Rose said.

"Ah." Anna put the painting down.

Rose moved to the door, opened it, and held a biscuit so that Cannibal had to sit up for it, which he immediately did.

"Your artwork covered the entire refrigerator when we were kids," Anna said.

You take over any space you are in, William had told Rose. That's why she didn't like to sail, he theorized; she couldn't have enough of her own space on the boat. But Rose didn't think that hypothesis entirely true. She thought it was the closing them out of her space that William and Anna had both minded. She needed a certain amount and kind of solitude that had been difficult for William to accept.

Maybe he understood that now, but there was nothing any of them could do to make it as it was.

"So, that way?" Anna said and she proceeded to the hall.

Rose stood in the open sliding door and gazed over the deck. Somewhere out on the bay was the *Ariel*. She hoped they were having a reasonable time, though she didn't like to think what the chances were. Miranda had been so distant and angry all summer, but Danny had made a difference.

Cannibal thumped his muscular tail against the deck.

"That's all, boy," Rose said. He trotted off toward the woods.

She slid the door closed and turned back into the kitchen, absentmindedly flipping through the magazine on the table. How much responsibility should she take for the failure of her marriage? It was true, she had needed to mark out a space for herself, to withdraw within the boundaries of a privacy where she could be free to work. In doing so, had she fatally altered her relationship with her sister and her husband?

She looked at her paintings, some of which she disliked, but all of which, cumulatively, were testament to her ability to survive, even thrive, without William.

And the fact was she was ready to be alone while William was in Scotland, even if their marriage had remained intact. The only difference now was that they would owe each other nothing.

Anna reappeared. She approached a

wide canvas covered in wavering lines of translucent color.

Rose identified the subject for her. "The colors of water."

"That's what you were painting?"

Rose nodded. "That was my original idea, but I soon realized I could never get the colors exactly right because they are never static. And in looking at water and light, I saw other things. Shapes. Patterns. So, I painted suggestions of all of that. Or rather, tried." Pleased with her summary, she made a mental note to write it down, her first articulation of a piece of recent work intended for the fall show at the New Works Gallery.

"It's entrancing," Anna said.

Always Rose's greatest fan, as a child, Anna had been forever asking her to draw castles and enchanted forests and exotic lands. And Rose had always complied, even when she hadn't felt like it.

Anna pointed toward the smallest, darkest of the paintings. "Rocks under water, at night? Is that a moon in the corner, stars reflected across the surface?"

"You make it sound romantic," Rose said. "Look at it, it's ugly."

Anna's expression was uncertain. She bit a fingernail, tearing a half-moon with her teeth. "What do you mean?"

"It's ugly," Rose insisted. "I know, as I painted it ugly. The murkiness, the asymmetry, the distortion."

Anna said nothing. She walked from one picture to the next as one would in a gallery. And suddenly Rose saw Anna as she had been that day, it was seventeen years ago, when she had brought William to see Rose's work. She had accompanied him to the gallery where Rose worked and then left him there in his baseball cap and his no socks. Anna had brought William to her, even though she herself had loved him.

Rose folded closed the top of the Milk-Bone box. "You gave me William," she said.

"But you gave him back." Anna turned away, banging her hip against a chair and cursing, then went out the sliding door onto the deck.

Anna had always gone outside to get away from things. And she had always needed to get away from something. No wonder she loved to sail.

Had Rose given William back? She thought of how she'd send her sister and her husband off together, weekend after weekend, so she could work. In her mind that was called trust. Anger roiled in her.

She took a bottle from the wine rack, one of the Spanish reds Luis had given her as a welcome gift. She grabbed two glasses and the corkscrew and followed Anna onto the deck.

It was the principle that had stuck its thorn in Rose; the idea that her sister and her husband would betray her hurt her more than the actual ending of her marriage.

Rose knew what passion was; she had felt it for William once, and before him for the high school boyfriend who broke up with her on graduation night. She felt passion for her daughter. For her painting. And now, maybe, she felt it for this place, for Shelter Island.

She knew she would say yes to Luis. And with that knowledge, her anger subsided.

Out on the deck, Anna was looking through the telescope Rose kept under the eaves, next to the fishing poles. She had set it up at the end of the prow. "What is that way out there," she asked, "sticking up out of the water near Gardiners Island?"

"The ruins?" Rose bent to look through the lens herself. "Yes, Fort Tyler, built during the Spanish-American War. I think they used it for target practice during

World War Two." She turned the eyepiece, back and again, adjusting it. "Oh," she said.

"What?"

"I'm fairly certain that's the *Ariel* at three o'clock."

She offered the telescope to Anna, who peered through, adjusted the eyepiece and laughed softly. "It is the *Ariel*," she said, a shade of possessiveness in her voice.

With the sharp end of her corkscrew, Rose began to peel the foil from the wine bottle. Then she grasped the bottle between her thighs, twisted the corkscrew into the cork and, with a small grunt, pulled it out. She poured the two glasses, the deep red liquid sloshing like waves in a blood sea, offered Anna a glass, and took the other for herself. She gazed out over the bay.

The birds were active now and noisy. The changing light of the lowering sun created new geometries on the lawn, and the air, cooling, released the scents of sunbaked grass. At the edge of the woods, a rabbit crept out to nibble dinner. Rose looked around for Cannibal, but he had gone off somewhere.

Anna sipped her wine. "I don't know," she said, continuing their previous conversation. "I've thought about it and thought about it. I don't think I knew what I was doing when I introduced you to William, except finding a way to keep him in my life."

"Right," Rose said. Anna was honest, at least. They still had that between them. She leaned over the railing, her eyes on the white dot she knew was the *Ariel*.

Anna continued, "I was shocked when you got engaged."

Rose felt herself go still for a moment, then she nodded. "At the time, it seemed you didn't like him much. I figured it was because he had been your teacher. Didn't he give you an A-minus?"

"Ha." Anna shielded her eyes. "Yes," she said. "I started seeing that guy Matthew, from the class, I suppose hoping William would notice."

The walls of Rose's stomach tightened. She knew that she should have known. That she had known and then had chosen not to. "He was cute," she said. "That Matthew."

Anna stared into her wine. "You always knew me," she said. "Even when I didn't know myself. How could you not have known how I felt?"

Rose shook her head. Her fingers traced

the bottom circle of her wineglass, around and around. "I don't know," she said. "Maybe I did. But I couldn't think that way." Images flashed in her head, scenes she had thought forgotten, she had chosen to ignore.

Rose had lost sight of the *Ariel*. She bent to the telescope. Gone. She didn't say anything about it.

"Do you think . . ." She paused. "Is it possible you took William from me because you felt that I'd taken Daddy?" The words made her slightly ill. She held on to the railing and breathed to clear her brain.

Anna drained her glass. "It isn't that you took him," she said, her eyes wet. "It isn't anything subconscious. It's that *he hit me*."

The words themselves were a slap.

Rose took Anna in her arms then, and they rocked together. "I should have done more to stop him," she whispered, and the sisters wept.

Later, when Gardiners Bay was empty save for the occasional small motor craft, Rose opened a second bottle of wine. Right away she felt warm and a bit dizzy and thought her face was probably flushed.

She leaned back in her deck chair, trying to sort through the decisions at which she had recently arrived. She would not go

302

back to Connecticut. She had forgiven Anna. She felt lighter, or anyway light-headed. "So," she said. "William is going to Scotland."

Anna nodded. "I know."

"Why don't you go, too, as you'd planned, to look for a puppy?" Rose said, surprising herself with her own munificence. But she couldn't stop. "You've always wanted to travel."

Anna held up a hand. "Stop it."

"No, I mean it." She refilled Anna's glass. "Maybe let this breathe a minute."

"What are you saying?" Anna leaned forward.

"To let the wine breathe?"

"No! You want me to travel with William?"

Rose rubbed the space between her eyebrows. "That isn't what I *want*. But neither do I want him back." She felt the crease in her forehead deepen. "I don't like the way things happened, but they happened for a reason."

"Or a number of reasons," Anna said.

Rose nodded. "Yes." She sipped her wine and thought about Anna giving her William and she giving him back. "But you only need one reason," she said. "If this is what you want, for once in your life, have the courage to go after it."

Anna's lips made a thin, hard line, then she opened them to speak. "Well, I'm doing something I've always wanted. I've signed up to crew on a sailing yacht."

Rose was stunned, relieved, and sad. She and Anna had just begun to acknowledge and accept each other, and now Anna was planning to leave. Seeing faraway places had always been her dream. "So, you'll travel at last."

Anna nodded gravely. "Yes."

"Send me a postcard," Rose said, and Anna broke into a smile.

Chapter 29

"Captain Kidd buried his treasure on Gardiners Island," Danny said. He had taken over the tiller and was close-hauled on the wind, sailing brilliantly.

Miranda watched his face, watched his eyes on the sails. "Yes, I know," she said. She loved the way these things made him happy. "And there's a stone marker at the spot saying the treasure is gone."

"He was hanged for political reasons," her father added, typically. He knew all the stories, all the connections between things.

"He was Scottish," Danny said. "William Kidd."

Miranda frowned. She lay back on the teak bench and hooked her heels over the toe rail.

"Indeed," her father said. "Watch, your jib is luffing." He moved forward to uncleat the jib sheet and trim the sails, his body shadowing her from the sun.

Miranda sat up. "Let's go ashore," she said. "Who would know?"

"It's private property," her father said. As if he obeyed the rules! The more she thought of it, the more Miranda decided to blame her father for her parents' separation. After all, he was the one who had broken vows.

"We could drop anchor off the cliffs," Danny said. A passing cabin cruiser sent a large wake rolling toward port. Miranda wanted to tell him to hit the wave at an angle, but she held back.

Her father, of course, didn't. "Wake to port," he said. "I'll let out sail."

"Aye!" Danny said, grinning as he pushed the tiller and the first big wave slapped the prow. "Woo-hoo!"

Miranda got sprayed.

"This is a beautiful boat," Danny said, and Miranda cringed, knowing what was to come, and she was right.

Her father launched into his favorite topic: *Nathaniel Herreshoff began building boats with his brother in Bristol, Rhode Island, in 1898.* He could talk forever about boats or myths, longer than forever about the two combined.

She tuned him out and thought about how much she had changed this summer, how she couldn't go back to her old school and her old self. She needed to talk to her mother, to plead to be allowed to go to school on Shelter Island. She'd been wrong to act so bitchy to her mom all summer. She had blamed her for the separation, for being so obsessed with her painting, but she was an artist, after all. Miranda was starting to wish she'd been more understanding.

She looked across the water and there were the ruins in the distance.

As soon as she got out of the Jeep she spotted the two of them with their wineglasses, her mother and her aunt on the deck where she'd left them, blathering as though nothing were wrong. How could her mother stand to breathe the same air as her aunt, when, obviously, Anna and her father had had an affair. They had come here together, and her father had practically spelled it out for her, so that had to be what was going on.

What if her mother didn't know?

Miranda had assumed the major cause of her parents' split was her mother's obsession with painting and her father's decision to teach in Scotland. She figured Aunt Anna had sided with her dad. Was it possible her mother thought that was the reason, too, even if it wasn't? After all,

Miranda had gotten that idea from somewhere.

Danny shut the car door. "I've got to go," he said. He extended his hand toward her father. "Thanks a lot, Dr. Campbell."

Her father took Danny's hand and grabbed his shoulder. "My pleasure, son." Miranda started walking Danny to his bicycle. Would her father have admitted to her something her mother didn't know? She couldn't believe that. She couldn't figure out what was true, except that her parents and her aunt were all freaks.

Her father headed toward the deck. Until today, her mother, her father, and her aunt hadn't been together in the same space for three months. She wondered whether Danny could tell anything was going on with them. Probably not. Boys never knew these things. Probably her father hadn't even realized his own sister-in-law was hitting on him until it was too late. Suddenly, Miranda knew that everything that had happened had been Anna's fault.

Danny drew her against him, his hands cupping her hips. They were out of view of the adults on the deck. "When?" he asked into her hair.

"As soon as it gets dark," Miranda said. "At the dock at the inn, at the dinghy."

"Won't there be people?" Danny asked, moving his hands up her waist, setting off tiny sparks along her nerves. His thumbs lightly pressed her ribs.

"You're tickling me," she said, twisting in his hands. He measured her waist with them. His fingers almost met.

"It's my father's boat," she said. "I have a right to be on it. Who cares about people?" She lifted her face to him.

"I can't wait," he said, and he kissed her with a soft mouth. "But I'd better go now." He kissed the tip of her nose. "Bye."

Miranda nodded, touching his chin with a finger. She couldn't bring herself to say the word, couldn't tell him good-bye. She *had* to talk to her mother.

Danny rode away, disappearing around the curve of the drive. Cannibal came around from the back of the house to greet her, and they walked together toward the deck. Even for the dog's sake, Miranda thought, they shouldn't go back to Connecticut. He couldn't run free there. What if he couldn't adjust? There was nothing good about going back to Connecticut. She never thought she'd ever say that, but it was true. Everything was different now.

No one was talking when Miranda stepped onto the deck. Her father was drinking wine from a blue glass. Anna was looking at the fishing poles against the house. Something was different about her, too. Not her hair, not her weight. She had always looked the same. Miranda squinted.

"Your mother has granted me permission to take you to dinner," her father said.

Miranda looked at her mother, leaning against the railing.

"Who says it's hers to give?"

Her mother raked her hair with her ringless left hand and said nothing.

"Miranda." Her father was using his warning voice, obviously for her mother's benefit. How full of shit he was, they all were. Everything they said and did was lies.

"What?" she said. "Why do I have to go to dinner with you? I don't want to."

"Miranda?" Her aunt Anna turned toward her, and her eyes looked really tired. "Would you have dinner with me? I so want to talk with you."

Her father and mother exchanged looks. What was going on in this lunatic asylum of a family? They were competing for her? She had wanted to talk to her mother, but she couldn't now. She felt like she would burst from her skin. "I don't want to have dinner with any of you. I don't want to talk to any of you."

She hoisted her tote bag and walked toward the kitchen door.

"Miranda." Now it was her mother. "Where are you going?"

"Where does it look like I'm going? Saudi Arabia?"

Her mother turned to her father. "What happened on that boat?"

He looked clueless, as always. "Nothing."

Miranda groaned. "Nothing happened, though the only reason I went was 'cause Danny wanted to. But now I just want to take a bath." She was going to try to calm herself. Nothing could ruin tonight, nothing.

Chapter 30

Anna couldn't look at William. Rose had told her to go to Scotland — not that she would — and she couldn't look at him or she would begin to think it possible. But it wasn't possible, was it? How could her sister condone it? Well, she hadn't, exactly, and Anna doubted she meant that she wished them happiness ever after. Rose was pushing them together the way she always had, but this time they'd admitted it.

"Would it be loutish for me to offer you both dinner?" William said. His crooked smile caused one eye to squint more than the other. Anna had liked to tease him that he looked like a pirate. She'd threatened to find him a rescued parrot for his shoulder.

"I don't know, but I have other plans," Rose said. She seemed to be thinking out loud. "I need to call Luis."

"Okay," William said. "Well, then, I'll phone Miranda tomorrow, if she'll speak to me."

Anna felt a surge of panic for what would happen next. Her blood thrummed through her veins, and her scalp tingled. She could feel her hair follicles.

She didn't know why at first, and then, Anna did know what she feared. She was afraid of herself, of accepting her sister's challenge, of finding out what she wanted. But didn't she already know? She was going to travel, to sail, to discover herself in discovering the world.

"Miranda's been difficult all summer," Rose said, and her voice carried none of the tight accusation it had earlier. "But she seems upset today."

William looked away, and Anna understood that he must have revealed something to Miranda; she had felt it earlier. Oh, no.

"Maybe it's about her boyfriend," Rose said. "She doesn't want to go back to Connecticut." She gathered up the corkscrew and her wineglass and the empty wine bottles.

"Right," William said. "He seems a nice fellow."

"He does," Rose continued. She lowered her voice, as though not wanting Miranda to hear. "I have decided to stay here on the island, since that's what she wants."

"Stay here?" William said, and Anna said, "Really?"

"Yes. I'll let you know about it after I speak to Luis."

"Good enough," William said. "That might change some things."

"Yes," Rose agreed. "It might."

He turned to Anna. "Are you going back to the inn?"

She nodded, not meeting his eyes. Her heart pounded.

"I'll drop you off," Rose said. She went toward the kitchen. Anna and William took up their own glasses and followed her. They set the things on the counter, and Rose lifted her purse from a hook.

Anna took one more look at the paintings against the wall. "You have a gift for translating emotion into form," she said. "And color."

Rose pressed her fingers to her mouth. "Thank you," she said.

The three returned to the deck. Without saying a word, they each stopped to look at the glittering bay, prolonging this moment, perhaps the last they would all spend together for a very long time.

"I have a friend you would like," Rose finally said to Anna. "She's a vet, and she's training an African grey parrot."

"Oh, what fun." Anna clapped her hands, a silly childlike gesture, and she felt her face flush.

Rose led them to the Jeep, and for a moment Anna wondered whether Rose, who had been drinking, would get into the passenger side and let William drive — he'd had only one glass of wine — but she didn't. She got in the driver's side and popped the latch for the rear door. William loaded the bike Anna had ridden from the inn into the Jeep. Anna climbed into the cramped backseat. William closed the door behind her and got in up front.

The car smelled so familiar. Anna had been here before, so many times. Although she had generally driven her own car to the marina when they went to sail, wherever else Anna went with William and Rose, they all drove together, in their car. This car, often with Miranda sitting beside her. Sometimes Anna had felt more like Miranda's sister than her aunt.

"So, I'll let you know about the *Ariel*," William said as Rose turned out of the driveway and onto the road.

"Okay," Rose said. She stared straight ahead, seeming distracted.

It occurred to Anna that if Rose were going to live on Shelter Island because that's what Miranda wanted, she and William could sell their house in Connecticut.

Couldn't they? And then perhaps William wouldn't have to sell the *Ariel*. Of course, the underlying issues were more complex than simple real estate allowed. She said nothing.

"I'm just going to ring Luis from the car when I drop you at the inn," Rose said. "He's staying there because I'm in his house."

"Of course," William said.

"Sometimes he stays with friends," Rose added, somewhat defensively Anna thought.

William turned his head toward the window, and Anna traced the dark line of his beard along his jaw. His neck was thick, his profile strong. Years ago, browsing through one of Rose's art books, Anna had found an allegorical sixteenth-century painting by Veronese, *Mars and Venus United by Love*, and she had been struck by Mars' resemblance to William. She wondered why Rose had never painted him.

"Oh, what's that?" Rose cried as something darted out from the trees into deepening evening shadow. "A fox."

Anna looked out the window. "And three deer." She pointed to the group, two females and a young one, motionless with their white flag tails raised, ready to run.

"I missed the fox," said William.

"There was a rumor earlier in the summer that somehow a coyote had gotten or been brought onto the island," Rose said.

"Perhaps it came over on the ferry," William said, adding, "I hope it paid the fare."

Rose frowned at him good-naturedly. "Ha ha," she said.

Anna experienced the disquieting sense that although everything had changed, nothing really had.

The sun was blazing low over the water as Rose made the turn into the Ram's Head Inn. The car lot was full, and she parked on grass near the woods.

Anna opened her door. What could she say in parting? William got out, and Rose pressed the rear latch release. William went around to remove the bicycle, and Anna followed him.

She had always been touched by his courtesies. She had missed them. She had missed him. She couldn't imagine her life without him; that was the difference between her and Rose. Rose could; Rose had.

"Thanks," she said to William, but he said, "I've got it," and bumped the bicycle over the gravel. They stopped at Rose's window. Rose was holding her cell phone in her lap, waiting for them to leave.

Anna opened her palms and then pressed them together in a gesture of uncertainty. "We'll talk again, I hope?" she said.

Rose nodded. The gray of her eyes was soft, like animal fur. "I know we will," she said.

Anna felt a surge of happiness then. She wanted to reach into the car and embrace her sister, but she felt too physically awkward. Instead, she reached in a hand and touched Rose's shoulder. "I'm glad we talked," she said.

Rose closed her eyes and nodded, and Anna knew she wanted them to go. "Thanks for the ride," she said.

William took his cue. "Yes, thanks, Rose."

She waved at him as they headed up the grass, then bent to dial her phone. Anna walked alongside William, the bike between them, around to the back of the inn.

The sun was setting over Gardiners Bay, and the clouds striped the sky with color, deep oranges and pinks and golds. The surface of the water looked purple. William parked the bicycle in the rack and locked it. He brushed off his hands and then rolled down his shirtsleeves. On the terrace, tables were filled with couples dining.

Anna knew she should say something neutral and leave. Go up to her room. Watch a video. Plan the rest of her life. Today had exhausted her.

But she didn't want to leave him yet.

"Are you starving?" William asked.

Anna didn't think she could swallow food just now. "No," she said. "Truthfully, not at all."

William buttoned his cuffs. "Could you go for another glass of wine?"

That question held the key to her destiny. Of course she could, but did she have the nerve?

William caught her forearm in his hand. "Let's watch the sunset from the *Ariel*."

Everything stopped.

And then, *wham!* Everything went fast, the blood pumping through her veins, the heart muscle thumping in her chest.

"There's that wine on board," William said.

"There is." Anna agreed and took a moment before answering. She watched two fair-haired children chase each other to the bottom of the lawn where a man stood taking pictures of a woman posing in the gazebo. In the distance, the *Ariel* rocked at her mooring, backlit by the setting sun. Anna should tell William about quitting her job to sail. On board the *Ariel* seemed the most fitting place.

"Okay," Anna said.

William pressed her forward, his hand flat and gentle against her shoulder. "And you will sail with me to Sag Harbor to-morrow?"

"Yes," Anna said, "I will. That will be the official good-bye." *The,* she had said, not *our.*

He stopped walking. Voices buzzed around them. He looked into her face. "Indeed," he said. "The official good-bye."

She didn't answer, only looked away.

They walked down the lawn, past the hammock and the tennis courts and the gazebo, to the beach and the little dock owned by the Ram's Head Inn. He held her arm. She wanted his arm around her.

Guests and passersby milled around, strolling along the rocks. Bicyclists stopped along the road, drank bottled water, and watched the sun immolate the sky.

William helped Anna into the dinghy, and she met his eyes over the touch of their hands. They both knew exactly where they were going.

He paddled out to the *Ariel.* The sun was slipping to the horizon now, a glowing coal. The water was a sheet of indigo.

"How did it go?" he asked. "With you and Rose? You seemed . . . okay. You're speaking."

Anna looked at him full in the face, and she knew that she loved him. She tried to exude it, to let him know. "It was intense," she said. "But, yeah, I guess we said a lot of stuff we needed to say." She didn't say, *Rose told me I should go with you to Scotland.*

William let out a breath as he lifted the oar. "You two have to be okay. I couldn't bear it otherwise."

"I know," Anna said. "We will." And she thought to herself that, yes, she and Rose would be okay, in whatever form that eventually took, though it would probably take a while. The idea of Rose and Miranda living in this new place was a good one.

They reached the *Ariel.* William leaned for the lifeline and looked back at Anna, and his eyes shone with the dark reflection of the sea.

Chapter 31

William opened the door of the antique anchor lantern and filled it with oil. He turned up the wick with the little brass wheel, lit it with a match, adjusted the flame, and smiled at the flickering light. This Davey lantern was two hundred years old; he'd bought it at the chandlery in England. For how many scenes of passion and drudgery and terror had it lit the way? He had rarely used it — and he knew Anna knew that. The lantern signaled an occasion, as of course this was — their last night, ever, on the *Ariel*. He closed the glass door and set the lantern on the cabin roof.

Though the sky was not yet dark, it would be soon. He turned the combination of the padlock to the companionway. Anna slid the lantern farther down the cabin roof and hoisted herself up to sit. She was lit gold, her hair, her skin.

"So, wine?" William asked. Her arm was inches from his face. He remembered that night, Memorial Day weekend, when she had stood so close to him he'd felt her heat.

She jangled her legs, clearly self-conscious. "Yeah," she said. "Okay."

"Good. We'll make a toast." The lock opened and he slid out the boards. "I'll get it."

He went below.

The cabin was nearly but not quite dark. In the shadows lurked the after-images of all William's years of sailing. His father, Rose and Anna, Miranda — all of them were here, would remain here, with the others whose presence he sometimes thought he could sense.

Anna and Rose had spoken and survived, it appeared, which meant they had begun to reconcile. Thank God for that. As though he'd been blind, he hadn't seen what either woman wanted, all along. He knew he hadn't, and he despaired for it.

He had wanted their happiness, always, but that hadn't been enough. When what one wanted was to trick himself, the odds for success were in his favor.

A bottle of wine, a corkscrew, and some plastic cups were packed in a cardboard box in the sink. He had cleaned out all of his belongings, except for the few things that would remain with the boat — the lifesaving gear, some spare engine parts and the ancient operations manual he kept carefully stowed in double plastic bags, a set of plastic dishes.

He uncorked the wine.

Next to the sink was the pull-down chart table; within its drawers lay the antique navigational tools he'd yet to make up his mind about. Should he leave them for the new owner — who surely, since he would choose this old ship over a new fiberglass model with a Japanese engine, would appreciate them — or should he keep the tools himself, as mementos of the ship he had loved? He put down the wine and opened the drawer that held the global positioning system, which would absolutely stay. Then he opened a second drawer. There were the old brass sextant, the antique parallel rules and dividers. The new owner wouldn't need them.

Anna appeared at the companionway. Her light T-shirt and shorts, her fair hair, her pale skin, the fading light — all served to make her appear wraithlike. If he blinked his eyes, she might disappear.

"The sunset is almost over," Anna said. She came down into the galley.

"Not yet," William said.

He recalled Memorial Day weekend, recalled her standing with her face tilted up to him, her sunburned cheeks radiating.

And then his name. She had looked in his eyes and said, *William*. And he had kissed her and he had felt the physical sensation of plummeting, as though the *Ariel* had taken a great swell and dropped.

William left the wine bottle in the sink and walked over to Anna, standing where they had stood that May afternoon. It seemed ridiculous not to kiss her.

Anna turned and vanished through the door that opened into the forward V-berth. William closed the drawers and the chart table. He would leave the navigational tools with the ship after all. He picked up the wine and followed Anna.

She was kneeling on the bed, opening the hatch above to let in air. William stood in the triangle of floor space. He wanted to touch her, but offered her the wine. She dropped down, sitting on her heels, looking at him. She took a small swig.

"Would you like to take some cushions up on deck?" he asked, but immediately he knew he'd said the wrong thing. He sounded like a social director, rerouting them inanely. He'd only thought to be under the stars with her.

Anna shrugged. She looked up through the hatch and he looked, too. The piece of night sky that they could see had stars in it.

The smoky aroma of burning oil wafted down.

"Look," William said, pointing. "See that bright star there? That's the constellation Lyra, the harp." Anna liked him to tell her about stars, he knew that. She never remembered half of what he said, but she liked it.

He leaned forward to kiss her at the same time she turned to speak, so that her chin bumped his mouth. "Sorry," he said. He was fifty-three and felt fifteen.

Anna rubbed her chin and leaned back to smile at him, holding his gaze. How many times had he imagined this, replayed it in his head, extended the torture of anticipation. And always, he'd imagined their lovemaking set here, on this boat — though somehow in his fantasies the quarters weren't quite so cramped.

He pulled her toward him by her shoulders; then unwound the elastic from her hair. He liked when her hair fell forward across her face and she looked up at him through strands.

He slid his hands beneath her shirt, along her warm skin. His fingers traced the edge of her bra, dipping into the moist warmth between her flesh, then up again across the curving silk, thumbs trailing lazily across the bumps of her nipples. The small, ragged moan of her response caught at his breath. Oh God, the rush of blood to his groin. He kissed her.

At last the taste of her. The plump and point of her tongue, the salt and sweet of her skin. The musk of her. The birdlike beating of her heart in her chest, against his. It was right. That's all William could think, and he whispered it to Anna.

"This is right."

Chapter 32

Danny hadn't asked her about birth control. Miranda realized this as she waited for him, leaning behind the entrance sign to the Ram's Head Inn. She had decided not to wait down at the dock in case her father might see her from the restaurant or the bar or something. It was nearly dark, but she didn't want to risk being seen. So she waited at the sign and worried.

They should have talked about it. She assumed Danny would have a condom with him. But what if he didn't? Part of her almost didn't want to do it anymore. Thinking about it this way made it seem kind of gross. But, no, of course she wanted to. She was just scared. Of pain, of awkwardness. What if she didn't please him? And she didn't want to have to bring up the issue of safe sex because he might find it insulting.

Why hadn't they talked about it?

One of the last e-mails Jai had written her was advice about how every teenage girl should carry a condom in her purse.

You never know when it might come in handy, Jai had said, implying experience, but Miranda couldn't imagine such a situation, having sex unplanned. And she couldn't imagine herself buying a package of condoms. At the Shelter Island Pharmacy? At George's IGA? Still, she wished she had one now.

It was dark. Where was he? What if he couldn't make it? How embarrassing would it be if he just didn't show? She could never face him again. Not that she would have to — since she was going back to Connecticut. Her mother still hadn't said so, officially. But it was stupid, at this point, to hope they would stay on Shelter Island. For some reason she had dared to imagine that her mother's lunch with Mr. Naufragio might have something to do with the decision. It was her last hope. Of course, Miranda hadn't stuck around to talk to her mother, not with *them* there.

But maybe she should have. She didn't have much time left in which to convince her mother to stay, and the alternative meant leaving Danny. Her stomach throbbed with the ache of it. Or maybe she was ovulating. Oh, no.

Headlights lit up the causeway, temporarily blinding her, and she felt a flash of helplessness. Then the car sped past, red, her eyes adjusted, and she saw Danny on his bicycle riding up the road. Her relief was physical; the muscles in her shoulders and chest and arms relaxed. She stepped out from behind the sign and waved to him, not sure he could see her.

He did. He called to her and crossed the road.

Over Coecles Harbor, a brilliant burst of lightning forked the sky. Miranda gasped, mesmerized, thrilled, terrified. Maybe she would write a poem about it in her journal, using some of her favorite words. She was embarrassed to admit to writing poetry in Connecticut. But here was different. No one knew who she was, so she could be who she wanted. She could be someone new here.

"Hey." Danny stopped in front of her. "How you doing?"

Miranda shrugged. "I don't know," she said.

"You're here, though," he said. "I wasn't sure you would be."

She searched his face in the tricky light. "Of course I am." She didn't tell him she had been afraid he wouldn't be here.

He moved his bicycle off the road, back into the shadows, and Miranda moved

330

with him. Trees blocked their view of the inn, as well as, she hoped, anyone at the inn's view of them. "So?" she asked.

"So, we haven't talked today. Your Dad was there and then we sailed and all that. So, tell me what's going on with you."

He knew her so well. She did need to talk. Maybe that was what was making her feel weird. She didn't know what to say about her screwed-up family. What could she possibly say?

"I don't know what's going on with them, really" was what came out. She pushed her hair off her forehead. The air felt suddenly thick. She knew lightning would flash again, and it did, to her left. She saw it out of the corner of her eye.

"When my mom split . . ." Danny shrugged his shoulders. He didn't ever talk about his mom. It was a given, his mom was gone, that was it. She'd left his dad and gone to South Dakota. Miranda wasn't exactly sure why. Danny used to go there every summer, but he didn't anymore. He went at Christmas. That was pretty much all he'd said about it.

"What?" Miranda asked.

"I don't know," Danny said. He turned to glance down the road, and his profile made her stomach clench. He was so gorgeous. Lightning flashed again, and this time a low rumble followed.

"Damn," Danny said. "Another storm's coming."

"Let's get to the *Ariel*," Miranda said. She righted her bicycle.

Danny didn't move. "Should we, now?"

A startling lightning bolt and nearly simultaneous explosion of thunder ripped the sky just above the harbor. The hairs on Miranda's arms bristled. Was he concerned for safety or having second thoughts, as she was? She wanted to lie in his arms; she wanted to smell his soap, to feel his warm skin. But. She wasn't quite as sure about the other. Or rather she was, but she wasn't sure about when. She wasn't sure about just now. Still, she wanted *him* to be sure. Why wasn't he?

There was no rain, no rain clouds that she could see. The air was still. Perfectly still but vibrating. *Thrumming.* A word for her poem.

"Yes," she said. "Let's go!" She turned her bicycle around and jumped on. Suddenly, she needed to rush. She needed to be on board the *Ariel*. The storm would make everything romantic. She imagined the scene. She couldn't wait.

They coasted down the side of the road

toward the water, Danny riding behind her.

The road dipped and then rose, and as she crested the hill she saw a light from the water grow bright and then dim, flickering. Perhaps a party boat was lighting fireworks leftover from the Fourth of July. In a moment she saw the harbor, a shining purple surface to the left — and then she saw the flames.

"Oh my God!" she cried. A boat was on fire.

The road veered and trees blocked the view, and then she was flying past the tennis court and she could see the smoke coming off the boat. It was the *Ariel*, on fire.

"Wait," Danny said. He stopped his bike and spun around, skidding up grass. Miranda stopped short ahead of him. They had nearly reached the beach, and she could see the dock. She saw the inn's tender but not the *Ariel*'s dinghy.

"Let's go up and call for help!" Danny shouted.

"Yes!" Miranda said, and he was off, standing up on his bicycle, pressing hard to ride uphill. Miranda got off hers and ran it up, her heart beating hard against her chest. The *Ariel* was in flames. If Danny had been on time, they might have been on it.

At the top of the hill, she climbed on her bike and bore down on the pedals. Danny had gone on ahead of her as fast as he could. His legs were so strong. He would get to the inn ahead of her and call for help.

She pedaled, her insides twisting. She hadn't seen how big the fire was; everything had happened so fast. She looked over her shoulder, but she was too far away to tell much now.

She turned a sharp right to cut across the lawn, riding too close past a couple in a pair of Adirondack chairs, bumping and crunching over something — a plastic cup? — left on the lawn. She was close enough to hear dishes clinking in counterpoint to the low din of the diners. She saw Danny dropping his bike, running into the inn.

And suddenly she realized where the dinghy was. Her father and her aunt Anna were on board the *Ariel*. She dropped her bike at the edge of the flagstone and ran as sirens began to scream.

Chapter 33

They lay together, legs entwined, her ear pressed to his chest, listening to the gradually slowing rhythm of his heart. He kissed her forehead. Their faces were wet with tears. He exhaled and drew her closer, and she thought her body had never before known such release, nor this deep calm. She blew out her breath against him. They hadn't spoken. Language seemed inadequate.

The scent of burning oil was strong. They had left the Davey lantern on the cabin roof above and lit the little electric lantern on the shelf down here in the V-berth. The rocking of the boat and the various light sources together surrounded them in a flickering dance of illumination and darkness.

She rolled onto her back and looked up through the hatch at the night sky. A low-slung crescent moon had appeared, its pointed ends blurred by their own glow. William pressed his head to hers and gazed up beside her.

"The old moon in the new moon's arms," he said. He kissed the curve of her eyebrow.

She smiled.

"Earthshine," William said. "Do you see how you can faintly detect a ghost of the rest of the lunar circle?"

"Oh." Anna laughed. "I thought . . ."

William nuzzled her. "You thought I meant us? Me, the old moon?"

A flash of lightning lit the sky, and Anna pressed her forehead against William's shoulder. Thunder rumbled. He cradled her, stroking her. "We should go soon."

She nodded, wriggling closer. She felt safe with him, a physical safety, as though because of him every inch of her skin was protected. Lightning would never strike while she lay beside him. She stretched her legs against the length of him, twitching her toes, enjoying the animal sensation of her muscles pulling. She stretched longer, feeling expandable.

She looked up through the hatch at the stars. Odd, to have thunder and lightning on such a clear night. Venus was especially bright.

William's lips moved against her cheek, his beard tickled. His voice was low and traveled from deep in his chest. "I have always loved you," he said.

Anna tried to memorize his face exactly as it was now. She had survived the last three months in a desolate, echoing cavern of waiting. Finally, she had given up waiting for love and decided to love herself. Time compressed: It was Memorial Day weekend and they had completed what they'd begun. Now she could say good-bye; now she had to.

"I have always loved you," she said, reaching for his hand. "But you're going away — and so am I."

William took her chin in his hand, and she knew he wanted her to look at him, at his dark eyes, into them. "What are you saying?"

Anna kissed him, gently. "I've quit my job and registered to crew on a classic boat, perhaps to sail to and from a regatta."

His eyes filled with astonishment. "My God!"

Smoke from the lantern on the cabin roof grew more intense. She started to rise, to look through the hatch to see whether the oil was burning too fast, but he pulled her down.

"Not yet," he said. "This is all I will have of you to sustain me."

She stroked his face, her heart about to rupture.

"How long do you plan to do this crewing?"

She shook her head. "A year?"

"Any chance your travels might take you to Scotland?"

She laughed. She had thought of that, hoping he would ask. "Not likely. But perhaps I may have some time to holiday in Spain or France."

"Hmmm." He hugged her to his chest. "You'll let me know, of course?"

"I'll send you postcards."

He groaned and nibbled her neck. "I'll live for them."

She sank into him, into the bulk of him, and knew that she must go to Scotland. She would write articles about Scottish wildlife, real and perhaps mythological, wild cats and loch monsters, and send them to the Nature Center newsletter. But she wouldn't promise him anything yet. For a time, at least, she must be on her own.

She pressed against the stickiness between them. William held her head in his hands and whispered her name in her hair.

And then she heard it, the unmistakable low roar, and she smelled it and shot up, leaping. William was up, too, grabbing for his pants. Anna snatched her shirt from the ledge. She smelled it for what it was now, fire. Oh God, the *Ariel* was on fire!

William rushed through the cabin, seizing the fire extinguisher from the bulkhead. Anna tugged on shorts, eschewing underwear, and ran after him, following him up onto the deck.

The staysail and the forepeak were ablaze, and almost immediately Anna understood what had happened. The lantern, which had rested on the edge of the hatch, had knocked over when Anna opened the hatch for air from below, probably an hour ago. The oil had dripped from the lantern's reservoir and soaked the cotton cordage that hung from the foresails.

William aimed the extinguishing foam at the club-foot spar.

And then in an instant the large, red fire extinguisher canister became a small, red cigarette lighter in Anna's mind. She was nine years old and looking up at her father's thick fist, his knuckles white, the hairs on them springy and black, like a bad man's. She was watching his thumb, flicking and flicking the lighter, and it failing to light, and him cursing, *Damnittohell,* as he waved his hand beneath her mother's yellow gingham kitchen curtains. He was trying to set them on fire, because he was angry with her, Anna, because she drove him to drink, because she didn't know the meaning of anything but the back of his hand.

The sky lit up again with double forks of lightning, and then Anna heard people. People running from the inn, pulling off the road, calling from the other boats. Shouting at her. For how long had she been shutting out the sounds?

Chapter 34

At the inn's front door, Luis kissed Rose good-bye on the cheek. He had an appointment in Water Mill. A rather late one, Rose thought. She had offered to make up for running out at brunch by taking him to dinner, but they only had time for a drink. She wanted to celebrate her decision: She would accept Luis's offers of job and house, and she would stop William from selling the *Ariel*. Instead, they could sell the house in Connecticut. Miranda wanted to go to school on the island, and Rose's painting had developed in surprising ways here; why shouldn't they stay?

It was time for Rose to leave Connecticut and her former life behind. Except for her years at college and a brief six months abroad, she had lived there all her life, tethered to her past. She hadn't realized it until she'd seen it from a distance.

William could keep the *Ariel* docked at Shelter Island. Boat slip privileges were associated with a real estate venture Luis was involved in, and he offered the slip to Rose if she paid the maintenance fees. She would have to discuss it with William, but she was sure he would be pleased.

Maybe Rose would sail the *Ariel* herself, she was more than capable, she and Miranda — and Danny; according to William, he had seemed to enjoy himself today. Danny knew these waters, which would be a plus. And if he were an enthusiast, Miranda would want him to have the opportunity to sail. Rose recognized that the *Ariel* might be the very means by which to regain her daughter's company.

At least another month or two of good sailing weather lay ahead. Rose looked forward to an unfamiliar array of autumn color. She was eager for the particulars, for waves of yellowing sea grass and beach plums big and scarlet as apples. She saw her palette shifting from blues and greens toward russets and pink-golds.

Luis promised to phone the next day to discuss their contracts, one for the rental of his house, one for her employment, by him on a per diem basis. They had hammered out the basics of her new job: Rose would work for Luis certain days, no fewer than three a week, and she would paint on others, and for the most part the allocation of days could be flexible.

Miranda would be happy when she learned they were going to stay. Perhaps she would begin to forgive her mother. Girls in love had soft, open hearts. Rose was eager for a chance to rebuild their relationship. Or to initiate a new sort. That would be fine, too.

"Good-bye, then," said Luis, and he turned and set off toward the front door. Rose didn't mind that he wasn't available for dinner. She had dined alone many times this summer and enjoyed it. She couldn't remember having done so in Connecticut, ever.

The front door closed behind Luis just as the back French doors blew open, and Danny was there, breathing hard, saying, "Your boat is on fire!"

He ran past Rose to the front desk, where he grabbed a phone from the startled concierge, pushed numbers, and began speaking. "I want to report a fire. Yes, it's on a sailboat moored in Coecles Harbor at the Ram's Head Inn."

Danny hung up the phone. "They're on their way," he said to the concierge. "Let's get as many fire extinguishers as we can and go down there."

"Sure," the young woman said. "From the kitchen." She hurried off. The volunteer fire department siren blared. Rose felt stricken in place.

A silver-haired man jumped up from his seat in the dining room near the hall and ran over to Danny. "Excuse me," he said. "I overheard you say a boat's on fire. Let me help. I have a tender with a motor." His blond wife rushed to join him. It was the familiar-looking woman Rose had seen earlier today at the inn.

"Sure," Danny said. The French doors sprang open and Miranda was there. She ran to him. "The fire department is coming," he said, clasping her hands. "And we'll take his tender." He turned to the silver-haired man. "The key? Mr. . . . ?"

The concierge reappeared with three fire extinguishers.

"John Vitulli," the man said. "And my wife, Marie." John slid his hand into his pocket and produced a single key on a chain with a miniature anchor.

Danny grabbed the key and he was off, pulling Miranda with him. John ran behind him and the concierge, and Rose and Marie followed. They ran across the flagstone terrace where voices were rising in panic.

A siren grew louder and closer.

In the distant dark, flames leapt from the deck of the *Ariel*.

At the tennis court, Rose caught up with John and Marie. Danny and Miranda and the concierge had run ahead to the tender, each carrying a fire extinguisher. Cars were stopped, parked along the grass, headlights shining into the water. People were shouting — *It's a boat fire! The wooden boat!* — streaming down the lawn from the inn.

Rose and the Vitullis reached the dock, panting, watching flames engulf the *Ariel*'s foresail. Danny and Miranda and the concierge had taken John's tender and were halfway across the water to the boat. Rose prayed that the *Ariel* would not explode: *Remember, O most gracious Virgin Mary, that never was it known that anyone who fled to thy protection, implored thy help, or sought thy intercession, was left unaided.* She hadn't said that prayer in thirty years.

John Vitulli squinted, as though doing so would help him see through the dark. A thin, white, apple slice of moon hung low in the sky, and the thunder and lightning had stopped. Thank God.

A burst of light caused Rose and the Vitullis and the people who had gathered on the beach and along the road to cry out as flames ran up the halyard and along the furled Egyptian cotton sails. Rose called out in panic, "No!" and Marie Vitulli took her arm.

Rose saw them then, William and Anna, as they emerged on deck, carrying what Rose knew had to be the fire extinguisher. The flames along the sail subsided, and relief surged through Rose like a paroxysm of love. Anna and William were okay. They hadn't been trapped below by flames or knocked unconscious or poisoned by gas. Everything would be all right.

And then Rose realized she wasn't angry that her sister and her husband were together; she was glad they were alive. She had finally made it up to Anna for being loved more, unreasonable or sick as that might be.

Danny boarded the *Ariel* to join William and Anna's fire-extinguishing efforts, and then Miranda and the concierge climbed aboard. A dark, damp smoke rose above the mast, spread across the silver sky and filled the air. The fire was out.

Chapter 35

John Vitulli was wearing sailing clothes today instead of golf clothes, white duck pants and deck shoes instead of pale blue poplin and wing tips — but it was either one or the other. He sailed or played golf every day. Now, as morning sun streamed through the windows, John cut his French toast into miniature, even pieces as though for a child or a magazine photo. William understood that John took pleasure in small felicities, including those he made toward himself. And he was grateful for his generosity and quick thinking of the night before.

"I phoned Tony before we came down to breakfast," John said. He patted his lips with his napkin, glancing at his wife. Marie smiled and sipped orange juice.

"Thank you," William said. John had promised to put him in touch with the top local yacht restoration man, Tony La Bianco, who would estimate repairs to the *Ariel*. He happened to work out of the marina where Luis Naufragio had given Rose access to a boat slip.

Last night, after the fire, when they'd all settled down, Rose had told William not to sell the *Ariel*, that they should sell the house in Connecticut instead. She had offered to look after the boat once it was restored, maybe sail it with Miranda. In the space of a few hours, William's world had altered completely. Despite the dissolution of his marriage, he felt fortunate indeed.

He sipped a Bloody Mary. Just one. He and Anna would motor the *Ariel* the brief distance to the boatyard. Then they would take the ferry to Greenport and the train, changing in New York, all the way to New Haven.

After that he didn't know. He would pack for his trip, she for hers. And someday, maybe soon, they would meet again across the ocean.

He looked at her across the table now and saw her with a new acuity, as though he'd pulled heavy drapes from a window and let light fall on her face. He had loved her from the start, and he had married her sister. He had much to contemplate during the long, cold Scottish winter months ahead.

Marie, who had been writing in a small leather notebook, ripped out the page now and placed it on the table beside Anna's water glass. The women were exchanging addresses.

Anna said, "Write the title of your novel, please."

"Just go to her Web site," John said. "Marie Macaire dot-com. Well-designed, if I do say so."

William smiled and swallowed a mouthful of eggs. John had redesigned Marie's Web site as a wedding gift to her. They had been married here, at the Ram's Head Inn, on Labor Day two years before, and returned for their anniversary. John had retired from a job in middle management after the sudden success of Marie's first novel.

Last night, long after the fire department had gone and the onlookers had dispersed and driven off; long after Miranda and Danny had taken off on their bikes for a celebratory ice cream from the Tuck Shop; long after Rose had astounded William by not only agreeing to keep the *Ariel* but offering to actually sail it while he was abroad. After all of this bizarre and miraculous day, he and Anna and the Vitullis had put away a few nightcaps together.

They had asked to be remembered in postcards.

Anna swabbed a forkful of blueberry pancake in a puddle of syrup and ate it, licking her lips. She speared a quarter of a sausage, dipped it in syrup, ate. God, this was good. She looked up at William, across from her, and grinned. She couldn't help it. She had been ravenous, and breakfast was, under the right circumstances, her favorite meal. These were the right circumstances.

Marie had gone outside for a cigarette. She was considerate that way. And generous: She had offered Anna and William the use of the condo she and John owned in Greenport. The two of them would be staying on here for another week, she'd said. *Take the key.*

But Anna had refused, with regret. William needed to get the Connecticut house in shape to sell. Nothing major, a few put-off repairs, some sprucing up. He had promised Rose he would see to it before he left. And Miranda had promised him she would come to Connecticut the next weekend to pack her stuff to bring back to the island and to see Jai.

Anna needed to attend to as much as she could before leaving the Nature Center in Theo's hands. He was more than capable of handling the job, but after so many years, Anna couldn't let it go without being certain all was well. Moving Theo up meant the Center would be short staffed for a bit until they hired and trained another person, and Anna would help as much as she could with that transition. But then she would leave.

She sipped her mimosa, savoring the contrast of sharp effervescence and sweet nectar. William and John were talking about the *Ariel*. She listened contentedly to their voices with no desire to join the conversation. She liked not having to speak. She had done more talking yesterday than she'd thought possible. And there was more discussion to come, she knew.

But for now, for this morning, all she could think about was that William loved her. How everything had changed so quickly. All because of a storm. What if the weather had remained fine? Would they have left the *Ariel* with the yacht broker, shyly fumbled to express their regrets to each other, and gone on their separate ways? What did it mean, that life could so easily turn one way or another, because of wind?

She knew William would explain their twist of fortune to her in mythic terms. In a low voice, his mouth pressed against her hair, against the skin of her neck just below her ear, he would tell her the story of them in the words of so many others.

Anna bent to sniff the stargazer lily in the vase on the table, and as she did she felt a brush of wing against the tip of her nose. As she pulled back from the flower, a bee buzzed out. She laughed, then bent to smell it again. The spicy fragrance filled her brain with pleasure.

Chapter 36

Cannibal was asleep on the deck, snoring. Miranda laughed, wanting to hug him but not wanting to wake him. She had never seen him quite so relaxed. Maybe he sensed they were staying. Maybe he could smell it or he had a doggy sixth sense or something. Anyway, he lay there, dead still except for an occasional movement behind his eyes or twitch of his paw. He was probably dreaming. What did dogs dream about? Sticks? Lobsters?

Last night she had dreamed about fire, but she hadn't been scared. It wasn't a nightmare because Danny had been with her in the dream, leading her through a tunnel of flames and emerging, she somehow knew this, at the edge of the world.

She had woken exhilarated. And the feeling was with her still.

She was going to stay on the Rock, keep her dog, attend Shelter Island High. Her mother had decided to take a job working for Mr. Naufragio, and they were going to continue to live here. They were even going to keep the *Ariel*. Maybe, eventually, her mother would buy a house of her own. Miranda didn't care what house they lived in, as long as it was on this island. As long as she could be with Danny.

Cannibal lifted his head and opened one eye to look at her. "Hi," she said, and he thumped his tail just once on the deck. The dog was a master of understatement, Danny had said when he'd first met Cannibal. Miranda felt her cheeks rise in an automatic grin, remembering that first evening Danny had ridden his bike over to the house to see her. She'd been surprised — and thrilled — to find him crunching up the driveway as she came up the stairs from the beach. She'd been carrying a bucket filled with gleaming, wet rocks.

Her mother had been using rocks in her paintings and Miranda liked collecting them. Danny had looked at them one by one as they talked, she remembered, and she had watched. It had been a way not to look at each other.

"Nice," he'd said, "this one's cool," and she knew he appreciated the same things she did.

Cannibal yawned, and Miranda dropped to her knees to hug him. They were staying, they were staying!

Her mother had been so nice last night; Miranda still didn't really understand it. She guessed it was because of the fire, that her mother had been scared for her dad and her aunt. There was something going on there, but her aunt was leaving on some sailing thing across the world. Miranda didn't understand, and she didn't think she wanted to. All she knew was that she was getting to stay here.

Maybe her mother really wanted to stay here, too. She had agreed to do some boring legal work for Mr. Naufragio. Plus, her mother had been painting a lot since they'd come here, and she was happiest when she was painting. So of course she wanted to stay. But she hadn't ever said so before.

Gardiners Bay was filling with sails, mostly white, and with cabin cruisers and the occasional speedboat. Miranda wished she and Danny could go sailing again. He had liked it so much, and she had liked it because of him. But the *Ariel* was burned pretty badly.

She was surprised at herself for caring, but she did. Well, Danny liked it, and, as he had said to her last night, it was a part of her history. A member of her family. Her weird family!

Cannibal lay his head down onto his

outstretched paws and went back to sleep. Miranda stood and walked to the edge of the prow deck. Maybe her father and Aunt Anna were out there on the *Ariel* right now. They'd be traveling under engine power, not sail, so it would be hard for her to recognize the boat, at least from so far.

She glanced down at the bench and saw the telescope, as though she'd wished it there. She lifted it and adjusted the eyepiece, focusing on a bright pink and yellow spinnaker at twelve o'clock. A dark-haired man and fair woman in bathing suits were hiking out the starboard side. Miranda looked away. She knew these people weren't her father and aunt, but she felt funny looking at them.

Could she bear to see her father and Aunt Anna together? Wasn't it disgusting, at least in principle?

She thought about Danny. About what it felt like to love him, the tenderness inside at the place where her throat met her chest, the sweetness of the ache. It wasn't the kind of thing she could make go away; it wasn't the kind of thing she wanted to ever live without.

Her mother had confessed she didn't feel that kind of love for her father anymore. Her aunt Anna, however, did.

Miranda could tell. She recognized signs she wouldn't have known before — the way Aunt Anna's eyes darkened when she looked at him, the way she paid attention to his words, listening instead of just hearing.

Miranda had to admit she understood, a little. She squeezed her eyes closed and buried her face in Cannibal's neck.

Rose looked around the kitchen and decided to make some changes. An entire bottom cabinet was filled with junk that could go in the basement. She could keep her paints and supplies in here. Maybe push the kitchen table to the wall — still plenty of table space for her and Miranda to eat, while freeing up floor space for her easel. She'd get some heavy vinyl to cover the tile.

She'd be able to paint outside for weeks yet, but she was eager to set up her permanent space in here. Well, as close to permanent as anything had felt for Rose in quite some time. A different home, but a home. When she spoke to Luis, she would begin divorce proceedings.

The light that poured into the room through the glass doors was pale and clear. She wondered how it would change as the seasons passed. She might base some of her work around the changing light as she experienced it. That was one idea. She had many. Several since last night, in fact.

What a roller coaster of a day Sunday had been. Joy and horror within the same frame. She hadn't had a day like that since childhood, and she had never experienced a day as horrible as some of Anna's. Not even the shock and anguish of Memorial Day weekend could compare with Anna's constant fear. And until yesterday, they'd never talked about it.

Rose's eye caught the glimmer of a silver pan on the stove, and she saw herself as a fourteen-year-old, frying eggs for her and Anna's dinner. She saw herself in the kitchen of their childhood house, the one that contained Anna's screams and tears and had paid for her condo and thus, in a sense, provided her the means to go off on her adventure now. How strange life was.

Her father had hit her sister with his belt that day because she'd cursed at him. He'd gone crazy, chasing her through the house. Rose hadn't seen the actual beating, but she had heard the sounds, and she'd had an ugly vision of his suit pants falling down when he removed his belt. Later, her father had said to her mother, *Either she goes or I go*, meaning Anna, because she had provoked him, and her mother had for once stood up to him. *Get out,* she'd said. *Get out.*

Rose had been so happy at that moment, happy and terrified both.

But her father hadn't left. He'd shut himself up in his room for a week or so and eventually everything went back to normal. And her mother hadn't stood up to him again. Maybe he'd threatened her; Rose didn't know. Her mother was mostly not around when her father went crazy on Anna. And it didn't happen that often. Those were her mother's words. *It didn't happen that often.*

Rose felt sick, recalling those words. But she knew that she had to allow herself to remember, that she'd carried the scars inside for too long, and that because of them she had kept a part of herself isolated. More than a part.

Anna had found a puppy that evening of the day she got hit with her father's belt, a small white terrier she named Lucky because she was so lucky to have found him — on the "luckiest day of her life," the day her father's belt raised thick, red welts from her ten-year-old skin.

He had picked Anna as the object of his

fury. Why Anna? Why not Rose? Why had Rose received the praise and Anna the pain? She had never understood, but now she thought perhaps she did. Anna had a fire in her, a fire that was dangerous but also enviable. It burned as defiance but also as passion, for living, and for living things. And she possessed a powerful dignity. Rose understood how William would love it. He had always loved Anna, and Rose had known and denied it.

She wished she knew what it was she loved, aside from her daughter and her sister and the way that light changed the color of things. She had spent her life observing and interpreting, appreciating or avoiding the spectacles before her. She knew it was time to let herself burn a little.

She laughed at herself, thinking of the *Ariel.* She rephrased her thought: It was time she let herself sail where the wind would take her.

She poured herself a cup of coffee and took it, black, out onto the deck. Miranda was hugging Cannibal.

"Good morning." Rose blew across the top of her mug. "*Beautiful* morning."

"It is," Miranda agreed, surprising Rose. "I'm going to ride over to the Ram's Head

Inn to say good-bye to Daddy and Aunt Anna."

Again, Rose was surprised. "You are?"

"Yes. They said they would leave after breakfast, around ten." Miranda looked at her watch. "It's nine."

"That's nice of you," Rose said, then hoped that didn't sound wrong. She sipped her coffee.

"Well, I mean, he's going to *Scotland*."

"Yes," Rose said.

"And she's going across the ocean on some boat she's never seen!" Miranda stood. "I mean, you guys are *freaks*, but you're my family."

Rose felt her eyes fill and burn. She looked away, toward the north.

"I'm going to leave now," Miranda said. She bent to scratch Cannibal's chest.

"Let's let him in the house," Rose suggested.

"Wow," Miranda said. She looked from her mother to the dog. "Now?"

Rose laughed a little. "Sure. Why not? Before you go."

"Do you think he will?" Miranda wondered.

Rose shrugged. "It's possible."

Miranda addressed Cannibal in a firm voice. "Come, boy!" She patted her thigh, and the dog got up. She backed toward the house. "Come," she said, softer now, and he followed without hesitation.

At the threshold of the sliding glass doors, he stopped as he always had. "Come on," Miranda coaxed. She made kissing noises. "It's okay, boy. Come on, I'll give you a bone." She walked backward into the kitchen, her eyes fixed on the dog.

Rose crossed the deck, rubbed past the dog into the house. "Come on, Cannibal," she said casually. "You're invited."

Miranda reached for the box of Milk-Bones on the counter, but Cannibal had already decided to come in. He made his way around the room, sniffing.

"Amazing," Miranda said. She set the box on the counter. "I thought we'd have to convince him."

"It will be nice to have a dog around the house," Rose said. She had never had one. Lucky had been dispensed with in a day.

"What do you think will happen?" Miranda asked.

"With Cannibal? I think he'll be fine. Maybe he'll chew something, but I'm not too worried." She drank more of her coffee.

"No," Miranda said. "I mean with Daddy and Aunt Anna."

"Oh." Rose looked around at the kitchen, which was still strange and not really hers. She put the coffee mug down.

Cannibal had gone to investigate the hallway and beyond. His nails clicked on the wooden floors. Then they hit the braided rug in the living room and were silenced.

"Aunt Anna has always wanted to travel," Rose said finally.

"I know," Miranda said. She grabbed her bicycle helmet from a chair. "So has Daddy."

Had he? "When will you be home?" Rose asked.

"Right after I say good-bye. Not long. Danny is working today."

Rose nodded. "Do you want to eat at Princi's tonight?" She had never before dared to ask.

"Yes!" Miranda's face lit up. She slid open the glass door. "I'll be back soon."

"I think they love each other," Rose said as Miranda stepped onto the deck. "And us. I do believe they love us, too."

"I guess," Miranda said, the light in her face dimmed. She stared at the dolphin toe ring on her left foot. Rose wondered whether it had been a gift from Danny.

"I don't know what will happen," Rose

363

said. "But they'll be where they are and we'll be here, and I think we'll all be okay. And then, we'll see."

"We could go over to Scotland for Christmas," Miranda said. She wiggled the dolphin, considering it.

"We could," Rose agreed.

"Okay," Miranda said, her voice soft and charitable, almost as though she'd said *I forgive you*. She hadn't said any such thing, of course, and she wouldn't, not soon. But they had gotten past something and survived. They were on the other side of something now.

Miranda skipped across the deck, waved, and disappeared around the house. In a minute Rose heard the crunching of her bicycle down the drive. Familiar now, a sound from her new life.

Cannibal reappeared and sat at Rose's side in the open doorway, looking out toward the water. Rose wondered whether he'd want to go outdoors again, but he didn't move, and soon she was asking him one last time to be sure he didn't want to be outside because she was closing the door; when she did, he followed her into the living room and lay at her feet on the cool stone of the hearth.

He gave a little sigh — a dog could get

used to this, Rose supposed. He looked like he belonged there, in that spot, and Rose imagined painting him there. She thought some day she would.

How inexorably we each become what we have been, never changed, never the same. Rose opened a window, and a breeze blew through the room. Perfect for a little fire in the fireplace, her first fire in this house, to honor the end of summer and all things past. Rose wouldn't paint it, not today, although another of her ideas was to paint fire reflected by water. She had so many ideas; probably many of them were bad ones. Today, she would just have a fire.

She looked around the room for wood, expecting to find a small stack, but there was none. Well, she could gather some outside. There were plenty of fallen branches in the woods. The fire didn't have to be large. She walked to the front door, not intending to disturb the dog, but he was immediately up and with her. They went out together.

Cannibal peed against a clump of browning azaleas and then trotted ahead of Rose. She was headed toward the woods, but as she came around the side of the house, the dog shot past her and beneath the deck. Rose followed him and stopped, crouching to check his water bowl while she was here. And she noticed his collection of small logs.

The water bowl was filled. Perhaps Miranda had taken care of it.

Rose looked at the dog, grinning at her, then at the pile of wood. Why did he scavenge it? Did he care if she used it? Did he want her to? She reached to take a piece, then another, and another. She slid out from beneath the deck, her arms full. Cannibal waited till she was up, and then he followed her back into the house.

It didn't matter why, it just was. Cannibal was a dog who collected wood. He certainly had not objected to Rose taking some; he'd seemed almost pleased. Maybe he was thanking her for letting him inside.

I'm losing it, Rose thought, and she laughed.

She dropped the pile of logs and sticks onto the grate in the fireplace and struck a long match. The dried leaves and pine straw she'd carried in with the wood ignited immediately. The smaller of the twigs caught easily, too, and before long the fire was underway.

Cannibal settled down on the floor beside the hearth, a bit farther away than before. He moaned a little, settling into himself, and then his muscles relaxed. Rose admired him, his fur partly striped like that of some prehistoric creature or medieval gargoyle. Its patterns seemed ancient. Yes, she would paint him.

As a delicate flame consumed a curled brown leaf, Rose thought of the *Ariel* on fire the night before, how frightened she had been, then how grateful to find everyone safe. Even the boat would be okay. She was glad the *Ariel* was saved, though a month ago she'd have watched it burn with glee. Anger could be that destructive. More than anything, Rose was grateful to have let some of hers go.

Last night, Anna had explained how the fire had been started when William's prized Davey lantern was inadvertently knocked over as Anna opened the hatch from below. Oil had spilled along the cabin roof, and a steady flame had burned its way to a coiled sheet, traveled to the foresail, along to the halyard, up the mast, and along the furled main. That had been the bright flash Rose had seen just before William arrived on deck.

What Anna hadn't explained was what she and William had been doing below during the course of this conflagration. She hadn't needed to. And that, the idea of that, the knowledge of that, did cause Rose pain — would continue to cause her pain. But she would get through it, she knew. The process had already begun.

Rose stirred the crackling twigs with the iron poker. The fire was small but burning nicely. She stood up, looking around at the room she'd rarely used all summer. She walked the circumference of the braided carpet, a circle of muted blues and greens. In the center of the carpet sat a glass coffee table, and in the center of it a dusty beeswax candle, its wick still white. She lit it.

She looked around the room and found a few more candles, which she arranged around the big white candle on the table. She lit them all.

The raw silk upholstered chair beside an open window beckoned her, and she lowered herself into it. She lifted her face to the moving air, the wash of it cool across her eyelids and nose. Her legs stretched toward the fire; she slipped off her sandals and warmed her toes.

Cool face, warm feet, a pleasant balance. That's what Rose craved. She wanted to let past poisons go. She turned her face to the window and looked across the water. A clear view. She could see Connecticut. Once, she had lived over there.

❖ *Conversation Guide* ❖

The Opposite Shore

Maryanne Stahl

This Conversation Guide is intended to enrich the individual reading experience, as well as encourage us to explore these topics together — because books, and life, are meant for sharing.

A Conversation with Maryanne Stahl

Q. What inspired you to write about sisters and betrayal?

A. Shakespeare's *The Tempest* is a favorite of mine, and my son happened to be reading it during the early stages of my thinking about this book. I love so much about the play, especially the character of Prospero and his shifting relationship to his art. I knew I wanted to explore the themes of love and betrayal, art and illusion, so I thought I'd borrow what I could in terms of plot and inspiration. I liked the idea that the novel would be in one sense an homage. Part of the pleasure of being a writer is having the means and the opportunity to acknowledge work that has meant so much to me.

In addition, I'd had a real-life story floating around the back of my mind for years, a situation concerning someone

371

whose own sister had stolen her husband. It was a horrible blow when she discovered them, of course, but in the end, the family reconfigured: The spouses divorced, the younger sister married her former brother-in-law, and the new arrangement was accepted by all. Painfully.

I knew very little of the particulars, but the story fascinated me. I couldn't imagine such a thing happening with either of my sisters, but I thought that losing faith in a sister would have to be even worse than losing a husband. Or would it?

Q. Were your characters based on these real people or on the fictional characters in the play, or did you imagine them once you had the basic situation?

A. All of the above. I started with the play, and immediately knew I wanted to write about two sisters rather than two brothers; I then decided the "usurped territory" would be a husband rather than a dukedom. Once I determined that, I recalled the story I had heard, and then I began to imagine characters. When I knew who they were, they led me to the story I finally wrote.

At first, they were difficult to understand, these characters. I couldn't see how any of the three adults could be made sympathetic, and in some ways of course they are not. But we are all flawed, and love is a powerful force. What happens when opposing loves collide?

I wanted to comprehend how such a betrayal could happen, how the people involved could be ordinary, even good, people, and yet wreak such havoc on those they loved. My first writing task became to learn as much as I could about Rose and Anna and William and Miranda, to understand who each of them was, what each one wanted, and how each of their lives had led them to this point.

Q. Why Shelter Island?

A. I knew that I wanted to set my second novel on Shelter Island because it is a place I love, an unusual place, a place about which I have long wanted to write. Contained and yet somehow unfettered, a small island is a kind of stage, an ideal place for a story to unfold.

My in-laws had a house there for many years, situated on a bluff much as Luis Naufragio's house is situated in the book, though their house was not at all like his. I spent many summers on the island and wanted to use some actual places, such as the Ram's Head Inn, as settings. Coecles Harbor, Mashomack Preserve, Sunset Beach — I wanted to celebrate all of them.

Q. Given the island setting, sailing plays an important role in the story. Do you enjoy sailing?

A. Yes, but I really haven't sailed in years. Before moving to Georgia, my husband and I kept a Pearson 26 in Port Washington, Long Island, and a two-person Laser in Shelter Island. We enjoyed sailing, but we never took the boat anywhere too terribly exciting, mainly day trips. Though I love the ocean, I'm not sure why sailboats keep appearing in my novels. Of course, they serve as metaphors for a spectrum of ideas, but in this case, I wanted the book to start as *The Tempest* started, with a vessel in a storm.

I actually wrote the second half of the book first, beginning with Anna and William on the *Ariel* en route to Shelter Island. "Boatswain (Bo'sun)!" is the first line of *The Tempest*.

Q. What are you working on next?

A. While researching the history of Gardiners Island for *The Opposite Shore*, I came across a historical account of a woman by the name of Goody Garlick who was tried as a witch in East Hampton in the 1650s. Witchcraft, witch trials, and witchery in various forms are an interest of mine, and I had hoped but not managed to include some of the magical element of *The Tempest* in *The Opposite Shore*.

East Hampton — another eastern Long Island beach locale — seemed a good place to set my next book, and I became interested in a story that explored the character of a misunderstood woman — a "witch." What if a contemporary woman lived in the house once belonging to Goody Garlick? How might their stories intersect? That's the question I have set myself for the next book. Though I've chosen another Long Island ocean setting, it will be a different sort of story and explore some new themes.

Q. Forgiveness is a theme in this novel as well as in your first novel, Forgive the Moon. *What is it about this theme that especially interests you?*

A. We all seek forgiveness and we all need to forgive. Because life is painful by its nature, we are inevitably in various states of emotional, psychological, and sometimes physical healing. Forgiveness — or letting go — is essential but so very difficult. Maybe I write about it to teach myself how to do it.

Forgive the Moon ultimately makes a different point. When the heroine realizes that trying to forgive her mother is like trying to forgive the moon, she accepts that some things are beyond forgiveness, that forgiveness is sometimes irrelevant. That paradox intrigues me.

Questions for Discussion

1. Rose is an artist. Has her painting caused her estrangement from William, and, by extension, Anna? Is it the antidote? In what sense has Rose "created" the situation in which she finds herself as the book begins? How is it significant that Anna introduced William to Rose by bringing him to see Rose's artwork?

2. Rose eventually begins to forgive Anna. Would you? Are some things unforgivable? Does it matter that Anna and William hadn't actually slept together? On the other hand, if you don't act on your feelings, as they didn't for so long, are you betraying yourself?

3. What do you think about the changes the characters make in their lives? Is Rose being fair to William when she kicks him out of their house? Should she consider reconciliation more than she seems to do? Should William fight harder to save the marriage for Miranda's sake? Do you think Anna's decision to travel is a good one? What, if anything, do you think

will transpire between Anna and William in the future?

4. As the story unfolds, we learn that, as a child, Anna was physically abused by her father, but Rose was not. What effect has this had on the sisters' relationship? Does it play any part in what happens to them as adults? Do you know anyone who has been shaped by a similar background?

5. Miranda and Danny plan to make love for the first time but are thwarted by the fire. Do you think they will go to have sex at the next opportunity or might they have second thoughts now that Miranda is going to stay on the island? Are a sixteen- and a seventeen-year-old too young for a sexual relationship? Does first love shape one's future relationships? Was William Anna's first love?

6. The book features strong natural elements — storms, fire, the sea, the stars. In what way do these relate to the emotional drama of the story or the inner lives of the characters? How does the Shelter Island setting contribute to the book? Why is Rose able to heal there? How is she more or less isolated on the island than she was in Connecticut?

About the Author

Maryanne Stahl, a native New Yorker who has spent many summers on Shelter Island, teaches writing at Kennesaw State University near Atlanta. When she is not writing, teaching, gardening, duck tending or chatting with writer friends on-line, she enjoys an alternate identity as a folk artist.

The Opposite Shore is Stahl's second novel. *Forgive the Moon*, her first, was nominated for the Georgia Author of the Year Award for a First Novel.

To contact her, read reviews and excerpts of her work, or check appearance dates, visit Stahl's Web site at www.mary annestahl.com

The employees of Thorndike Press hope you have enjoyed this Large Print book. All our Thorndike and Wheeler Large Print titles are designed for easy reading, and all our books are made to last. Other Thorndike Press Large Print books are available at your library, through selected bookstores, or directly from us.

For information about titles, please call:

(800) 223-1244

or visit our Web site at:

www.gale.com/thorndike
www.gale.com/wheeler

To share your comments, please write:

Publisher
Thorndike Press
295 Kennedy Memorial Drive
Waterville, ME   04901